SENTINELS OF TZURAC

VENGEANCE

Books written by James Raven in the Sentinels of Tzurac saga

Terra Major Under Threat
Zarkwin's Revenge
Retaliation
Vengeance

International Film Festival Awards for
Script adaptations on first edition books:

Silver Award – Terra Major Under Threat
Gold Award – Zarkwin's Revenge
Gold Award – Retaliation

California Film Awards:

Gold Award – Terra Major Under Threat

James Raven

SENTINELS OF TZURAC

VENGEANCE

Inspiring Publishers
P.O. Box 159, Calwell, ACT Australia 2905
Email: publishaspg@gmail.com
http://www.inspiringpublishers.com

A catalogue record for this book is available from the National Library of Australia

National Library of Australia The Prepublication Data Service

Author: James Raven
Title: Sentinels of Tzurac:
          Vengeance
Genre: Science Fiction

Paperback ISBN: 978-1-923449-06-0
ePub2 ISBN: 978-1-923449-07-7

FOR her dedication in supporting and editing my writing,
I want to express my deepest gratitude to my partner, Julie.
I am also grateful to readers who inspired me to write a fourth book.

INCARCERATION

ENDLESS years living in a prison farm located on an isolated dead planet knowing there was little hope of escape was enough to break the spirit of the enslaved. It was especially so when the prisoners were labouring long hours on little sleep in a parched, dust-filled quarry, barely surviving on half rations of depleted nutrition and always with a rumbling, hungry stomach.

This was the punishment dealt to rebels and enemies who attempted to destroy the Federation of Planets and Tzurac's Sentinel soldiers charged with securing its safety and ensuring peace throughout the Universe. The Tzuracian Senate sentenced offenders to hell for life on the dustbowl planet Lokar.

Lokar was one of the many smaller planets located amongst the asteroid belt in the Western Quadrant's Pandark Star System known as the 'Dead Zone', where no craft ventured other than Tzuracian transporters. A permanent canopy of grey dust created by constant dust storms and whirlwinds blotted out the sky and choked out all natural life and moisture. The landscape was flat, uninhabitable and uninviting with temperatures of searing heat during the day and freezing cold at night. It was an ideal location for keeping highly dangerous, unwanted criminals out of the way

– it was harsh and isolated and at the same time useful because the Tzuracians could put prisoners to work there excavating hard stone used for constructing roads and buildings back on Planet Tzurac.

Among the prisoners on Lokar were one hundred and twenty Treldarian soldiers in faded prison orange, looking tired and bedraggled and a far cry from their former proud and disciplined selves. The Tzuracians had captured them six years ago in a major, all-out assault on Tzurac's capital city, Khazor. They had been convicted and sentenced to life imprisonment and transported to Lokar along with the leaders of the remaining defeated allies, the shiny-headed Kyroni, each with a distinctive long plait.

And all had received an antidote designed to permanently reverse the enhanced effects they'd once gained through a powerful Xytrinium infusion. The counter-acting injection had decreased their artificially powerful strength, slowed down their agility and suppressed their aggression, allowing the Sentinel guards – all with the advantage of Xytrinium enhanced DNA – to control the prisoners more easily as they performed their laborious tasks.

The Treldarians had been Tzurac's archenemies for centuries, and the Sentinel guards on remote Planet Lokar didn't much care whether these murderous prisoners lived or died. They were satisfied that, like other hard-core prisoners sent there, the Treldarians would eventually succumb to premature deaths from the extreme harsh environment. But they were learning that Treldarians don't die easily …

The Treldarians' forefathers lived on Treldar, a ravaged, weather-beaten planet in the Grekadian Star system with scorching landscapes travelled by nomadic tribes. They were acclimatised to a hot, dry and dusty environment, and they were survivors. In the protracted interplanetary Grekadian Wars in centuries past, the strongest and fiercest of their race had banded together to fight against the Sentinels of Tzurac. Although they had ultimately been defeated, their resilience to harsh environments, food deprivation and inflicted pain had been passed down from generation to generation, along with a deep-seated hatred of Tzurac and the Federation.

They had rallied again six years ago after procuring the secret to the Sentinels' amazing strength and abilities – the blue crystal, Xytrinium. The Treldarian army had received enhancements from a powerful Xytrinium infusion before going into battle, but again were ultimately defeated. Those who survived were injected with an antidote to diffuse their strength but they survived on Lokar thanks to their already inherent tolerances.

Despite the oppressive conditions on Planet Lokar, the tall and once well-built officer with the distinctive dark features and black ponytail of a Treldarian, Lieutenant Tykran Vark of the Second Legion, Eastern Quadrant remained an inspiration to the captured soldiers. And it was pure hate that kept him from losing his will to live.

Before being sent from Tzurac to the prison farm, he learned that his father, General Khuram Vark of the Second Treldarian Legion, along with General Rokan of the Third Treldarian Legion, had been executed by order of the Tzuracian Council of Elders for their part as leaders of the attack on Tzurac. Tykran had not been permitted to see his father and hold him in his arms for the very last time to say his final farewell, and this had intensified his hate towards the Tzuracian Senators and its Sentinel army.

The relationship between father and son had been distant and strained after years separated by hierarchy in the military. Tykran had rebelled against his father's constant high expectations and engaged at times in reckless, youthful behaviour with drink and women. But the rebel Treldarian Blader, Captain Ramlok, who had been sent to Orkharn and inspired Tykran's father to go to war against the Tzuracians, helped Tykran find his feet as a responsible soldier and begin to rebuild the bond with his father.

Tykran loathed being deprived of his only opportunity to finally tell his father how much he'd grown to love and respect him. And he resented the humiliation his father suffered when the Tzuracians executed him after the trial, rather than letting him die like a warrior in battle with his sword in hand. He saw it as a disgrace to his family and the Treldarian soldiers' code of honour. Tykran Vark wanted revenge.

Over the last few weeks, Tykran felt the fire inside him fuelling his aggression. It was growing stronger each day, along with his increasing strength. Other enhancements he'd acquired following a Xytrinium infusion years ago, including sharpened eyesight and amplified hearing, were also gradually returning.

And Tykran observed the same was happening to his soldiers. They had been docile when they first arrived on this hellhole, but they were gradually becoming more aggressive day by day. The effects of the counter-acting injection were wearing off and Tykran could finally see an opportunity to make their escape.

* * *

One night after the guards had routinely locked the Treldarian prisoners into their shared sleeping quarters, the young but worn Lieutenant gathered them together and advised them to keep their rediscovered enhancements hidden until the time was right to use them.

'My comrades-in-arms,' he continued in a strong and confident tone, 'I share in your despair. This is *not* how we'd want to end our lives, labouring like beaten dogs for an enemy we swore to destroy. But I have *not* abandoned your needs to break free from this enslavement. Like you, I've not given up hope there will come a time when we'll once more return to the glorious days of victory, proud to be Treldarian warriors like our forefathers who fought for our freedom to go where we please, take what we want and share in the spoils of war without consequences.

'Like all of you, I would prefer to die in battle than grovel in the dirt and dust of a Tzuracian prison and die without dignity and honour on an unknown, forgotten planet in an unmarked grave. I want our ancestors to be proud of who we are. Follow me and I'll give back to you what you crave – your freedom, your dignity, and a safe return to our family and friends, and the lifestyle we had back on Planet Orkharn.'

Tired but not defeated, the Treldarian prisoners gave a muffled cheer, raising their arms with clenched fists and greeting Tykran with wide grins of optimism. They were with him all the way. It wasn't just that he was their superior officer. He had proven himself to be a strong, worthy leader who respected and protected his soldiers and who in turn had earnt their respect. They would follow his orders without question.

'Yes, Captain,' cried one of the soldiers and the title 'Captain' echoed from voices around the room.

Tykran smiled in appreciation. He would accept the unofficial promotion, realising he was now fully in charge of all the soldiers who remained in the Treldarian army.

'Sergeant Krag,' he called, beckoning to his loyal and faithful comrade, who had also survived the Treldarian defeat with a minor injury, 'we need to talk.'

Like his Lieutenant, Krag too was tall and solid with a square jaw. He had a weathered face, piercing dark-brown eyes under thick eyebrows, and a deep husky voice. He wore his long and now untidy black hair pulled back loosely revealing an unkempt black beard.

A close, trusting friendship and camaraderie had grown between the two soldiers long before their incarceration. Back on

Planet Orkharn, in the lead-up to the last invasion of Tzurac, they were the first to be infused with Xytrinium by Captain Ramlok, the rebel Blader and General Dranz's first Lieutenant in the rogue Fifth Legion. Ramlok was commanded to search for the Second Legion and persuade them to join forces against the Federation. Vark and Krag were chosen to train the newly enhanced Treldarian army and then to accompany Ramlok to recruit the Third Legion living on the Moon, Mankro. There, once again, Tykran and Sergeant Krag together with Ramlok, were ordered to train General Rokan's soldiers after they too were infused with the powerful Xytrinium.

In fuller and more serious discussions with Sergeant Krag, Tykran informed his comrade of his plans. His current plan was simple. Although the prisoners were overseen by Sentinel guards equipped with laser weapons and electric prodding lances, the prisoners were left unshackled. There was nowhere to escape and the thinking was they could work more effectively and efficiently excavating the granite blocks if they were not encumbered with cuffs and leg chains. After all, the guards had been assured the antidote infusion these prisoners had been given made them permanently passive and weaker than the Sentinels guarding them. With their strength and agility now returning without the Sentinels yet being aware, Tykran could see he and his soldiers had the advantage to easily overpower their captors when the time was right.

But, if they were to escape from this hellhole, Tykran required a means of transport that would prevent the Tzuracians rapidly hunting them down. The Tzuracian supply ships were ill-equipped for an escape. Sure, they all had hyperdrives, but only to Level 4 power. *And who would want to commandeer a rock hauler?* he thought. He needed at least Level 8 hyperdrive power and a fully armed ship if he were to outrun or confront Federation spacecrafts.

'Captain' Vark had his father's DNA and the intellect of a war strategist passed on from father to son. As much as he was anxious and determined to seek his vengeance, he had learnt to control his impatience, thanks to his unlikely late mentor and friend Captain Ramlok who had started out as a renegade Blader pirate. He had to plan carefully.

Several thoughts crossed his mind. He could bide his time waiting for the right spacecraft to land on Lokar. But knowing these visits were few and far between, with no routine scheduled flights, he realised he and his soldiers could be stranded on this hellhole for another year.

Or, he and his soldiers could cause a devastating incident such as blowing up the planet's power source. This would force the surviving Sentinel guards to send an emergency distress signal to Tzurac and the Federation would dispatch a rescue team in one of their larger, high-powered ships to prevent a breakout and save their Sentinel guards, engineers and horticulturists. But it wasn't an ideal plan since destruction of the power source would leave them without hydroponic food or water normally produced in the artificial greenhouses while they waited indefinitely for the rescue mission to arrive. It would jeopardise the lives of his own soldiers.

He determined a better alternative would be to capture the guards and force them to send a desperate, pleading message *making out* there had been a life-threatening explosion on the planet which had cut-off their power source, leaving them with limited stored food and water supplies. Captain Vark and his unit would lay in wait, fully armed with weapons confiscated from the guards. Using these weapons, his soldiers would then commandeer, by negotiation or by force, the Tzuracian spacecraft dispatched to help the guards on Lokar.

Sergeant Krag nodded with excitement. There was a gleam in his eyes Vark had not seen in his comrade for a long time. 'I like your plan, Captain,' Krag said enthusiastically in his deep voice. 'With their renewed enhancements and weapons in hand, I'm confident our unit will be successful. And we can do this with few injuries unless the Sentinel guards foolishly attempt to stop us. Mind you, many of us wouldn't hesitate to kill all the guards for the satisfaction of payback for how we've been treated for these last three years.' He spat on the ground in disgust.

Tykran cautioned. 'I understand how they feel, Sergeant, but if we're to escape we must be a disciplined force and fight for a cause with honour and dignity. We're not like our brethren, the bloodthirsty Bladers who enjoy killing just for the sport. Nor are we like the barbaric Kyroni who have no respect for anything. We're Treldarian soldiers with morals, and I'll not have our soldiers kill unarmed Sentinels in cowardly acts. We may be enemies but we're not murderers. We give enemy soldiers the respect they deserve for serving in the military. Remember, they're only following orders from their superiors.'

It was true. The Treldarian Bladers of the Fifth Legion, had been bloodletting mercenaries who plundered the crafts of innocent space travellers, raping the females and enslaving the males since the Grekadian Wars. But the Second and Third Legions had maintained a military code and fought only those who raised arms against them. They treated their prisoners of war with respect.

Krag nodded. 'I agree, Captain, as much as I loathe our enemy. So, when do you plan for this coup, sir?'

'Soon, Krag. We need to wait for just the right moment when we know where all the Sentinel guards are positioned. We must hit them simultaneously when they're most vulnerable.'

Krag listened in silence, intently analysing the whole scenario as his Captain spoke with confidence, occasionally stroking his thick and unkempt black beard and raising an eyebrow or two.

'We know they change from the night shift to the daytime crew at exactly 0600 hours. And they usually have five guards overseeing each of our four working groups in the corners of the excavation site. What I want is to take them soon after we start our labouring in the quarry. With just over a hundred of us, we'll easily be able to overpower them, taking their weapons as well as their Sentinel Pledge rings to prevent them from transmitting any signals.

'After we've captured, gagged and bound them, we'll herd them into their barracks where the other Sentinel guards are sleeping. Taking the other shift guards by surprise, it should be easy to confiscate their weapons and rings. Before gagging and binding them, we'll strip forty of them and change into their uniforms. We'll use their helmets to hide our black hair and we'll remove our beards. We'll lock up all the Sentinels, with the exception of the one we'll use to send the distress signal to Tzurac. The rest of our soldiers will remain in hiding until the Federation rescue craft arrives.'

He paused for a moment, allowing Krag time to take in his strategy. 'We'll inform the rest of our soldiers of our plan tomorrow night. What say you, Sergeant?'

'What about the engineers in the Control Tower who have camera surveillance over the whole quarry? Surely they'll be monitoring all this. Won't they set off the audio alarms immediately, alerting the other shift guards? And won't they send a riot message to Tzurac?'

'You're right, Sergeant,' said Tykran, thinking quickly on his feet. 'Who's your best soldier in speed and stealth?'

Krag responded without hesitation. 'Corporal Jhakmar, sir. He's the best all-rounder with blades, guns and martial arts, and you'd never see him coming. He's fast and he's efficient.'

'Excellent. Inform him he's been chosen for a crucial part of the operation. The Sentinels' med-bay is in the same building as the Control Tower. He needs to be ready to fake an illness or injury tomorrow night to get him into that facility. Before sunrise the following day, he needs to get to the Tower and disable the guards, then send a signal to us by flashing the floodlights in the quarry on and off a couple of times. This will give us the 'all-clear' to begin our assault. Our very lives and future depend on this happening, and you need to stress this. Do you think he can do it, Sergeant?'

'Without any doubt, sir. I stake my life on it.'

'That's exactly what you *will* be doing, Sergeant – we *all* will be. I want you to quietly spread the word, but emphasise we want these guards captured quickly and silently with no lasers fired. We don't want to alert the other sleeping guards.'

ESCAPE PLAN

AS soon as the guards bolted the cell doors locking the prisoners down for the night, Vark and his Sergeant began passing word to the others of the proposed escape. There was whispering and murmurings as the message passed from bunk to bunk in the darkness of the huge barracks.

Sergeant Krag sat on Corporal Jhakmar's bunk in the dimly lit room. Pale light from one of Lokar's two moons filtering through the dusty grey atmosphere streamed through narrow window slits high up on one of the walls. Even in the pale light Jhakmar's hulking physique was impressive, his broad shoulders, solid chest and taut biceps exposed from his sleeveless prison overalls. He'd persisted in staying in shape despite the poor conditions on Lokar.

Krag watched the expressions on the Corporal's face as he gave him his orders. 'Once you've taken out those in the Control Tower you need to send a silent signal to all of us by switching the floodlights in the quarry on and off a couple of times. Are you up for it, soldier?'

'You don't have to ask twice, Sergeant. I've been looking forward to this opportunity since the enhancements started to kick in again.' Jhakmar turned over to the edge of his bunk, lifted a corner of the thinly padded, flat mattress and pulled out a slither of metal about four inches in length, with a sharp point on one end.

Krag looked alarmed, but before he could comment, Jhakmar whispered, 'I was saving this for one of the guards. It's easily concealed and just long enough to pierce through to a lung or heart if it can get past their Xytrinium-meshed uniform.' He chuckled wickedly. 'It's perfect for what I have in mind to get me to the med-bay. Sergeant, I want you to slice a two-inch cut across my left forearm vein.'

'You're not serious are you, Corporal? You'll bleed to death before the guards come to assist you!'

'Not if you lot hammer heavily on the doors and yell and scream just before slicing me. Cutting *down* the vein I'd definitely lose too much blood too soon and that's when it becomes *really* serious. But a shallow incision *across* my vein will rapidly release a large quantity of blood and give the impression I'm bleeding to death. If they bandage it within ten minutes of the cut, it'll be enough time to stop the bleeding. With our renewed enhancements the wound will heal before dawn breaks. So, when do we do this?'

'Now if you're ready.' Krag was keen for action. 'Just give me a minute to confirm with Captain Vark and if he gives the go-ahead, we'll commence the countdown. Go stand by the door and wait till I return.'

'Okay, Sergeant, will do,' said Jhakmar waving a tight-fisted arm across his chest in a formal Treldarian salute.

'What have we got to lose?' was Vark's answer. 'Let's do it!'

Krag was soon standing beside the Corporal with metal spike in hand and some of the inmates had gathered in readiness to start thumping the doors and yelling. Krag gave the order to commence and within seconds, amid the din, he began to cut Jhakmar's vein carefully like a surgeon with a razor-sharp scalpel.

Blood spurted out and the Corporal muffled a yelp of pain and doubled over. Krag held the Corporal's tormented torso while lowering him slowly to the floor and quickly concealing the sharp metal spike in Jhakmar's boot. Warm, dark-red blood began to seep from the wound forming into a large, wet and sticky puddle around his arm.

Three minutes was all it took for bright lights to flood the barracks. Seconds later the doors flung open. Twenty fully armed guards stood fast, pointing their laser weapons in the prisoners' direction. Instantly the prisoners' raised their arms in surrender.

'Stand down!' yelled the Sentinel sergeant in command. 'Return to your bunks. All of you!' Then he sighted Jhakmar's body lying motionless on the floor just inside the door with a large pool of blood around it. 'What's going on, Krag?'

'I'm not exactly sure, sir. In the half-light I could hear shuffling. I saw one of my men stagger towards the door and then suddenly collapse. I rushed over to him and saw his arm was bleeding profusely. I couldn't stop the flow of blood and he needed immediate medical attention. So, we bashed on the doors hoping to get attention. I've no idea what caused the injury. Perhaps he was injured at the quarry earlier?'

'Right, all of you get back to your bunks!' the Sentinel sergeant ordered again, waving his laser gun back and forth at the group who began moving slowly towards their bunkbeds.

Seeing them start to turn and move away from the door and realising they were of no immediate threat, the Sentinel sergeant called out to his troops. 'You two, pick up this prisoner and take him to the Med-bay immediately!' He waved his gun back and forth menacingly at the prisoners and threatened, 'The rest of you cretins will have to do his share of the work until he returns to the quarry. But you won't be sharing his food rations if that's what you're thinking. Now get back to sleep. You'll need it!'

Within minutes the guards had bolted the barrack doors once more. Before the lights were turned out again, Krag turned in the direction of Vark who was smiling and raising a clenched fist. The Captain was delighted his plan was starting to take shape.

Most of the prisoners, anxious about taking back their freedom and escaping from their never-ending nightmare, had a restless night. It was hard to contain mixed emotions of fear, anger and excitement at the thought of breaking away from the monotonous, tiring routine of labouring in the quarry, lorded over like livestock by their archenemy.

Rising before the light of dawn to the morning wake-up alarm of a high-pitched pulsing siren, the prisoners sat poised on their bunks in expectation of things to come. They knew the same daily mindless routine of being herded to the washing troughs, then to the breakfast benches to eat their bowl of slop, and then marched off to their allocated workplaces in the quarry, would not end the same as every other day. Today was the day they would take back their freedom and restore their rightful places as Treldarian soldiers.

By the time the sun crept above the rugged, ash-grey mountain range on the smoky horizon of the dead planet, the stage had already been set. Five Sentinel guards with long-barrelled laser guns slung casually over their shoulders were milling around the outskirts of the prison in each corner of the huge, dug-out cavity which was the mine. They watched lazily with one eye on the prisoners going through their laborious motions of cutting, dragging and loading the heavy, rough-hewn stone blocks into small metal carriages. And they were too preoccupied with casual chit-chat to be aware something was about to happen. But, out of the corner of *their* eyes, the labouring Treldarians focused keenly on the high posted floodlights, waiting anxiously for them to light up.

Tykran was feeling a little anxious because Jhakmar hadn't yet executed the scheduled sunrise ploy. His mind began churning over all the things that might have gone wrong. *What if Jhakmar had lost too much blood and hadn't recovered from last night's injury? What if he'd been unable to break into the Control Tower's operation room this morning? What if he'd been caught in the process and the mission thwarted?*

Standing close by, Sergeant Krag could see his Captain becoming agitated by the delay. His impatience was making him careless. In anger and frustration, Tykran began lifting the heavy stone blocks above his head and heaving them in the direction of the carriages forgetting the watchful eyes of the guards.

Krag rushed over to Tykran and grabbed his arm to prevent him from repeating his actions. In a low whisper and with strong intention, he caught the ear of his superior. 'Be *patient*, sir, or you'll draw attention to our restored enhancements. Then we'll *all* be shackled and it will ruin any chance of ever escaping! I have faith my soldier will come through. Just give him a little more time!'

Before Tykran could respond, the floodlights surrounding the complex suddenly began flashing. Simultaneously, all of the one hundred and twenty prisoners, armed with an assortment of excavation tools, rushed the Sentinel guards with speed and stealth. The unsuspecting guards were outnumbered and before they could unshoulder their weapons to fire a blast, they were easily overpowered by the new-found strength and agility of the Treldarian soldiers. It was all over in an instant.

After confiscating the Sentinels' weapons and Pledge rings, the Treldarians gagged the Sentinels, bound their hands, and marched them to the corner of the quarry where Tykran and his Sergeant were waiting. Hand-signalling them to suppress any sounds of excitement, Captain Vark directed all of them to head towards the Sentinel barracks in single file to help dampen the sounds of trampling boots.

But just as they were about to head off, one of the guards managed to break free and bolted. Vark's reflexes were astounding. Before the guard could reach the building complex, he cut him down with a quick laser blast from one of the confiscated pistols.

'I'm not a cold-blooded killer,' he said in a quiet but strong tone, addressing the shocked Sentinel guards, 'but if any of you test my patience by trying to warn your comrades, I won't hesitate to put you down, *permanently*! Now *move*!'

Vark's soldiers formed an escort in a parallel line, aiming the confiscated weapons at the captured guards as they marched. Before long, they reached the Sentinel barracks, a building resembling a small hangar closed in with a wide, metal sliding door. No-one was guarding it. Sergeant Krag who was leading the group, hand-signalled to halt with a gesture to maintain silence. Then he signalled to four of his soldiers, directing them to the front of the line to raise their weapons in readiness for when he opened the door.

As soon as they were in position, he yanked on the metal handle. It was the loud, high-pitched screeching metal of the door sliding along its old rusty guide-tracks that instantly woke the sleeping Sentinel guards. Daylight streamed into the wide cavity, temporarily blinding those who staggered out of their bunks still half asleep. Before they could come to their senses, Krag bellowed a threatening warning in rough Tzuracian dialogue, 'Stay where you are, Sentinels! Do *not* attempt anything foolish. I won't hesitate to shoot if any of you give me an excuse.'

Just as he finished his threat, one of the guards to his right reached for a laser gun hanging from his bunk. Instantly, the Sergeant swung his weapon and fired with a speed reflex and the guard slumped to the floor with a smouldering hole in his chest.

There were gasps of shock from the other Sentinels in the crowded room and all of them raised their arms indicating surrender.

His face contorted with anger, Krag spoke loudly once more. 'I keep my word!' He raised his arm and ordered several of his soldiers to bind the guards' hands and herd them off to be locked up in the cells.

'And collect all their weapons as well as their Sentinel Pledge rings,' Vark added before signalling Krag to join him. 'I don't want them using their Pledge rings to forewarn those on the rescue ship.'

Captain Vark spoke quietly, with urgency in his voice. 'As planned, I want you to select soldiers of similar size to these Sentinels and have them change into their uniforms, including helmets. Have them shave their facial hair to remove any sign of our black colourings. You and I will do the same and prepare to receive the rescue ship. By the time the rescuers are close enough to notice the difference, we'll have already captured them. Time is of the essence, so do it with haste, Sergeant!'

'Yes, sir. Understood.'

'And,' Vark said, drawing breath, 'I want you to identify who is the communication operator amongst the Sentinels as he'll be the one making the emergency transmission under duress. After you've locked the Sentinels up, have two of our soldiers stand guard outside the barracks just in case they attempt an escape. Finally, I want you to build a huge pile of rubble close to the power source using materials that will send out billowing, black smoke. We'll set it alight a couple of hours before the rescue ship arrives. Then we'll wait to greet the rescuers at the landing bay. I'll get you to place our armed soldiers in hiding strategically around the bay ready to surround the Sentinel rescuers as they disembark.'

Krag nodded. 'Okay. Hope it all goes according to plan, sir, but we've got nothing to lose if it doesn't. I for one don't want to spend another day in the quarry of this hellhole! I'd rather die trying to escape.'

'I think we all feel the same, Sergeant.'

* * *

Everything was arranged within a few hours and they were ready to send the transmission. While Vark and Krag escorted the reluctant chosen Sentinel to the Control Tower, the remaining Treldarian soldiers milled around the complex, tasting their first experience at being set free from the hard labour and deprivation they had endured for the last six years. They even made up for the food they'd been denied by gorging themselves on the overstocked canteen supplies and fermented wine usually reserved for the Sentinel soldiers and Tzuracian staff. The taste of freedom was not only quenching their hunger and thirst, but also igniting their spirits for war!

Vark and Krag cautiously entered the Control Tower, nudging their Sentinel captive in the back to take the lead, while clutching their laser weapons at the ready in case Corporal Jhakmar hadn't totally secured the complex. There was an eerie silence as they traversed the passageways leading to the lift well. As they passed the clear glass walls to rooms on either side of the walkway, they could see why. Bodies lay lifeless on the floor, some in green workers' uniforms, others in white, medical lab coats, and all with blood stains visible on their torsos. All were dead.

Vark turned to Krag and spoke sarcastically, 'It appears your over-zealous Corporal takes his missions seriously!'

'He's an expert at what he's been trained to do,' replied Krag, slightly overwhelmed himself, 'but as I mentioned before, sir, he's fast and he's efficient.'

'Yeh, perhaps *too* efficient. I'm glad he's on our side! But I'm not exactly happy he's killed innocent Tzuracians. It's given us confidence about our immediate safety, but when the Tzuracian rescuers find these corpses, they'll want to execute all of us if we're caught.'

When they made it to the top floor of the Control Tower, they encountered Corporal Jhakmar with several more dead Tzuracians who were still slumped in their seats at the control panels in blood-stained clothes. Jhakmar had already started celebrating the coup by downing a couple of bottles of alcohol he'd obviously pilfered from the supply store in the complex, the discarded empties lying on the floor under his chair.

On seeing Vark and Krag he staggered to his feet and gave them a half-hearted salute, still holding onto a half-finished bottle in his other hand, his forearm partially bandaged. 'Corporal Jhakmar reporting, sir,' he slurred, in his inebriated state. 'Control Tower secured; no prisoners taken!'

Tykran scowled at Jhakmar. 'Sergeant Krag, take this soldier to a washroom and sober him up. Obviously, he's successfully completed his mission and the cut to his arm is on the mend. Under the circumstances I'll overlook his unruly behaviour and unnecessary killings, but you must bring him into line. Report back when you've sorted out this drunk and don't waste too much time. You have your orders, Sergeant.'

Krag saluted with a 'Yes, sir!' and headed out the automated sliding door dragging Jhakmar by his good arm.

As the two disappeared, Vark, who had kept his weapon trained on the Sentinel recruit throughout, gave a direct order in Tzuracian using a threatening tone. 'Remove one of those bodies and set yourself down at the control panel!'

Seeing what had happened to his comrades and fearing for his life, the Sentinel moved without hesitation.

'What's your name, soldier?'

The soldier managed to get his words out with a dry, croaky voice. 'C-C Corporal Grydah.'

'Okay, C-C Corporal Grydah,' said Vark waving his retrieved laser pistol inches from the Corporal's face and speaking in a threatening tone, 'I want you to send an emergency distress signal to your Command Headquarters on Tzurac. Tell them there's been a life-threatening explosion here on Lokar which has seriously damaged your power source. Some of your comrades, including your Base Commander, Captain Rhumark, have been seriously injured and need urgent medical attention. You have limited food supplies and fear the prisoners may riot and break out of their containment. You need immediate help. Got it?'

He pointed his pistol at Grydah's head and spoke in an even more threatening tone. 'Don't attempt to expose the real situation or you may find yourself greeting your fellow soldiers in the afterlife. I'll be watching you closely and remember, after six years of living with you lot, I can read and speak Tzuracian fluently. Now send it!'

The Sentinel, now looking pale, his eyes shifting nervously, confirmed with a nod, acknowledging his precarious situation but remaining silent. Sitting beside him at the console Vark watched the Sentinel's trembling hands depress the small, luminous-green buttons on the control board as the message began to present itself on the blue, fluorescent screen at the back of the console. The message completed, the Sentinel signed off and waited for a response.

Within minutes a reply appeared on the green, fluorescent screen.

'Message received. Will alert Security. Rescue ship will be launched and should reach you within forty-eight hours.'

'Good!' Vark gloated. 'Now we wait.'

There was an uneasy silence in the room for some time as Vark sat guarding the anxious Corporal and anticipating the next steps.

The silence was broken when Vark heard the sliding action of the door behind him. He whipped around at once in a reflex action with his weapon raised ready to fire.

Krag and the Corporal entered the room. 'Easy, sir!' the Sergeant cautioned with an outstretched arm, his hand raised in a stop position.

Jhakmar, now sobered up and looking more like a soldier, approached his Captain, halted within arm's length and saluted, his right arm reaching across his chest and thumping his clenched fist above his heart. Then he quickly lowered his arm smartly to his side. 'I wish to apologise for my drunken behaviour, sir. It won't happen again.'

'In these extreme circumstances I understand your behaviour. So, I accept your apology, soldier. But what I can't forgive is the bloodbath you caused in this complex. Want to explain yourself?'

'Yes, sir. I was only following Sergeant Krag's orders. He said, quote "Once I've taken out those in the Control Tower," which I thought meant kill them, all of them.'

Vark turned to face Krag seeking an explanation.

'He's right, sir,' the Sergeant responded, holding out his open arms and shrugging his shoulders, 'I did say that to him, but I didn't mean for him to *kill* them all.'

There was an uneasy silence for a moment. Vark turned back to the Corporal, slowly shaking his head from side to side. 'Very well, Corporal. I accept your reason but if the Tzuracians catch us now, they won't return us to the prison farm. Instead, they'll execute us all. Next time an order is given, it needs to be clear as to precisely what's intended. Right, Sergeant? Right, Corporal?'

'Yes, sir,' both responded in unison.

'Corporal, gag this Sentinel, tie him to his chair and stand guard while the Sergeant and I organise our Unit in the compound. If I'm not here when the rescue ship contacts the Control Tower, alert me via one of their short-wave communicators. I see they keep them on that storage shelf over there.' Vark pointed with his left hand to the far corner of the room. 'Sergeant Krag will synchronise the frequency channel before we leave. And *do not* attempt to injure or kill this Sentinel. I need him alive and undamaged. Do I make myself clear, Corporal?'

'Yes, sir, perfectly.'

'Good. And while you're waiting, have some of the soldiers remove the dead bodies in here and take them to another room out of sight. Sergeant Krag, follow me.'

RED ALERT

DEAFENING alarms suddenly erupted throughout the Citadel Headquarters located in the Tzuracian capital Khazor. In the Control Room amplified, high-pitched screeching pulsed loudly through the speakers as red lights dashed across the control panel throwing the operator into a frenzy. Containing his adrenalin rush, the Communications Officer stabbed at the panel trying to quell the noise and the flashing colours. He was unaccustomed to the turmoil.

On the green, fluorescent screen in front of him, a luminous-red digital message came to life as line after line spurted out information about a crisis situation.

LOKAR PRISON FARM...

LIFE-THREATENING EXPLOSION CAUSING DAMAGED POWER SOURCE...

SEVERAL PERSONNEL SERIOUSLY INJURED INCLUDING THE BASE COMMANDER- NEED URGENT MEDICAL ATTENTION...

HAVE LIMITED FOOD SUPPLIES ...

FEAR PRISON RIOT AND BREAKOUT OF THEIR CONTAINMENT...

NEED IMMEDIATE HELP.

.... CAPTAIN RHUMARK, LOKAR PRISON.

Startled by the message and realising the urgency, the Communication Officer immediately forwarded the message to General Ehrane Dakhar, Commanding Chief of Military Operations, or CCMO, for the Northern Quadrant.

General Dakhar, a distinguished soldier with deep blue eyes and the blonde features of a Tzuracian Sentinel, was in his office when he received the Red Alert message. Never one to panic in such situations, he calmly pressed the intercom button to his aide who was located in the adjoining office and spoke in an authoritative tone. 'Call Admiral Okerahm and tell him a Code Red Alert has just been initiated. Have him report to my office immediately! And contact Captain Nazhark and request his attendance as well!'

'Yes, sir!' came a nervous voice on the receiver, the aide sensing something was up.

Dakhar was the most senior and experienced Sentinel leader on Tzurac. He was aware of the seriousness of the situation and his mind raced. *Without power to the base on Lokar, the prisoners could overpower his Sentinel guards, killing them to make the rations last, while trying themselves to repair the generator, or holding the Sentinel guards to ransom their freedom should a Sentinel craft arrive in time. Was this going to be his first real test after returning home?*

After defeating the Treldarians in the fierce battles on Tzurac and Terra Major six years earlier, Dakhar had been appointed CCMO in charge of the Western Quadrant stationed on Terra Major. He had transferred there from Planet Tzurac with his wife Tajhira and young son Kyrah, and a daughter had been born while they were living there. He enjoyed life on Earth and would happily have remained there for longer, but recently the Senate had ordered him to return to Tzurac as soon as he had his affairs in order. His good friend, Admiral Harzan, had passed away from natural causes and the Senate voted unanimously to appoint Ehrane to Harzan's vacant position as CCMO for the Northern Quadrant. Now, Dakhar was again permanently stationed at home on Tzurac with his family and they'd been living there for the last six months.

Within minutes, both Admiral Okerahm and Captain Nazhark filed through Dakhar's office door. The Admiral stood several inches taller than the captain and commanded a presence of authority. His short-cropped, sterling silver hair and matching, well-groomed, thick beard and sideburns suited his navy-blue and silver-buttoned dress uniform. He had piercing, steel-blue eyes which maintained a zeal in spite of his veteran years. Nazhark on the other hand contrasted in size and appearance. He was somewhat shorter, half the Admiral's age and was dressed in keeping with the Sentinel military maroon uniform minus the blue and maroon cape, his long, blonde, plaited hair flowing from the nape of his neck over his costume.

'Please be seated, comrades,' said Dakhar indicating with his hand to the two dark leather padded seats in front of his desk. 'I've just received word of a distress signal from the prison farm on Planet Lokar.'

The two visitors, now seated, leaned in closer to Dakhar with worried expressions on their inquisitive faces.

'According to the transmission we received, there's been an accidental explosion which has destroyed the power source, leaving all on the planet isolated without sufficient food and water supplies. There's also fear of the prisoners escaping their cells, creating havoc and threatening the Sentinels' lives. They've requested immediate assistance to restore the power and quickly contain the situation.'

'Have any Sentinels been injured from the explosion or by unrestrained prisoners, sir?' asked Captain Nazhark.

'Yes, unfortunately. Several Tzuracians including the Base Commander have been seriously injured. I need both of you to act on this as a number one priority.' Dakhar's voice was serious and had a tone of urgency.

'Nazhark, you need to fuel an Advanced Destroyer II Class 10 Carrier, and load supplies of food and water for the journey there and back, as well as extra supplies for the personnel on the planet. Include a portable generator to replace the one that's been destroyed. Take a unit of fully armed Sentinels with you. Let me know when you're ready to leave, ideally within the next three hours.

'Admiral, I want your air base to remain on high alert with other spacecraft at the ready in case the need arises for back up. Keep me posted on your progress. You have your orders, gentlemen.'

Rising from their seats, the two visitors saluted, moved quickly out the door and hurried down the passageway, sharing reactions with animated gestures.

As soon as they left, Dakhar alerted the Senate, advising the arrangements he'd put in place and confirming he was waiting for word when the rescue team was ready to depart.

The incident triggered Dakhar's memories of the events which had occurred just over six years ago when the Treldarians and their allies failed in an attempt to defeat the Tzuracians and the Terranians. It had been an all-out war too close for comfort and the attack on Tzurac had almost succeeded in annihilating the Federation and allowing the enemy to take total control of rich Xytrinium deposits for their own selfish needs. Dakhar was all too aware that if the rebel armies had succeeded then, there would have been no peace in the Universe. Chaos would now reign and there would be terror and fear throughout the known planets.

Almost three hours passed before Dakhar was suddenly snapped out of his thoughts by the buzzing of the handset on his desk. 'Dakhar!' he barked after tapping the illuminated incoming call button.

The screen on his desk displayed the caller. 'Admiral Okerahm, sir! We're set to go. Captain Nazhark is at the helm and is awaiting clearance.'

'Good. You have my permission to launch, Admiral. How long before Captain Nazhark reaches Lokar?'

'Approximately five days at full hyperdrive speed.'

'Right. Keep me posted, and may the Ancient spirits protect you. Dakhar out!'

* * *

Retiring for the day, General Dakhar returned home with heavy thoughts on his mind about the Red Alert. He was consumed with questions about the danger of the rescue mission. *Five days was a long time for Sentinel guards to survive without power to the prison base. Would their supplies last? What if there'd been a prison break and his Sentinels had been captured, or even killed?*

He was also aware that General Vark's son, Tykran, would be harbouring hateful thoughts to avenge his father's execution. He recalled the last words Tykran had shouted as he was marched from his cell with the other Treldarian prisoners to the awaiting transport ship bound for Lokar. The threat echoed in Dakhar's mind like a blood-curdling death curse, *'You'll all regret what you've done to my father! I'll have my revenge on the Senate and the Sentinels who serve them. You'll wish you had executed me while you had the chance!'*

Although he knew the death penalty for General Vark and General Rokan had been severe, and Tykran Vark was furious about it, Dakhar was confident it had been justified. The Tzuracian Senate had decided this drastic measure would set an example for those who considered conspiring against the Federation in the future to disrupt the peace.

It was nightfall when Dakhar arrived at the magnificent mansion bequeathed to him by his father. It was situated on a crest overlooking several acres of lush green pastures and scattered clumps of thick forest. His domesticated herds freely roamed beside the slow-winding river which ran through the middle of his property. The stone heritage building was illuminated by numerous surrounding bright security lights. Shadows cast on the age-old sandstone structure, projected an image resembling a looming castle without the battlements and flying banners.

Dakhar put aside his concerns and alighted from his sleek and shiny, grey hover-vehicle, anxious to embrace his loving wife Tajhira and his two adorable children. As soon as he opened the thick, carved, wooden front door and before he had a chance to put down the items he was carrying, his two children came racing towards him down the wide, polished wooden staircase. 'Daddy! Daddy!' little Terrazah called out as she pounced and then clung to him with Kyrah right behind her.

'Hello, children,' he said greeting them with a broad smile, and patting them on their heads. They had grown so tall. Kyrah, now twelve, stood almost shoulder height to his father though he was still wearing his junior cadet uniform. Dakhar's young daughter, Terrazah, now six years old was waist high. They were excited their father was home to have their family dinner gathered around the table.

'Hi, Ehrane,' Tajhira called from the kitchen. 'Dinner won't be too long.'

'Thanks.' Dakhar turned to his children. 'Why don't you two help your mother set the table while I change. I'll be back in a minute.'

As he changed for dinner, Dakhar thought how good the move to return to Tzurac had been. *Over the last six years living on Terra Major Tajhira had increasingly grown homesick for Tzurac. She wanted to see her family and Tzuracian friends again after a long separation and have their daughter Terrazah, named in honour of her second home on Terra Major, meet all of her relatives. She seemed settled back on Tzurac.*

He smiled widely as he returned to his family in the dining room. Tajhira was a beautiful, royal Urgellan with wispy flaxen hair, violet eyes and a slender body. Kyrah had been blessed with his mother's looks including the violet eyes and his younger sister was blue eyed with blonde hair. And the meal Tajhira had prepared using recipes handed down from her mother was tasty as always. Although Ehrane had been raised on Tzuracian meals, he'd developed a real palate for Urgellan cooking. *How lucky am I*, he thought.

During the meal Ehrane asked the children what they'd been learning during the day. Kyrah was bubbling over with enthusiasm, but his sister was more withdrawn. 'What's wrong, Terrazah? You seem worried about something?' her father asked.

With her teary, blue eyes, she spoke about how her teacher was always asking her for the answers to questions instead of asking the other students.

'Were you able to answer the questions correctly?' enquired Tajhira, cutting in.

'Yes, I always get the answers correct.'

Dakhar cleared his throat. 'Then perhaps she asks you because you set a very good example for the other pupils by studying your subjects and completing all your homework on time. I'm sure your teacher is very proud of you, just as your mother and I am. Tell you what, I'll go to see your teacher and ask what's happening. How does that sound?'

'That would be great, Daddy,' said his daughter, now smiling. 'Thanks.'

After the table was cleared and the children were tucked in for the evening, Ehrane and Tajhira retired to the comfortable lounge chairs to relax with a glass of wine.

'Is something bothering you?' said Tajhira in a concerned voice, noticing her husband's worried frown.

'What makes you think so, my darling?'

'I can tell when you have something on your mind.'

'Is this your Urgellan psychic sense reading me or the intuitive mind of a female?'

'Both.'

'And I thought as a trained Sentinel I could hide my thoughts.'

'Maybe from your enemies, but definitely not from your wife.'

'Okay! I surrender.' Dakhar paused and took a deep breath. 'There was a Red Alert at the Citadel today.'

Tajhira raised her eyebrows and placed a hand over her mouth waiting to hear the worst.

Ehrane continued. 'At this stage there's no danger to Tzurac, but we're all remaining vigilant. There was an explosion in the compound on the prison planet Lokar and I've dispatched a rescue ship with a unit of Sentinels.'

'So why are you so concerned, my love?'

'Because amongst those prisoners is General Vark's son, Lieutenant Tykran Vark. He threatened to avenge the execution of his father if he ever escaped. I'm hoping all the prisoners are contained and it's only a case of attending to the injured, dropping off supplies and repairing or replacing the generator. But we won't know the status until the ship reaches the planet in five days' time.'

Tajhira and Ehrane exchanged a knowing glance. For Tajhira, this was the downside of being married to the Commanding Chief of Military Operations for the Northern Quadrant.

SEIZURE BY DECEPTION

ENTERING the Pandark Star System after five days travel at hyperspeed, the rescue ship *Piken* reduced its speed to Level 1 and cruised with caution in orbit above the Planet Lokar. The spacecraft had arrived during the day and the planet's barren landscape was clearly visible on the screen.

'Officer Marzhan, open the communication channel to Lokar's Sentinel Headquarters,' ordered Captain Nazhark, 'and put me on visual.'

'Aye, Captain.' With a quick stab on the console the large screen at the front of the bridge snapped to life exhibiting the Control Room in the Sentinel Headquarters. 'Go ahead, sir.'

Sitting at the desk in the Control Room was a Sentinel whose face exuded tiredness and stress. His eyes twitched nervously as he manipulated the controls on his console. The room appeared empty but hidden out of view Captain Tykran Vark and Sergeant Krag were present, their laser weapons trained on Corporal Grydah.

'Ahoy, Sentinel. This is Captain Nazhark, Commander of the Tzuracian rescue ship *Piken*, requesting permission to land at your base. May I speak with your Base Commander, Captain Rhumark?'

Vark raised his laser pistol higher, pointing it directly at the Sentinel Corporal's head with the intention of blasting the weapon if the Corporal made any wrong move or said anything that would arouse suspicion.

'Ahoy, Commander,' the Corporal said, putting on a brave face and steadying his voice. 'This is Corporal Grydah. Thanks for responding so quickly to our urgent request for help, sir. My Commander sends his apologies. He's still in sick bay recovering from serious injuries, but he's given permission for your craft to dock in the vacant hangar, which is illuminated near the large cell block in the eastern corner of the complex. We'll have a unit standing by to escort you and your crew to our Headquarters.'

'Thank you, Corporal, descending now. Out!'

As the ship began its slow descent, Captain Nazhark's screen on the main bridge, depicted billowing black smoke rising from one of the main buildings.

The ship's PA system suddenly came to life. 'Attention Sentinels and medical crew,' the Commander's voice resounded. 'Gather your equipment and weapons and be prepared for any unexpected events as we still don't know whether there've been any prisoner breakouts. All the prisoners have been injected with a serum reversing the effects of the Xytrinium enhancements, so they should be non-aggressive and depleted of super strength. But stay alert just in case. We're here to attend to the injured, replenish the food supplies and restore power. The sooner we achieve this, the sooner we can leave. Out!'

The *Piken* descended slowly through the open cavity of the flood-lit hangar, landing gently with its four extended, stabilising shafts on the hard-surfaced floor. As the engines powered down, the thick, sliding hatch doors at the side of the craft opened, expelling a noticeable rush of pneumatic decompressed air.

No sooner had the automatic set of metal stairs unfolded to the ground, than the unit of twenty fully armed and helmeted Sentinels in maroon and blue uniforms disembarked. They immediately lined up in a precision two-line formation facing each other either side of the landing, laser rifles at the ready. Commander Nazhark followed and half-a-dozen medical staff and technicians carrying equipment and small metal cases of various sizes and shapes brought up the rear.

Now assembled and all on alert, Commander Nazhark soon spotted a welcome party approaching from a large sliding door at the end of the hangar. But Nazhark and his entourage were unaware those approaching were escaped prisoners disguised as Sentinels, and they had no idea they were being surrounded by another forty of Tykran's disguised Treldarian soldiers with laser guns drawn and pointed at the Commander's assembled unit.

The welcome party met the arrivals face-to-face without detection before the leader, Tykran Vark, acted. 'Don't make any sudden moves, Commander!' he yelled in an accented Tzuracian voice, while removing his helmet to expose his long, faded-black hair. 'Or my soldiers will open fire!'

Nazhark immediately recognised the Treldarian face of General Vark's son, and instinctively reached for the laser pistol at his right side. But before he could release the weapon from its holster, one of Tykran's soldiers fired his weapon, badly searing the Commander's right shoulder. Nazhark silently slumped to the ground, semi-conscious but still breathing.

It was futile to resist. When the two lines of Nukwar's Sentinels dropped their laser rifles and raised their arms, the entourage followed. They dropped what they were carrying and raised their arms above their heads in surrender.

'Collect their weapons and their Sentinel Pledge rings,' Tykran ordered his soldiers. 'And two of you pick up the Commander!'

Judging by the serious contortions on his face, Nazhark was obviously in excruciating pain. But Tykran demanded answers. 'Who else is onboard, Commander?'

'I don't answer to convicts,' Nazhark responded defiantly.

Tykran raised his laser pistol and pointed it at one of the Sentinel guards. 'You may not value *your* life, but I'm sure you wouldn't want to see your soldiers die one at a time as you refuse each of my questions!'

'There are two pilots at the helm,' the Commander answered quickly.

'And are there more rescue ships on the way?'

Nazhark was alert, mentally numbing his pain the way Sentinels are trained to do in a crisis. He decided to bluff his captor, stalling for more time. 'Yes. Control intended despatching the Security Forces within 24 hours after we departed Tzurac to make sure the Treldarian prisoners hadn't escaped their containment.'

Tykran had spent enough time imprisoned on Tzurac awaiting his fate to know that the Tzuracians follow strict protocol and leave nothing to chance. He would need to vacate this hellhole as soon as possible to get a head start on the pursuing Tzuracian Security Forces known as the TSF.

'Then call your pilots out to join your unit, Commander!' ordered Tykran.

The pilots inside the ship heard Tykran's order and the higher-ranking pilot looked at her co-pilot and whispered urgently. 'We must remove our Pledge rings and stow them in the hidden compartment under the seats in case they do a body search. Hide your enhancements and don't let them know we're Sentinels. The less they know about us the more chance we have of surviving.

We look like Tzuracian fleet pilots in our navy blue uniforms, and we'll act just like that. Okay?'

The co-pilot nodded and quickly did as ordered.

On Nazhark's order, both pilots emerged from the craft. Tykran and his soldiers looked in awe at what they saw – two beautiful, young, blonde-haired Tzuracian females in tight-fitting, dark-blue fleet uniforms that outlined their slender and curved bodies. Their laser weapons were drawn and aimed at Tykran, but they hesitated when confronted with a sea of armed Treldarians dressed in Sentinel uniform.

'Drop your weapons unless you and your Commander want to die,' Tykran yelled loudly.

When mumbles of lust sprang from the surrounding Treldarians who'd been deprived of female company since their imprisonment six years ago, he added, 'And quiet, men!' The soldiers ceased their mumblings, their penetrating eyes still fixed firmly on the two attractive pilots.

The two females had no choice but to bow down and drop their weapons knowing that Treldarians usually shoot first and ask questions later.

'What are your ranks and names?' commanded Tykran while pointing his laser pistol within arm's length at the head of the senior pilot who was the taller of the two and the one showing more attitude.

Unshaken, and with a resentful expression on her porcelain face, the senior officer spoke abruptly. 'I'm Captain Jharryn and this is my co-pilot Sub-lieutenant Rhamak. You're making a grave mistake!'

'Well, I'm Captain Tykran Vark and the only mistake I'm making is keeping you two alive. You'll be flying me and my soldiers off this hellhole just as soon as we've locked Nazhark and his unit safely away.'

He turned to his Sergeant. 'Collect their weapons and shackle their wrists. I'll escort them back to the Control Centre. Lock the rest of the rescue unit in the cells and meet me back there. Make haste, Sergeant. We don't have much time!'

'Aye, sir,' Krag replied as he saluted. He turned to his soldiers and in a raised voice, gave the order. 'Right, you lot. You heard the captain. Now move!'

MANKRO REVISITED

SIX years had passed since the exiled Tzuracian Sentinel, Yarron Blandhar and his Treldarian partner, Bhalar Rokan, settled together on Bhalar's home planet, Mankro. Mankro was one of the three moons of the dead planet Dunkor, located in the Clavistoq Star System, Southern Quadrant. The friendly Treldarian community on Mankro had fully embraced Yarron, who had initially come to their planet in disguise as Armel from Planet Urgellan, after he liberated them from their enslavement by Bhalar's ruthless father, General Rokan of the Third Treldarian Legion.

Bhalar explained to her people that Yarron had disguised himself as an Urgellan soldier in order to uncover what her father and his soldiers were intending. And, as Bhalar predicted, Yarron was even more appreciated when he informed the villagers he was a Tzuracian Sentinel, although now honourably discharged from their army. The Tzuracians were archenemies of the Treldarian military, but the Treldarian civilians themselves were a peaceful and amiable race, and not warmongers. They welcomed Yarron knowing if they ever got into trouble again, Yarron could potentially call upon the Tzuracians for assistance.

As bequeathed by law, Bhalar had inherited her father's house and she with Yarron, who now looked more like a Tzuracian Sentinel with his long, blonde, pony-tailed hair, moved in without any protests from the villagers. They made a handsome couple and Bhalar was still beautiful with silken tanned skin, shiny black hair, and dark piercing eyes. Their first priority was to remove all remnants of her father's existence. Bhalar wanted no reminders of her horrible, suffering past.

With Sentinel blood, Yarron was determined to train the peaceful villagers to become fighters in the event of any future invasions by unwanted intruders. And Bhalar wanted to be involved. So, together, they trained the males and females in hand-to-hand combat, and in weaponry including the use of swords and daggers, as well as in survival tactics.

Yarron established fortifications and sentry posts around the complex, arming them with warning devices gleaned from the scraps of wreckage previously salvaged by Bhalar. The power source used to operate this equipment was the stored Xytrinium left over from when General Vark's Second Legion supplied volatile crystal to fuel General Rokan's spacecrafts for the long voyage to attack Terra Major.

Yarron wanted to advance the community's primitive ways of living and Bhalar agreed with his long-range plan. In his first year on Mankro, Yarron negotiated with the Tzuracian Elders to have their scientists and engineers construct power generators to supply both Xytrinium power and hydroelectricity to the village and to introduce agricultural techniques and animal husbandry. Yarron also established a formal council, comprising Bhalar and six elders to administer and oversee the development of these remarkable changes.

Knowing the remaining stocks of Xytrinium would soon be depleted, Yarron was desperate to find more of this valuable resource, whether on Mankro or on the other moons of Dunkor. He'd learned of the past that when the universe was created, most planets contained Xytrinium deposits. Yarron wanted to learn more about his new home and to discover the rest of this moon. And Bhalar, who had been confined for all of her life within the village walls, wanted to join him. So, they decided to explore the vast terrain of Mankro together and look for any signs of the valuable blue crystal.

It was the beginning of his second year on Mankro when, much to their surprise, Bhalar broke the exciting news that she was pregnant. Yarron had always wanted children, but assumed Bhalar being Treldarian, could not bear offspring with him due to their DNA incompatibility. He loved her deeply and had been willing to forfeit that gift.

'That's impossible but incredible!' he exclaimed, jumping for joy, picking up Bhalar and dancing her around the room. 'I was told Tzuracians and Treldarians were unable to conceive. And yet, here's a miracle.'

'I'm just as surprised and delighted as you are, Yarron. Maybe when I was infused with the Xytrinium, it changed the reproductive biology allowing Tzuracians and Treldarians to mate and conceive?'

'If that's the case, I'm overwhelmed and overjoyed,' Yarron said with a huge grin.

Eight months later, after a lot of wondering what this unique union would bring, twins arrived – a boy and a girl. Both of the tiny babies were perfectly formed. The boy had the features of a Tzuracian with blonde hair and blue eyes, while the girl looked very much like a Treldarian with jet-black hair and deep, dark eyes. Yarron was there for the delivery and was emotionally overcome with the joyous event. Bhalar, much exhausted after the delivery, cuddled a baby under each arm, looking very proud, while Yarron held his beloved partner with his arm around all of them, smiling.

'Have you decided on the names for our beautiful babies?' he asked.

She gushed with joy. 'I'd like to name our baby girl Jelkah, after my wonderful stepmother. She would have loved to see our babies.'

'That's a beautiful name and a great tribute to her memory. I think I'd like to name our baby son Zentar, which means great warrior. What do you think?'

Yarron's exploring had been put on hold for the next two years while he supported Bhalar with their new family and helped the villagers with their community farming activities and their ongoing self-defence training. Yarron taught the males and the females as well as their children the skills of staff combat using long sticks carved from the hardwood of the forest trees. Then they advanced to sword techniques using the blades stored in the small armoury left by Bhalar's tyrant father and the sleazy Captain Chekhmar, the officer who'd once been in charge of the Treldarian soldiers. And, during the times in between weapon training and farm chores, Yarron instructed the villagers in hand-to-hand combat. Eventually, after two years of training, Yarron believed they were proficient to defend the village against enemy soldiers.

By this time, the twins were two years of age and old enough to be minded on occasional days by the family's close female friend, Grenham, also a young mother, who helped with their education. Military training for the twins would not start until they reached the age of five. On the days Jelkah and Zentar were being cared for, Yarron and Bhalar continued their explorations, still searching for signs of Xytrinium.

Mankro was smaller than the planet Tzurac, in fact only about half the size, but quite dynamic in its geographic landscapes.

Rotating on its own axis Mankro had a gravity similar to Tzurac as well as similar landforms and geographical structures. The weather conditions created dense forests, long deep rivers, high mountain ranges and moderate seasonal temperatures. The seasonal changes were created by the rotational plane of the dead planet Dunkor. However, to the far north and deep south, the cooler temperatures produced polar caps and snow-covered peaks, making these areas almost inhabitable.

In the fourth year of their exploratory excursions, Yarron and Bhalar came across an ancient, deserted city amongst thick forest trees on the far side of the moon. At least fifty buildings – some two and three stories high, others low-lying – constructed of crumbling stone walls, were partially engulfed by thick, twisted vines and blue-green moss which grew rapidly on both sides of the walls.

Several of these ancient buildings still had heavy, black wooden doors that were now rotting and hanging loosely from red-rusted metal hinges and, what looked like thatched roofs that had caved onto the dirt floors long ago. Over centuries, the jungle had eventually reclaimed its own and the animals had made use of the sanctuary by building nests on the grounds and in the corners of the high walls.

When they ventured inside the ruins, Yarron and Bhalar found it hard to breathe in the dank atmosphere caused by rotting undergrowth and tropical heat. The overhead sun streaking through the forest canopy allowed enough natural scattered light to illuminate the interior walls. Strange symbols, like some form of primitive writing, were carved into some of the walls to tell stories. And there were colourful painted drawings of figures in fighting positions holding ancient weapons like bows and arrows and spears. Others stood holding swords and pistols and wearing helmets and armour.

Bhalar jumped back in fright with a gasp when she examined the paintings. Thinking she'd been attacked by one of the strange jungle creatures nesting in the room, Yarron ran to her aid, rapidly drawing his short-staff and turning it into a two-bladed sword.

'What's wrong?' he cried out, his eyes darting in all directions. Bhalar said nothing but pointed at the wall with a shocked expression on her face. He could see for himself what had caused her to react. The armoured figures in the wall paintings had symbols of bright red scorpions emblazoned on their black chest plates. 'Treldarians!' he exclaimed aloud.

'Treldarians,' repeated Bhalar quietly. Both stood dumbfounded for some time before Bhalar broke the silence. 'They must have attacked the natives who lived on this planet! But for what reason?'

Yarron didn't answer straight away but contemplated in wonder while slowly stroking his thick beard with his left hand. Then he turned his sword back into his short-staff and began to follow the continued pattern along the wall using the light on the tip of his staff to illuminate it. Bhalar followed behind, clenching her now-unholstered laser pistol also closely examining the coloured etchings. The intricate drawings depicted what appeared to be a long battle showing figures, mainly natives, lying on the ground with dark red ochre pouring from their bodies.

Suddenly, Yarron stopped in his tracks and pointed to the wall for Bhalar to see. They both stared in awe. What they saw was a shape the size of a small fist, sculptured like a cut diamond. It was multi-faceted and dark blue with long spears of white paint shooting out from it. Yarron and Bhalar instantly reached the same conclusion – the blue diamond shape was Xytrinium, and the battle had been fought with the natives over this valuable prize.

'Did your father know about this?' Yarron asked.

'If he did, he didn't tell me or any of the villagers anything about it. Otherwise, we wouldn't have lived in such a primitive way, burning oil lamps and lighting wood fires to cook.'

'Well,' said Yarron excitedly, 'we now know this planet has deposits of Xytrinium. The problem is, where's the mine?'

Bhalar thought for a moment. 'I'd say the artist who painted this story was the last survivor. The native may have left more clues on the wall.'

'Or not,' said Yarron. 'If the natives fought and died to prevent their invaders from possessing the Xytrinium, I'm sure they wouldn't give them a map to easily locate where the mine was.'

'Yes, you're right. So, what's the plan for finding the mine in a thick jungle like this on such a very large land mass? It would take years to look for it!'

Yarron smiled at Bhalar, his eyes sparkling while gently nodding his head with raised eyebrows. 'I have a plan that would locate the mine within days. But you may not like it …'

'I'm listening,' she said, folding her arms across her chest in mild defiance, eyes fixed rigidly on Yarron.

'My people have scientific equipment which can detect deposits of buried Xytrinium to a depth of one thousand metres. All things created have a unique specific vibration or energy wave, a frequency. Our Tzuracian scientists have defined the frequency of Xytrinium and all they have to do is send out the dedicated signal while flying low and slow over the landscape. If the signal strikes a Xytrinium deposit, its signal bounces back to the machine in the craft.'

'Would your people be willing to help us find the Xytrinium? And, if they did, what would they want in return?'

'I believe they would help us in return for a very small percentage of the mined Xytrinium. And they'd let us use their special excavation machinery to carefully extract the volatile crystal. Hopefully, over time, they'd show us how to use this precious substance for medical treatments, farming implements and vehicles both for use on the land and for spacecrafts. This would ensure a future for the people of Mankro.'

After listening intently to him, Bhalar folded her arms tightly across her chest. 'I suppose the Tzuracians would want my people to join the Federation of Planets!' she said in a mildly defiant manner. 'We would again be suppressed, this time under Tzuracian law. We would lose our newfound freedom and independence, going from one tyrant to the next! I speak for my people and I believe we would rather live without this precious crystal in spite of all it could do to change our primitive way of life. We just want to live a quiet, peaceful life without any interference!'

'Okay, okay,' cried Yarron, raising his arms in protest. 'I understand where you're coming from, and I completely agree. First of all, I don't think they'd ask us to join the Federation seeing as they excommunicated me from their army of Sentinels. Second, the Treldarians living on Mankro would not be accepted by the Tzuracian Senate. It would cause too much uneasiness amongst the other planetary members given the havoc and devastation Treldarian armies caused in the past. And third, we don't have the equipment and know-how to retrieve the Xytrinium ourselves, and we need it to power our spacecraft, our new heating, lighting and cooking as well as our refrigeration. We've come to rely on Xytrinium as our power source, and I don't think the villagers would want to return back to their primitive ways when the remaining stores of the crystal are used up.'

'Then,' exclaimed Bhalar, 'I suggest we consult with our new Council and put it to the vote.'

After returning to the village, Bhalar called the council together to inform them of their findings and the issues she and

Yarron had discussed at the old ruins. As Yarron predicted, the Council were in favour of contacting the Tzuracians to help find and mine the volatile blue crystal, but with conditions. The Tzuracians would receive no more than a twenty-five percent share of the mined crystal each year and Mankro would remain independent, not to be administered by the Tzuracians and their Sentinels. Finally, the Tzuracians would assist the villagers in implementing medical equipment and developing farm machinery powered with Xytrinium.

Within days of the unanimous decision, Yarron activated his Sentinel Pledge ring and made holographic contact with General Ehrane Dakhar. He hadn't spoken with the General since his banishment from Tzurac four years earlier and he feared the Tzuracians, though perhaps not Dakhar, still had mixed feelings about him.

To most Tzuracians, Yarron was a traitor and a fugitive who had breached his Sentinel Code of Honour. In the past he had become infatuated with the beautiful, female Sentinel prisoner Khaneera Zarkwin he'd been guarding, and she had persuaded him to steal the Xytrinium infusion formula, a secret which had been highly guarded for centuries. In helping her escape Tzurac with the formula, he had allowed Tzurac's enemies to acquire the same super abilities as the Sentinels and fight them on more equal terms.

He would have been executed for the crimes he committed, if it had not been for the fact he later redeemed himself. Realising his unforgivable mistake in time, he was secretly able to relay information about an impending, massive invasion planned for Tzurac and Terra Major by the enhanced Treldarians and their rebel forces, and by doing so, help the Tzuracians win the war. During the battle on Terra Major, Yarron also helped save the life of Dakhar's Sentinel Lieutenant and close friend, Kyron Tyros, by acting as a human shield, and saved the capital city of Washington from destruction.

There was a mutual respect between Dakhar and Yarron, although many Sentinels still mistrusted Yarron and he'd been exiled from Tzurac for his own safety.

Dakhar was surprised but curious when Yarron's hologram suddenly appeared in civilian attire and he spoke in a strong and disciplined tone. 'Why have you contacted me after all these years in exile? I let you keep your Sentinel Pledge ring to enable *us* to contact *you* if we needed to call on your assistance. So, I assume you have a very good reason for this visit!'

'Yes, sir, I have. Recently, while exploring Mankro, Bhalar and I discovered evidence there is a Xytrinium deposit buried somewhere here. We don't have the expertise or the equipment to find and mine it. Would you consider helping us by sending some Tzuracian engineers and scientists with the necessary equipment?' Yarron continued to pass on what the Treldarian Council had proposed in return, and the suggested terms of this arrangement.

Dakhar responded, this time in a more lenient tone. 'Thank you for approaching me with this good news. We're always on the lookout for new deposits. I'll inform the Council of Elders straight away of your news and your proposal, and I'll let you know the outcome.'

'The Senate or Council of Elders!' Yarron complained in a bitter tone. 'I contacted you because they were the ones who sentenced me to be executed. They didn't rescind their decision until you and Kyron came to my defence by giving evidence of my efforts to save Tzurac and Terra Major. I hope they can see past this.'

'I understand your concerns and will do my best to convince them. Until then, I bid you farewell.'

Pressing his Pledge ring, Dakhar watched Yarron's pale-blue holographic image fade away.

TASTE OF FREEDOM

CORPORAL Grydah was the last of the Sentinel guards on Lokar not yet locked up. He was still sitting slumped over the main console under the guard of two Treldarian soldiers when Tykran burst through the doors of the Control Room, laser pistol in hand. Sergeant Krag and his Treldarian soldiers trailed behind Tykran with the two Sentinel pilots. The pilots' wrists were cuffed and two of Tykran's soldiers were holding the two females firmly and tightly by the arms.

'Right, Corporal, I have another job for you!' shouted Tykran who was now standing beside the Corporal and looking very serious. He shook the Corporal roughly and pointed his pistol at the Corporal's head.

Corporal Grydah roused immediately, turned his head around and looked nervously into Tykran's eyes. He wondered what this Captain had in mind.

'No need to fear for your life, Corporal, unless you do the wrong thing.' Tykran twirled his laser pistol several times for effect, showing who was in command. 'I want you to send a transmission to the Tzurac Control Centre using these words.'

Corporal Grydah turned slowly back to the console and began pressing buttons with slightly trembling hands, to start sending the transmission. He was taking no chances with Tykran observing his every movement. 'Communications opened and ready to start transmitting your message, sir.'

'Here's the message,' said Tykran deep in thought, carefully choosing his words so as not to arouse any suspicion on the part of the Tzuracians when they received it. 'Rescue ship has arrived. Prisoners still locked up with no escapes. Injured being attended to. Captain Rhumark needs medical attention back on Tzurac. Generator needs replacing. Will take two days. Will depart Planet Lokar in two days' time. End.'

As Corporal Grydah finished entering the message he turned to look at Tykran awaiting further instructions.

'Transmit the message now!' ordered Tykran.

Without hesitation, the Corporal hit the glowing red 'SEND' button and the light turned green. 'Message sent, sir.'

'Good. You've saved your soul and you can now join the others.' Tykran turned to Krag. 'Sergeant, have your soldiers escort Corporal Grydah to the cells and then report back here.'

As Sergeant Krag vacated the room with his captive and two of his soldiers, Tykran ordered his remaining soldiers to bring the two pilots over to where he was standing and to seat them in the chairs at the console. Captain Jharryn and Sub-Lieutenant Rhamak defiantly shrugged off the soldiers' firm grips, Jharryn elbowing in the stomach the one who had been restraining her, causing him to yelp and double over with great pain. As the two pilots paced over to the console chairs and slumped into them, Tykran grinned at Jharryn's defiance.

'Now,' said Tykran, his eyes darting back and forth between their faces, 'I have a proposition for you, which involves a choice.'

Jharryn and Rhamak stared poker-faced, showing no emotions, waiting silently in anticipation.

'First of all,' Tykran said in a soft, mellow voice, leaning closer and glaring into their faces as if there was no-one else in the room, 'I'd like to know what your first names are?'

'Why do you need to know that?' asked Jharryn adamantly.

Tykran smiled sarcastically. 'Because Captain, if we're to travel very long distances together in a confined spacecraft, it would be nice to communicate on a first name basis.'

'Why would *we* want to travel with convicts like *you* on a long voyage?' Jharryn cursed.

'Well, here's where my proposition and your choice come in,' he said, waving his pistol from one to the other, before glaring at Captain Jharryn. 'Either you pilot this Advanced Class 10 Destroyer …' He paused momentarily for effect. '… or I'll shoot the Sub-Lieutenant in the leg. And if you still refuse, I'll shoot her in the arm. Then I might give her to my soldiers to play with and let you watch. And then, I might start on you. What do think about that? You have ten seconds to make up your mind!'

Jharryn replied coldly without hesitation. 'My name is Kharmyne and she is Sharne.'

'Very sensible answer – a decision which will benefit both of us.' Tykran lowered his pistol to his side and stood upright. 'You'll live while I hold you two hostage as a bargaining chip, and you'll pilot my soldiers and me to my chosen destination.'

'And where will we be going?' asked Jharryn in a more indignant tone.

'I'll instruct you once we're all onboard and the homing device on the Advanced Destroyer has been permanently disconnected.'

Just as he finished speaking, Sergeant Krag burst through the doors with his soldiers. 'All secured and locked down, sir,' he blurted, saluting his captain.

'Thank you, Sergeant. Now I want you to round up everyone and have the soldiers change into Tzuracian uniforms taken from the Sentinel guards as a precautionary strategy in case we encounter any Tzuracian patrols on our travels.' He pointed to the pilots. 'And keep these two under close guard. I'll explain why in due course. On your way out, have some of your soldiers incinerate the whole Control Room to prevent the Tzuracian Sentinels sending a distress signal to Tzurac, or to anyone else for that matter.'

'Aye, aye, Captain.' Krag was enjoying the action and was excited by the new venture.

* * *

It was nightfall by the time all the Treldarian soldiers and the Sentinel pilots were aboard. Tykran commanded Captain Jharryn to permanently dismantle the homing device, threatening her again with his laser pistol and reminding her of the consequences if she tried anything stupid. Fearing the consequences, she complied reluctantly with his demands.

'Sergeant!' Tykran called from the cockpit. 'Give the soldiers something to eat from the stores in the pantry – it should be well stocked on this rescue ship. But limit rations as we have a long journey ahead of us and we can't predict the unknown. And also ration the alcohol. We need to maintain discipline on this craft and not have a drunken rabble onboard. We're not out of danger yet. Then get them seated until we blast off. But before you go, escort Sub-Lieutenant Rhamak to one of the sleeping quarters with a lock on it.' He smiled smugly at Rhamak, saying, 'If she's wise, she'll get some sleep.'

'Aye, Captain,' Krag said, saluting again.

Sitting in the co-pilot's seat, Tykran could see all the controls clearly and keep a watchful eye on his Tzuracian pilot. 'Now, Kharmyne, I want you to set the co-ordinates for Mankro.'

'You can address me as Captain, out of respect for my rank!' Jharryn said in a stern voice with a severe look on her face.

Tykran smirked. 'Alright, *Captain*, if that's your wish.' He was quite surprised by her attitude and admired her brashness. She was very different from the more pliant and docile Ludaxian women back on his own planet, Orkharn. There the women had mild temperaments.

'Thank you. I've never heard of this planet Mankro. Where the hell is it?'

'It's not a planet. It's one of the moons orbiting the Planet Dunkor in the Clavistoq Star System, Southern Quadrant.'

'Then, lucky I've heard of the Clavistoq Star System.'

Jharryn rapidly punched several switches on the console and a small hologram of a galaxy suddenly appeared before their eyes. It showed a swirling, luminescent nebula of coloured hues, streaked in greens, blues and violet. Hitting the console switches again with her right hand, the hologram magnified a hundred times in size showing a sun with a large red planet circling it. The planet was surrounded by three moons of assorted sizes and colours.

Tykran pointed to each of the masses in turn. 'This large red planet is Dunkor. It's a dead planet with no atmosphere. This sand-coloured moon is Ancrod, inhabited by savages. This pale green one is Nujhar, populated with a slightly more advanced race of green-skinned natives. And this pastel blue-green moon is Mankro, until recently ruled by the Treldarian Third Legion.'

'What beautiful colours,' Jharryn said, fascinated temporarily and watching with awe.

'Alright, Captain. Chart a course and give me an estimate now of how long it will take to get us there.'

Jharryn rapidly pressed her nimble fingers on several switches across the console which illuminated them in bright green. Within seconds the coordinates flashed onto the screen above the console showing a list of coded numbers with degrees assigned to each string of numbers. After silently reading and processing the results, Jharryn turned to Tykran. 'The distance to Mankro is approximately one hundred and fifty light years. Cruising at Level ten hyperdrive speed, we should be there within four to five days.'

'Excellent! Thank you, Captain. But do we have enough Xytrinium in reserve for the trip?'

'Just enough, if we don't take any detours or use the shields.'

'Great!' exclaimed Tykran in a burst of excitement, raising his arms with clenched fists in the air. 'Engage the engines and let's get off this shitty rock. You and Sub-Lieutenant Rhamak will alternate shifts. And one of my soldiers will always sit in the co-pilot's seat to make sure you stay on course and send no transmissions unless directed.' He looked at her provocatively. 'Not that I don't trust you personally, Captain Jharryn – I just don't trust Tzuracians.'

Jharryn sneered.

As soon as Krag returned, Tykran yelled loudly in Treldarian to him. 'Come up to the cockpit and bring one of the soldiers who knows about spacecraft navigation!'

Three minutes later, Krag was at the cockpit entry with another soldier. 'This is Corporal Heltz, sir. He used to pilot our Scorpion fighters and he has a good understanding of aerodynamics and navigation.'

'Alright, Corporal, I want you to sit in the co-pilot's seat and closely monitor everything Pilot Jharryn does. Make sure she doesn't deviate from the coordinates to the Clavistoq Star System.'

'Yes, sir,' the Corporal responded, saluting by wrapping his right arm across his chest.

'And you, Kharmyne or should I say, Captain Jharryn. If you try any tricks your partner Rhamak will be the first to suffer the consequences! Do I make myself clear?'

Jharryn swivelled her head and responded harshly with a fierce look on her face. 'Yes Captain Vark, very clear.'

'Sergeant, follow me.'

Krag followed Tykran to one of the empty cabins at the back of the craft, where Tykran closed the door for privacy.

'Now, Sergeant, I suppose you have some questions for me regarding our voyage to the Clavistoq Star System?'

Sergeant Krag had formed a very close friendship with his captain and thought he knew him well enough to predict his moves. But he *was* surprised that Tykran had chosen to travel to the Southern Quadrant when their own planet Orkharn was in the Eastern Quadrant, and closer. 'Yes, sir, I do. Why are we going to this star system instead of heading home? Why are we wasting time and fuel?'

'First of all, it's only a matter of time before the locked-up Sentinels break free from their cells and notify Tzurac we've escaped in their rescue ship. Or before the Sentinels on Tzurac figure out something's gone wrong. When they do, the Tzuracians will assume we've headed straight for Orkharn and focus their hunt for us in the Eastern Quadrant. They'll assume we'd exhaust our fuel if we were to travel anywhere else, so they'll send most of their patrols into that sector. We'll have at least a five-day advantage before they call a Red Alert.'

Krag nodded to confirm his Captain's logic.

'Remember, Sergeant, when we were preparing to attack Tzurac six years ago we stored a large supply of Xytrinium on Mankro. It was part of the Treldarian agreement with General Rokan as payment for his own use on his return from our expected victory. Well, as we were defeated and Rokan was executed, the

Xytrinium should still be there for us to retrieve and refuel this Destroyer.'

Krag nodded again.

'And I've also got a personal score to settle with that deceitful Sentinel, Yarron Blandhar.' Tykran's mood changed to anger, his face tightening and his eyes narrowing. '*He's* the one who divulged our strategic plan to the Tzuracians, foiling our surprise invasion of Tzurac and Terra Major. *He* was the cause of my father being captured and executed. And he now lives with General Rokan's daughter, Bhalar, on Mankro.'

The Sergeant's eyes opened wide in surprise. 'How do you know all this?'

Tykran clenched his right fist in anger. 'When we were captured and thrown into the holding cells on Tzurac General Rokan told me, just before he was executed. He said Yarron, disguised as an Urgellan under the fictitious name of Armel, infiltrated his army and secretly sent information about our proposed two-pronged attack to Tzurac on his Pledge ring. We could have defeated the Federation if they hadn't been warned in advance by that conniving snake.

'Yarron was exposed as a spy by General Rokan prior to launching our attack. But before they had a chance to torture and interrogate him, the General's daughter Bhalar helped him escape and left Mankro with him in his spacecraft. She betrayed the Treldarian army as well as her own father and I want revenge on her as well.'

Krag was impressed by his Captain's intel. 'And where are we going after we visit Mankro? To Orkharn?' He looked to Tykran for confirmation. *Surely it had to be home.*

But Tykran's response was a shock. 'Perhaps, Sergeant. But I have a few ideas I'm still working on and they involve gathering a major force to fight the Tzuracians and help me seek vengeance for the execution of my father. We may have to go beyond the Eastern Quadrant to find them.'

Krag wasn't persuaded. 'But, sir, we couldn't destroy the Tzuracians before with combined armies of Treldarians, Kyroni, Diunons and Nujharenes. Our force proved ineffective against the might of the Tzuracian forces and the robot Diutrons. What makes you think we can defeat them this time?'

Tykran stared directly into Krag's eyes and spoke firmly and confidently. 'Sergeant, last time our armies were divided with the aim of conquering both Terra Major and Tzurac. That was a strategic error on my father's part.'

He became angrier. 'The other weakness in my father's strategy was underestimating the use of those robotic Diutrons, which our enemy reprogrammed to turn against us.' He raised his clenched fist and with a determined look on his face declared, 'We'll not make the same mistakes as before and we *won't* fail this time.'

Realising his captain was now on a mission, Krag simply nodded. He could see Tykran's reasoning and was loyal to his leader though he still wondered where this major fighting force would come from.

'I'll keep you informed of my plans, Sergeant. But the first thing we have to do is stay clear of the Tzuracian patrols until we make it to Mankro. I want you to keep the soldiers on their toes, keep them training and in fit condition. Make sure their confiscated weapons are in top condition. This will keep them occupied for the journey. Understood, Sergeant?'

'Aye, aye, Captain!'

WANTED DEAD OR ALIVE

FIVE days had passed since General Ehrane Dakhar received the message from Planet Lokar informing him no prisoners had escaped and the rescue ship *Piken* would be leaving for Tzurac in two days' time after repairs to the generator were completed. He had rescinded the Red Alert on Tzurac and was sitting quite comfortably at his desk believing all was going according to plan and expecting the rescue ship to return soon.

He was taken by surprise when a hologram suddenly appeared before his eyes in the form of a Sentinel. It was Captain Nazhark wearing his right arm in a black sling.

'General Dakhar, sir,' said Nazhark as he gave a respectful salute with his left arm, 'I need to inform you what's happened on Lokar. The initial distress message requesting urgent help was sent as a trap, and my crew were ambushed on arrival here. Tykran Vark and the rest of the Treldarian prisoners seized the *Piken* after locking us up and taking our pilots hostage. It's taken us all this time to break free of the cells only to find all the communication equipment had been obliterated. They had confiscated our Sentinel Pledge rings, but we eventually found them hidden in the Control Room. They have a six-day head start, sir, and we don't know in which direction they're heading.'

Dakhar was shocked by the news, seriously concerned about his soldiers and horrified to learn that Tykran Vark was on the loose with his Treldarian followers in a Tzuracian Advanced Destroyer. 'Have any other Sentinels been injured or killed, Captain? And how did they manage to overpower you?'

'Unfortunately, they killed six of our guards, and injured several others, sir. The Treldarians have regained their super strength and enhancements. It's obvious the serum to reverse the Xytrinium powers was only temporary and it's worn off.'

Dakhar reeled in disbelief covering his eyes and his forehead with his right hand and cursing under his breath. Then he bowed his head and rubbed his forehead for several seconds to regain composure. When he raised his head, his face showed a sincere, sad expression for the loss of lives. 'Thank you for reporting the circumstances as soon as you were able to, Captain. I'm sad to hear about the loss of lives. Are you well enough yourself to travel back to Tzurac?'

'Yes, sir.'

'Good. I'll order another spacecraft immediately to rescue you and your crew and arrange to have cryo-tubes on board to bring back our lost soldiers for military funerals. Please send through the list of those who have passed away so I can let their families know of their untimely deaths. See what can be salvaged from the Control Room and report to me on your return to Tzurac. I'll take care of the hunt for Tykran Vark. Keep well and may the spirits of the Ancients protect you.'

Captain Nazhark saluted as Dakhar watched the image slowly fade.

Without hesitation Dakhar gave orders for another rescue ship to be sent at once to Lokar with a team of medical personnel and the required number of cryo-tubes. Then he arranged an urgent meeting with the Senate in order to inform them of the situation.

Within the hour the Council of Elders was assembled in the Senate Chambers, awaiting news from General Dakhar. The heritage building which housed the Senate Chambers was one of the oldest establishments in the capital, Khazor. It was also the largest building and very ornate with its solid, smooth stone blocks standing forty feet high and huge, carved, wooden double front entrance doors guarded by four thick, evenly spaced, round-raked, temple pillars. On top of the building was a spire clutching a royal red waving flag proudly displaying the Tzuracian emblem of a round, dark, shimmering metallic blue shield with a vertical gold sword in the middle. Although the structure looked slightly out of place amongst the surrounding modern towering glass and metal obelisks, it maintained an aura of justice, tradition and authority.

'Well, General Dakhar?' said Senator Ghalbrak, the most senior senator and highest authority amongst the ten members. Draped in a pure white robe matching his flowing white hair and long white beard, with aged lines etched into his wizened face, he exuded an aura of wisdom. Surrounding him were the other elderly senators in their distinguished crimson and purple robes all focused on the General. 'Why the urgency?'

Dakhar rose from his seat at the end of the long, solid white marble table, took a sip of water from the supplied goblet, and cleared his throat. He noted the serious expressions on all their faces as he informed them of the latest crisis. Momentarily, there was shocked silence, and they all looked at each other with deep concern.

Turning his head to face Dakhar and still calmly composed, Ghalbrak spoke on behalf of the senators. 'Well, as Commanding

Chief of Military Operations for the Northern Quadrant, what strategy do you propose, General Dakhar?'

'Senator, I have a number of recommendations to implement with the Council's approval. The first is to reinstate the Red Alert status and raise our protective dome over Khazor until further notice. No doubt Tykran Vark will have interrogated the captured pilots and discovered the arsenal he has on board the rescue ship contains Xytrinium war head torpedoes. And we're all aware of the devastation that was caused last time a Xytrinium warhead fell on our city ...'

There was an anxious murmur among the senators.

'The second recommendation is to mount a full-scale search and, if necessary, a search and destroy mission in the whole Eastern Quadrant with most of the Tzuracian Fleet. I suggest we keep in reserve a quantity of Advanced Destroyers Class 10 to guard the city and the Citadel in case Vark, having nothing to lose, mounts a suicide mission.

'Third, we should alert all the planets in the Federation and advise them to remain on full vigilance until further notice. If Vark is out for vengeance, there's no telling where or when he may strike. My thinking is the craft he's procured won't have enough fuel to reach his home planet Orkharn. So, he'll need to refuel. But we're unable to track the craft as Control Centre informs us he managed to disconnect the tracking device. I assume he forced our Tzuracian pilots to show him how. At this point we're in the dark.'

Raising his hand in a gesture to quieten mumblings among the senators, Ghalbrak turned to Dakhar. 'Thank you, General. Please be seated while the Council members deliberate on your proposed recommendations.'

Rising from their seated positions the senators filed into a small room on the far side of the hall and closed the heavy, dark wooden door behind them. All Dakhar could do was wait.

Emerging after twenty minutes or more, the senators returned to their respective seats awaiting Ghalbrak to present their decisions.

'General, the Councillors have unanimously agreed with most of your recommendations. However, we consider there's no need at this stage to raise the Red Alert or the protective dome over Khazor as the early warning systems we have in place hidden on our moons will immediately activate any threat of incoming missiles or enemy spacecrafts entering our atmosphere.

'You can start making arrangements to hunt for Tykran Vark and his crew immediately and contact the other Federation Planets advising them to maintain a high alert until these extremely dangerous escapees are found and captured. Keep us informed of your progress, General.'

'Thank you, councillors,' Dakhar said, though he was not entirely pleased with their decisions. 'There's one other thing I forgot to mention. The injection given to reverse the effects of Xytrinium DNA infusion and neutralise the enhancements on Vark and his Treldarian soldiers has worn off and they have increased powers once again. If this serum is to be used again, our scientists need to revisit their research to ensure the counteracting injection produces a permanent reversal. I'll take leave with your permission and commence operations.'

Dakhar saluted and strode towards the exit as the senators contemplated this last piece of unwelcome news. Vark and his escapees were not a weakened army, but a force to be reckoned with.

After arriving back at his office in the early afternoon, Dakhar launched into action. His first, urgent priority was to send out the Tzuracian fleet to start hunting down the *Piken*. Pressing the intercom direct line to his orderly next door, he gave his first command. 'Corporal Markhaz! Contact Commodore Morkhan

Tarhdok and tell him I request his attendance in my office at once.'

While waiting for the Commodore, Dakhar clicked a button on his desk and a hologram of the four quadrants of the universe appeared instantly before his eyes. It portrayed a kaleidoscope of colours highlighting the four current planets of the Federation – Tzurac, Armonus, Urgellan and Terra Major. It also showed other important planets and star systems, with planet Lokar in the Western Quadrant, planet Orkharn in the Eastern Quadrant and Moon Mankro in the Southern Quadrant.

A gentle knock on his office door distracted Dakhar's focus, and he turned in the direction of the noise. 'Enter.'

The door opened slowly and there stood Dakhar's dear old friend, Fleet Commodore Morkhan Tarhdok. He was six-foot tall and dressed immaculately in a dark-blue uniform trimmed with gold piping, his trousers tucked into his mirror-polished, knee-high, black boots and his gold-braided peaked cap covering his cropped, blonde hair. It had been over six years since Dakhar last laid eyes on him, but Morkhan still maintained a hardened expression with his clean-shaven square jaw line and his burning, steely-blue eyes. The Commodore was a well-respected leader not only because of his honesty and directness as well as his intolerance of weak excuses, but also because he was a truly remarkable war strategist.

'Hello, Ehrane, my friend,' he said, removing his cap as he entered. 'It's good to see you again.' His deep and mellow voice was very familiar.

'Welcome, Morkhan. I've missed you.'

The two exchanged a vigorous and warm Tzuracian arm shake.

'Now,' said Tarhdok, 'what's this all about?'

'Before I start, would you like a drink? Tea, wine, water?'

'Water will be fine, thanks, Ehrane.'

Dakhar reached for the jug on his desk and poured some water into a goblet. As he handed the goblet to the Commodore, he gestured for him to take a seat in front of the hologram map.

'You're already aware of the rescue ship we sent to Lokar.'

Tarhdok nodded, acknowledging that he was.

'But you've not heard what happened on their arrival.'

Dakhar elaborated while Tarhdok listened intently, raising his eyebrows and shaking his head, his eyes now set in a serious, burning stare. He couldn't believe such a simple rescue had turned into a major threat. 'This is unbelievable. How could the Treldarians overpower our Sentinel guards on Lokar when their enhancements were neutralised prior to their imprisonment?'

'There lies the problem, my friend. It appears the serum to reverse the effects of the Xytrinium infusion has worn off after six years. And, not only are we now dealing with the vengeful son of General Vark and his crew with regained superpowers, but also our commandeered Advanced Destroyer, the *Piken*, is armed with Xytrinium torpedoes and has its tracking device disconnected.'

Tarhdok sat in silence, his fists clenched tightly, his eyes staring blankly at the hologram. He reached for his goblet of water and raised it in dry humour, saying, 'Do you have anything stronger?'

Dakhar couldn't help but smile even under the circumstances. 'I'll get you something stronger after we've discussed a strategy and then I'll join you in sealing our plans. Here's what I propose, but feel free to intervene as I'm open to suggestions.'

Dakhar drew Tarhdok's attention to the hologram and began outlining his proposed strategy. 'Tykran may be trying to reach his home planet Orkharn.' Dakhar pointed to the location on the hologram. 'But he'll need to refuel to get there. To refuel, the only planets where there's stored Xytrinium crystals are Terra Major, the Earthlings' refuelling station on planet Alkmene, and the moons of Terra Iota and Mankro. There's also one other planet frequented by unsavoury criminal types which has no jurisdiction and no law enforcement, Planet Krima, where he could barter for black-market Xytrinium crystals.

'I want to notify all the Federation Planets of the escape using my Pledge ring and send most of our fleet to search the whole of the Eastern Quadrant. I emphasise from now on, all communications when in the field, must be through Pledge rings so as not to alert the *Piken* of our intentions. What do you think, Morkhan?'

Morkhan stroked his chin with his right hand, spreading his fingers from the thumb. He was deep in thought as he looked more closely at the hologram map. 'The problem is, my friend, covering the whole of the Eastern Quadrant with the Fleet would spread our crafts too thinly and allow the *Piken* to slip through large gaps. It would be more practical to narrow the coverage to the top half of the Eastern Quadrant which includes Diunon and Kyronis, giving a more concentrated force. They may be headed there looking for support among their allies. The resources of Terra Major could cover the lower half of the Eastern Quadrant with Mankro and Krima in that territory. Can you ask Terra Major to join in the hunt?'

'Yes, I can, and I think they'd rally to the cause without hesitation. I agree with your strategy. Let's proceed at once. I already have the Senate's permission to implement a strategy to capture the *Piken* and all onboard though it will be a delicate operation trying to save our two Sentinel pilots.'

'And trying to avoid blowing up the *Piken* with the Xytrinium torpedoes and destroying everyone on board ...,' the Commodore added. He stood as if making ready to leave.

'I have faith in your judgement, Morkhan, and the power of the Ancient spirits to guide and protect you. But, before you go, I promised you something a little stronger than water. And we might need it!' Dakhar reached for his drinks cabinet. It was only after toasting to the plan with a vintage fortified wine and wishing his friend good luck, that Dakhar began to contact all the Federation planets using his Pledge ring for security.

First, he contacted General Kal Zawkon, who had replaced him as Commanding Chief of Military Operations, Western Quadrant, on Terra Major. The rugged, blonde-haired, blue-eyed veteran was surprised when Dakhar's hologram suddenly materialised in his office at the Citadel. He hadn't seen or spoken to Dakhar since his promotion to Brigadier-General, two years ago at a ceremony on Tzurac.

'Greetings, Kal. I hope I'm not interrupting something important.'

'Not at all, sir. It's good to see you,' Zawkon responded warmly before sensing trouble. 'But something tells me this is not a social call.'

'Please call me, Ehrane. After all we're now of the same rank and we've been friends for a very long time. And yes, you're quite right, it's not a social call, but a matter of great urgency.'

'You have my undivided attention.'

Dakhar explained everything that had happened since Tykran's escape from Lokar in the Destroyer *Piken* with two Tzuracian pilots held hostage, and the strategic response plan he'd formulated with Commodore Tarhdok.

'Tarhdok suggested that you place Terra Major on full alert until further notice and asked whether you could join forces in tracking down Tykran Vark in the lower half of the Eastern Quadrant, ranging from Terra Major through to the distant Planet of Krima. Keep in mind the *Piken* has Xytrinium torpedoes. So, if you find it, you'll need to tread very carefully. Oh, and would you also contact Planet Iota, as they have huge stockpiles of Xytrinium and little security or protection against an attack by Vark.'

'I'll alert Terra Major's World Assembly,' said Zawkon, 'and contact General Blake at ASPECT to request his space fleet join the hunt immediately. We'll only communicate by Pledge ring during the search as you requested, sir, I mean, Ehrane.'

The powerful General Blake was still in charge of Earth's Aero Space Exploration Colonisation and Transportation program, ASPECT, and had gained another star pip on his uniform. He was now Zawkon's father-in-law, Zawkon having married the General's only daughter, Lauren, who was now in charge of MERIC – Mining and Engineering Resource Industrial Company – the largest interplanetary mining company on Earth.

General Blake and his daughter had a very close bond which had grown stronger over the years since Lauren's mother passed away. He was proud of his daughter and he was proud to have Zawkon as his son-in-law, knowing his daughter would be well protected. But he worried that, at some time in the future, the couple might leave Terra Major to live on Zawkon's home planet, Tzurac. Although he understood his daughter now had a life of her own, he still found it a little hard to accept.

'Please keep me informed of your progress and I thank you for your assistance, Kal. May the Ancients protect you.' With these words Dakhar's hologram began to fade.

Dakhar also needed to forewarn the unit of Sentinels who were enforcing martial law on Planet Orkharn. He contacted the Base Commander there informing him of Tykran's escape and directing him to be on extreme alert in case Tykran returned to his home planet. 'So, if you encounter the escaped prisoners, use your Pledge ring to contact the Communications Centre at Headquarters in the Citadel on Tzurac.'

Dakhar's next move was to alert Yarron and Bhalar on Mankro where large reserves of Xytrinium had been extracted by MERIC over the last two years and stockpiled for gradual distribution. Dakhar needed to warn Yarron and advise him to be prepared.

Things were heating up.

OUT FOR BLOOD

DAKHAR'S hologram materialised without warning from Yarron's Pledge ring when he was in the Site Office of the Xytrinium mine on Mankro. The red-haired and bearded Irish engineer Grant Thompson had been contracted by MERIC to implement mining operations there and he was also in the office checking on mining operations.

'Holy Mother of Jesus!' Grant blurted out in his lyrical Irish dialect. 'I 'aven't seen a Sentinel hologram since the Terra Major war, be it six years ago. Looks like a bit o' trouble brewin' again, me lad?'

Seeing the serious look on Dakhar's face, Yarron waited for him to speak.

'Greetings Yarron and to you Grant.'

'Greetings, General,' they responded.

Then Yarron took the lead. 'I'm surprised to see you. It must be two years since we last spoke. As you're aware, we're fulfilling our agreement and continuing to send the required quota of Xytrinium to Tzurac each month. I hope nothing has changed?'

'No, Yarron, we're very happy with your progress, but there's a more urgent situation you and Bhalar need to be aware of.'

Yarron and Grant looked at each other with alarmed expressions before turning back to Dakhar.

'Six days ago, Tykran Vark escaped from Lokar with his Treldarian inmates in one of our rescue ships, an Advanced Destroyer Class II Carrier, taking two Tzuracian pilots hostage. The Destroyer is equipped with Xytrinium torpedoes and we don't know where they're heading. If Tykran is trying to return to his home planet, he'll need to refuel somewhere that has a supply of Xytrinium crystals. I suggest you stay on full alert and arm yourselves in case he comes to Mankro. And you need to know that the injections we gave the Treldarian prisoners before they were incarcerated to neutralise the Xytrinium enhancements have worn off – the Treldarians have regained their super strength.'

Yarron was shocked and angry. 'Six days ago!' he spluttered in a raised voice. 'Why didn't you inform us sooner? Grant and I have been here at the mining site for the last two days. It's on the far side of our planet and, for all we know, they could already have landed on Mankro.'

'I'm sorry for the late notice, Yarron, but I received the hologram from Planet Lokar less than twenty-four hours ago. The Sentinel guards on Lokar had been locked up and their Pledge rings confiscated. It took time for them to break free and when they finally did, they discovered the communication control centre had been obliterated. They were lucky to find their hidden Pledge rings, and eventually call me.'

Yarron collected himself. 'Alright. Sorry for sounding angry, General, but I fear for my young family and the innocent Treldarian community.'

'I understand your anger, Yarron, so I'll leave you to return to them in haste. And Grant, I want you to return to Iota as soon as possible and resurrect the Diutron robots stored there. Inform the Base Commander you have spoken with me and tell him to communicate only with his Sentinel Pledge ring direct to General Zawkon on Terra Major. Yarron, we all must keep tight security so as not to alert Vark and the escapees of our plans.'

'Aye, sir. To be sure,' said Grant nodding his head.

'Stay safe and may the Ancients' spirits protect and guide you.'

As soon as General Dakhar's image faded, Yarron wasted no time. He bolted through the Site Office door and ran to his black Advanced Destroyer, powering it up within seconds.

After flying at high speed over the terrain, Yarron arrived home an hour later only to find he was too late. The view from the air showed the devastation. Thick, black smoke was billowing from inside the village, some of the palings on the fortification fence were missing and others were charred and hanging loose or scattered like discarded, half-burnt matchsticks, and the huge wooden entry doors were swinging off their broken iron hinges. Numerous bodies were lying lifeless on the ground, while other villagers were limping around or holding their injured limbs and battered heads with bandages to different parts of their bodies.

Yarron hovered over the village before setting down his craft as quickly as he could. Then, drawing his laser weapon, he ran at full speed towards his house, fearing the worst. *What had happened to his beloved Bhalar and the two little ones?*

A pungent odour of wood-smoke mixed with blood, sweat and seared skin wafted through the dense atmosphere. His heart was thumping heavily, his pulse racing and his face was in a cold sweat. Tears caused by the thick smoke were streaming from his eyes leaving him with partially blurred vision. But as he approached, he could see his house was mostly intact, with little damage other than splintered doors and broken glass windows.

'Bhalar!' he screamed at the top of his voice. 'Bhalar, where are you? Jelka! Zentar!' He sped rapidly through the lower floor, opening every door and calling out as he searched frantically. There was no response. He began to worry himself sick with a gut-wrenching pain, his mind a mixture of fear and hate.

He turned and raced back to the stairs leading to the second floor and bolted up them, two steps at a time, before running through the whole area, calling out their names loudly. Still no answer.

Overcome with shock, tears streaming from his eyes and rolling down his now-flushed red cheeks, Yarron collapsed in a heap on the floor. 'No, no,' he repeated out loud over and over, while continuously shaking his head.

Suddenly, he was interrupted by a noise behind him. He swivelled instantly, at the same time pointing his laser pistol in readiness to fire on the intruder. Through blurred eyes he recognised the figure instantly and froze. It was Grenham holding hands with Jelka and Zentar, tears flowing from all of them.

'By the Gods, you're here!' said Yarron with relief written all over his face. He scrambled to his feet while holstering his pistol. Quickly wiping his eyes with the back of his hands, he charged towards them and both children ran to him with their arms outstretched, calling out, 'Papa! Papa!'

He hugged his children so tightly they could hardly breathe. 'I'm so happy to see both of you. I was so afraid something had happened to you.'

Before they could say a word, Grenham spoke with a shaking voice, her face pale and distraught, her eyes puffy from crying. 'I'm so sorry, Yarron, but I couldn't save Bhalar.'

Yarron's eyes widened in disbelief. He was at once distraught, his heart thumping. 'What's happened to her? Where is she?' he asked, pressing her for answers.

Grenham spoke in a quivering voice, trying to catch her breath. 'They took her with them. It was Tykran Vark. They were disguised as Sentinels but I recognised him from when he came last time to see General Rokan. He had at least a hundred soldiers with him. We were caught off guard. They started shooting and waving their blades, blowing up huts and demanding everyone tell him where the Xytrinium was stored. With the training you gave our people, they put up a good fight, but they were outnumbered. With some villagers killed and others injured, we had no choice but to surrender.'

Yarron shook his head from side to side in denial as Grenham elaborated. 'Bhalar and I watched cautiously from the house, in horror. Then she asked me to hide the children while she left the house and confronted Tykran. I tried to stop her, but she was determined. Such a brave and courageous woman. She showed no fear.

'Two of Tykran's soldiers grabbed her tightly, while he questioned her. I could hear him saying that if she didn't show them where we kept the Xytrinium left in storage from their last visit, he would kill us all, one by one. So, to save all our lives she led him to the small storage hut. I think they were unaware of our recent mining operations and had no idea about the Xytrinium we'd mined and stored elsewhere over the last two years.'

'Go on, Grenham,' Yarron pleaded.

'Tykran's soldiers began to load the Xytrinium onto their spacecraft. And after it was all loaded, he spoke to one of the villagers. After they left, the villager came to tell me Tykran had taken Bhalar as a hostage. He said if anyone tried to attack his ship, she would be killed.'

Yarron seethed with anger. *The bastard.* And then he embraced his children more closely. *How could he do this to our family?*

Grenham continued. 'Tykran knew you were living here on Mankro, and he wanted to know where *you* were. I don't know what Bhalar told him, but I fear he's taken her to question her further, may the Gods forbid, under torture.'

Yarron's fear for Bhalar instantly turned to revenge. 'How long have they been gone? Did they say where they were travelling to?' he asked Grenham sternly.

'They left about four hours ago and didn't say where they were going.'

'Well, I need to get her back,' Yarron said with determination in his voice. Then he spoke more gently. 'Thank you, Grenham, I'm in your debt for saving our children. Can you please look after them while I attempt to rescue their mother?'

'Yes, of course, Yarron,' she said sympathetically. 'Please be careful and bring her safely back home.'

Yarron kneeled down to speak to Jelka and Zentar. He tried to smile as he spoke in a soft and very compassionate voice. 'I love you both and want to stay with you, but I must try to save your mother and bring her home to us. Will you be good and help Grenham with everything until I return?'

'Yes, Papa,' they replied simultaneously.

Yarron hugged and kissed them before springing to his feet, waving goodbye.

He was in a hurry as he made his way across the village and didn't have time to stop and console the injured. He just hoped they would understand.

After reaching his craft, Yarron strapped himself in and powered up the engines. After switching on the tracking equipment and flipping the lever to 'Heat Sink Recognition', he waited for feedback. Within seconds the green, fluorescent screen on the console glowed to reveal a charted map with co-ordinance figures in degrees and the direction of a Tzuracian Destroyer with the time of its departure. It showed that four hours ago the craft had headed in the direction of Planet Orkharn. Yarron checked his fuel and found he had full reserves with more in storage on board. It was enough for the long trek. 'Got you Vark, you swine!' he exclaimed in anticipation.

He engaged the engine thrusters, reaching the outer atmosphere in seconds before changing the power to Level 10 hyperdrive following the heat sink trail.

Hearing a high-pitched whisper, Grenham looked towards the sky to see a short streak of white light before it disappeared. She clasped her hands in prayer.

After placing the craft on autopilot, Yarron activated his Pledge ring and began sending a message to Dakhar.

'Greetings, Yarron,' said Dakhar gazing at the hologram vision before him. 'What have you to report?'

'As I feared, Tykran has attacked our village on Mankro today. After killing and badly wounding some of the villagers he's confiscated the small amount of Xytrinium which was stored here before the assault on Terra Major. He's taken Bhalar hostage as a means of preventing Tzuracian spacecrafts firing upon the *Piken*. The heat sink trail I've detected shows he's heading for Orkharn and left here just over four hours ago. I'm in pursuit to try and save my wife.'

'Thanks, for this vital information, Yarron. Well done. I'll direct some of the Terra Major fleet at once to intercept the *Piken* and warn them not to endanger Bhalar. But I order you to remain on Mankro and let the TSF deal with Vark.'

That was not good enough for Yarron and his reply was abrupt. 'Sorry to disappoint you, Dakhar, but I'm no longer under your command, and this is *my* wife I'm going to rescue. I'm taking this as a personal threat and when I catch up with Tykran, I'm going to kill him. I'll keep you posted of developments. Yarron, out!'

Dakhar punched his right fist into his left palm and gritted his teeth, furious at Yarron's defiance. After composing himself, he contacted Commodore Tarhdok on the direct comms visual line to discuss the change of plan.

'Yes, Ehrane, any news?' Tarhdok asked, hoping to hear something positive. He watched Dakhar's serious expression on the large screen that hung on the wall directly in front of his desk.

'Yes, Morkhan,' Dakhar replied after taking a deep breath. 'The news is I've just received confirmation Tykran Vark is heading to Orkharn in the *Piken* after attacking the colony on Mankro and raiding their Xytrinium reserves.'

'Well, I'm relieved to hear we've tracked Vark down and know where he's going, but I'm sorry to hear about the attack on Mankro. Was anyone killed or injured?'

'Unfortunately, there were several. The other bad news is Yarron's wife, Bhalar, was taken hostage and Vark has threatened to kill her if the *Piken* comes under attack from our fleet. And to make matters worse, Yarron has decided to take matters into his own hands. He's defied my orders and is already in pursuit.'

'So, what do you propose we do now, Ehrane?'

Dakhar paused for a moment. 'Keeping in mind that Vark vowed to seek revenge for the execution of his father, he may try to raise another army to attack Tzurac and try to decimate the Sentinels as well as the Federation of Planets. Last time they raged war on the Federation, the Treldarian rebels deployed Xytrinium torpedoes and almost succeeded in destroying Khazor.

'I suggest we recall half our fleet to Tzurac and, with the remaining ships, set up a defence line evenly spread out between Tzurac and Planet Orkharn in the North-Eastern Quadrant. Our heat sensors and long-range sonar should detect anything coming towards Tzurac, leaving enough time for those spacecrafts to retreat and regroup around Khazor. I'll contact General Zawkon and request he call back his Terra Major fleet and prepare their defences. I'll keep you updated with progress reports as we hear more.'

The Commodore nodded his agreement. 'I think that's a sensible idea. We don't want to rush in and attack Orkharn, and risk killing and maiming innocent inhabitants, not to mention our own pilots and Yarron's wife. We have a window of opportunity to prepare for a possible onslaught. If Vark is trying to recruit allies, it will take him some time to gather a large army. There are most likely a small number of young Kyroni warriors left on Kyronis, though not enough to be a threat. And there are no Diunons to build more Diutrons as most of their soldiers were either killed in battle or imprisoned. I'm not sure about the status of Nujhar, but they may have soldiers. I'll follow through with your orders and keep you posted. Is that all, Ehrane?'

'Yes, thank you, Commodore. Talk soon.'

After ending the conversation, Dakhar projected his hologram to General Zawkon. 'Recall your fleet. We've just heard that Tykran Vark attacked Mankro and has taken Yarron's wife, Bhalar, with him as hostage. He's headed for Orkharn. I've asked Grant Thompson to resurrect the Diutrons in readiness for another potential attack on the Federation of Planets. Advise General Blake to prepare his aircraft and mobilise his armies in case there's an invasion on Terra Major. We just don't know what Vark's plans are or where he'll strike.

'And, Zawkon, although it was supposed to be a permanent fix, the antidote we used on the Treldarians and Kyroni to neutralise the Xytrinium infusion has worn off. Vark's soldiers have regained their enhancements. I'll leave the war strategy on Terra Major to you, Kal, but we have a challenge on our hands.'

'Very well, Ehrane. I'll make these arrangements and let you know when we're ready. Kal, out.'

Dakhar's next task was to call together the Council of Elders to inform them of the developments. This time it took only a brief consultation with the other members before Ghalbrak advised,

'We support your decision to retrieve the fleet and prepare for a possible Treldarian invasion. Prepare to mobilise the army in the Citadel and to increase the strength of Khazor's protective dome to repel Xytrinium torpedoes. And we suggest sending an emissary to Queen Tarune on Planet Urgellan asking for their aid once again. Remember, the Urgellan army had their DNA enhanced with Xytrinium to match the powers of the Sentinels, and they'll be a real asset to us in the fight.'

'Agreed,' said Dakhar. He smiled to himself, knowing this was already part of his plan.

A NEW PLAN

TYKRAN finally reached his home planet eight days after his escape from Lokar only to be confronted by a company of a dozen armed Sentinels. He hadn't expected his planet to be under martial law when he quietly landed the *Piken* at the space terminal in the capital city of Bharkaz. But Dakhar had forewarned the Sentinels.

As he stepped out of the side hatch of the craft it was déjà vu in reverse. This time Tykran and his soldiers walked into a trap similar to the one he had planned on Lokar for the Sentinels aboard the Tzuracian rescue ship. The Sentinels emerged instantly from their hiding places with their laser rifles aimed directly at the Treldarians dressed in Sentinel uniform without helmets revealing their dishevelled long black hair and eight days' stubble.

'Surrender your weapons and stand fast!' ordered the sergeant in command of the Sentinels using his translator transponder.

While Tykran and most of his soldiers deliberately responded very slowly as a delay tactic, several of Tykran's soldiers still inside the Destroyer ducked low and crept out of the rear hatch unnoticed, silently working themselves around and behind the Sentinels. Suddenly they opened fire, their comrades diving to the ground, anticipating what was to come. It was all over within minutes. The noise stopped, the smoke from the burning bodies cleared, and all the Sentinels lay dead on the ground.

'Good work, soldiers,' said Tykran now smiling smugly. 'They thought they'd catch us off guard, but we outsmarted them. So much for their superior fighting force! Dispose of the bodies and bring out the pilots and Bhalar and lock them in the cells. The rest of you, follow me for a celebratory drink at our old haunt!'

Tykran and the rest of his one hundred and twenty were excited to be back on home soil. As they made their way through the main thoroughfare to the taverns and the relaxing hot baths, the town's community cheered and waved their arms from their colourful market stalls, rejoicing at the return of their army.

Soon the wine was flowing and the soldiers wasted no time in catching up with the Ludaxian beauties who provided 'entertainment'. The exotic perfumes of the female hosts, the aromatic spices of the rich cuisine, and the whiff of alcohol were, to say the least, intoxicating.

Above the noise of the loud music and cheerful singing by inebriated soldiers, Tykran beckoned Sergeant Krag to his table. He needed a word before things got out of hand. 'Sergeant, I want all the soldiers on the parade ground first thing in the morning for a seven o'clock roll call. We need to maintain discipline if we're to be ready for the coming battle.

'After you arrange the morning meals with the Mess Hall cooks, organise with Supply for a fitting of new uniforms and issuing of laser pistols. Then prepare a schedule for training on a daily routine. We need our soldiers to be sharp and alert. We've a lot to accomplish within a short space of time before the Sentinels come hunting for us. And we need to strike first and catch them off guard. I'll discuss our strategic plans with you tomorrow.'

He leaned in toward Krag, adding, 'And Sergeant, one more thing.' He smiled widely. 'I'm promoting you to Lieutenant, for your loyalty, your service and your counsel. Congratulations! Choose one of the soldiers you think would make a perfect sergeant to replace you and have the ranks sewn onto your new uniforms.'

Standing at attention, Krag saluted Tykran with a straightened raised right arm, his face beaming. 'Thank you, sir, I'll not disappoint you.'

'And when you've finished for the day, go and enjoy yourself. You've earned it.'

As Krag walked off, the salacious Ludaxian, Shanowah, sidled seductively up to Tykran, enticing him to join her. Tykran had always fancied her and although she'd sometimes had eyes for others – including the rebel Blader Ramlok – she'd always admired the handsome Lieutenant, now Captain Vark. It was no surprise they ended up sharing one of the hot baths together and indulging in wine and each other for the rest of the day and evening.

Shanowah hadn't changed in the seven years of Tykran's absence, but she noticed the battle scars on his taut torso. 'Tell me what happened to you after you left to fight the battle?' she whispered in his ear.

But Tykran didn't want to talk about the battle, the defeat and the disgrace, or his father's execution. His mind was on other things and he spoke with a smooth, silver tongue. 'Tonight, I want to forget all that's happened since I was last here. I just want to immerse myself in your sweet company, feel your soft delicate skin, kiss your soft rose lips and feel the warmth of your tender body.'

'Then your wish is my command. I'm all yours,' she said.

Tykran woke as the early rays of the sun crept through the flimsy sheer pink drapes shading Shanowah's private boudoir. His head felt heavy from the wine he'd consumed through the night. It was not only his disciplined military regime and the years of prison routine that forced him to rise. He was also driven by a diehard determination to finish what his father had failed to accomplish and, by a more personal quest for revenge on Yarron and the Sentinels.

It was 06.00 hours and he was feeling dehydrated and famished from the night's sexual and alcoholic indulgence. After quickly dressing in the Sentinel outfit he'd been wearing when they made the escape from Planet Lokar, he left Shanowah sleeping soundly and returned to his own quarters. There he couldn't wait to discard all trappings of the enemy Sentinel and replace the outfit with his familiar black Treldarian uniform. Now he felt at home again.

Feeling more comfortable, he headed for the Mess Hall to see all his troops back in their working outfits, eating heartily as he entered the noisy hall. It was obvious Lieutenant Krag had herded them here before attending roll call on the parade ground.

Grabbing a large plateful of the culinary delights on offer, he headed to Krag's table at the back of the Hall, looking for some privacy. But before he could find a seat, the new Lieutenant called out loudly, 'Officer on Deck!' The clutter ceased and there was a sudden silence as all the soldiers stood rigid and saluted.

Tykran was quite overwhelmed. 'As you were, soldiers!' he ordered, and the troops returned quickly to shovelling breakfast into their hungry mouths. He grinned thinking, *Six years of cold, bland, tasteless gruel was a long time to be denied a tasty, wholesome Treldarian breakfast.*

'Good morning, *Lieutenant* Krag,' Tykran said as he sat down. 'Sleep well?'

Krag smiled. 'Yes, sir, the bunks never felt so good after what we had to endure in that Tzuracian shit hole. And you, sir, did you enjoy the comforts of home?' he asked with a smirk.

Tykran responded with a satisfied smile. 'Yes, Lieutenant, as a matter of fact, it was just what I needed.'

Between mouthfuls, Tykran issued more orders. 'I want to address the soldiers on the parade ground. As you know, the War Council no longer exists and I'm the only authority left in charge. Our fleet of war crafts and battle cruisers were all destroyed in our assault on Tzurac and General Rokan's ships were also destroyed. We've lost all but one hundred and twenty soldiers, and our planet is now technically under the control of the Tzuracians. We only have about eight days until a battalion of Sentinels come hunting for us to find out why the Security detail they left guarding our Capital Bharkaz haven't reported in. They'll know we're here, that's for sure.'

'So, what are your plans, sir?' Krag interjected.

'We can't talk here. After we've all had our new uniforms fitted, I want you to report to my quarters – my father's office – to discuss what I have in mind. Have your new sergeant, who I hope you've selected well, take the soldiers to the training ground to practise their target shooting and their hand-to-hand combat skills. Then have them clean their weapons and load up the Destroyer with weapons and munitions as well as food supplies for a month. All good, Lieutenant?'

'Yes, sir, all good. I've chosen Corporal Jhakmar as our new sergeant. Remember, he's a good all-rounder, proficient in a range of weaponry and fighting skills and he's got brains. He'll try hard to prove his worth after you chastised him back on Lokar for being *too* efficient.'

'Good. I approve. Call him over here.'

Jhakmar was taken by surprise at his new promotion. He was quietly overcome and couldn't help but smile at the good news. He thought Captain Vark had not forgiven him for killing all the administrative staff in the Control Room on Lokar. But this was a reward, rather than a punishment.

Tykran rose, saying, 'Well done, *Sergeant* Jhakmar, and now it's time to get everyone moving.'

Krag instructed his new sergeant to have the soldiers march to the Supply Depot for new uniforms. And, after quickly coming to his senses, Sergeant Jhakmar gave the order. 'Let's go, soldiers!'

After donning their new black material uniforms with red piping on the collars and sleeves, the soldiers were issued new, knee-high, black boots and the pièce de résistance, new blades and new standard regulation laser pistols. The excitement was clear.

Lieutenant Krag and Captain Vark had extra dark red epaulets on their jacket, denoting their rank and they made an extra stop in the Supply Depot to have gold studs implanted in their ears. Following protocol, three gold studs for a captain and one stud for a lieutenant.

After they were all kitted out, Sergeant Jhakmar ordered the soldiers to assemble on the parade ground. Within minutes the soldiers were all in lines, standing silent and at attention, organised by the new sergeant's shouting and bellowing commands.

Tykran stood facing them marvelling at the transformation after prison orange.

He began his address. 'Stand easy, soldiers. I know you're grateful to be free and home again. And I know you'd all like to stay here and recuperate for another week after being incarcerated for so long. But as I said last time I spoke to you, I wasn't going to die in prison in an unmarked grave without honour. I'll go out fighting with sword in hand and, if it's my destiny, die like a warrior with dignity and glory.'

He paused a moment allowing them time to recall his words. 'To regain our dignity and honour we'll not be running from our enemy like cowards, only to be caught and imprisoned, or executed like my father. We'll face them as proud warriors, doing battle with the Tzuracians, and hopefully be the victors taking home the spoils.

'To accomplish this, we'll be travelling to the outer regions of the Eastern Quadrant, far beyond our boundary, to recruit a new army, bigger and better equipped than our archenemies the Sentinels. So, after six years in prison without regular army training, we need to prepare ourselves for battle by improving ourselves both mentally and physically with determination and discipline.'

Tykran paused again and surveyed the troops. All eyes were focussed on him, and all faces were looking proud. 'Are you with me?' he cried out.

'Yes!' they called back, in unison.

'Will you follow me into battle?'

There was a resounding 'yes'.

'Then we leave in five days, so make the most of your time here. Hone your skills and enjoy the luxuries. Dismissed.'

Lieutenant Krag then gave the order for Sergeant Jhakmar to take the soldiers to the training grounds, while Tykran and Krag made their way back to General Vark's quarters.

Arriving at the huge stone building, Tykran immediately called a staff meeting with the twelve administrative staff, including the kitchen staff, to announce his new authority. All the staff arrived and congregated in the spacious ancient courtyard.

'Thank you for coming to this impromptu gathering,' he said with a sombre expression. 'As you may or may not be aware, my father along with General Rokan was executed by the Tzuracians for crimes against the Federation and for inciting a rebellion. Along with Lieutenant Krag and one hundred and twenty of my soldiers, I was imprisoned for the last six years on planet Lokar, but we managed to escape eight days ago.

'All the War Council members were either killed or captured in the battle, which leaves me, as the General's son, now in charge.

I thank you for looking after the Headquarters and maintaining everything. You'll receive your regular payments for services so let me know if there's anything you need, or if there's anything that concerns you. I'll be using my father's sleeping quarters now I've returned and will keep the usual routines for meals and guests. Are there any questions?'

One of the senior clerks dressed in a light-blue uniform, raised his hand seeking permission to speak. Tykran recognised the clerk's familiar aged face, 'Yes, Lazark, you may speak.'

'Sir,' he said with a sad face, 'I know I speak for all of us. We would like to offer our sincere condolences for your loss. If there's anything you need at any time, please let us know.' The others nodded in silent agreement.

'Thank you all, I appreciate your concerns. Now please return to your duties.'

The gathering dissipated quickly as Tykran and Krag headed for the passageway to General Vark's office.

As Tykran opened the thick wooden double doors he felt quite strange and a slight shiver ran through his body. There was a slight musk odour hanging heavily in the air and fine flecks of dust reflected from them as they permeated in the sunlight streaking through the small, high windows. He felt he was intruding. The only time he'd entered this room in the past was when he was called from the barracks by his father, usually to be reprimanded for rebellious or disgraceful behaviour. Nothing had been moved in this spartan room and it was as if it were only yesterday that he'd been in his father's den.

Hanging from the grey stone walls were weapons of war — long-bladed swords and metal shields, long bows, cross bows and spears of different lengths, together with an assortment of sharp-spiked weapons. The oversized wooden table and its surrounding wooden chairs covered with shiny black material were still in place.

Tykran gestured for Krag to take a seat at the table while he reached for a large, scrolled map made of old parchment from his father's antique, wooden desk drawer. He pulled out one of the heavy chairs beside Krag, seating himself, and gently brushed the dust and tiny cobwebs off the outside of the scroll with the back of his hand. After undoing the leather ribbon ties on either end, he carefully unravelled the scroll. To weigh it down, he placed on each corner a heavy, dusty metal goblet from the dust-covered metal tray in the centre on the table. The scroll revealed a map of the Eastern Quadrant stretching far beyond the known boundary of the Treldarian empire.

Krag was surprised. 'I've not seen this map before,' he said while keenly studying the intricate markings and dark-inked patterns of strange star systems and scattered planets.

'No. It hasn't been looked at for at least four hundred years.'

Intrigued, and impatient, the new Lieutenant quizzed Tykran for an explanation. 'Why are we looking at this old chart? And what has this got to do with trying to gather an army? Shouldn't we be contacting our old allies like the Kyroni and Diunons?'

Tykran shook his head in the negative and then smiled. 'We may still need them as reinforcements, if there are any soldiers left on their planets, but they won't be enough to conquer the Federation. What we need is a superior force with the aggression, the numbers and the fire power!'

Krag sat back in his chair, puzzled. 'There are no armies of that sort to my knowledge, sir.'

'Well, Lieutenant, you're about to learn something.'

Tykran rose from his chair and walked to the wine cupboard. Choosing two silver wine goblets and extracting one of the dark bottles from a group on the shelf, he set them down on the table and poured them both a large drink. Then, after taking a sip, he began to describe his proposed plan.

'Just as the Two-Hundred-Year War began, the Second Legion broke away from the Treldarian army and travelled to the far reaches of the Eastern Quadrant, settling on Planet Orkharn. From our fortified base we decided to expand our territory and conquer other worlds in order to discover new resources, new supplies of produce, and new raw metals.

'When we reached this area here …' – Tykran stopped and pointed to the map where the boundary line was drafted – '… we encountered a fierce warlike race from a planet called Rozak. After several battles, and more casualties than we could afford, a truce was made. We discussed terms before we were all wiped out by their superior weapons and resilience. It was agreed the Treldarians would stay this side of the boundary and the Rozakian race would stay on their side. And that agreement has remained in place for over five hundred years.'

Krag sat in silence, staring at the parchment, trying to take it all in. 'But how did you learn about this?'

'My father shared this information with me in secret.' Tykran was momentarily lost in thought, recalling the conversation with his father, General Vark. He could see his father's large imposing figure, his hair tied back in the familiar Treldarian style, streaked with silver-grey like his moustache and his well-groomed beard. And he could see a thinly grooved burgundy scar running vertically from his father's forehead across his right eye and halfway down his cheek. Then he sealed his thinking. 'My plan is to contact this race and persuade them to join forces with us to crush the Sentinels.' He paused. 'Well, Lieutenant, what are your thoughts?'

Krag turned to look directly at Tykran, while taking a large gulp of wine. He wasn't convinced. 'That's a bold plan you propose.' He hesitated and shook his head sceptically. 'Why would these fierce warmongers want to join forces with us after all these centuries have passed? What would be incentive enough to entice them to risk their lives?'

Tykran too took another swig of wine and then smiled smugly. 'Why, Lieutenant, the very same incentive that brought the Kyronis and the Diunons, as well as the Nujharenes on board last time. The power of the blue crystals!'

MOBILISE FOR WAR

FORTIFICATIONS had commenced on Khazor, including reinforcement of the protective Dome, and mobilisation of the armies. The early warning satellite beacons hidden on the three Tzuracian moons of Khelzar, Wurtah and Jorhan had been upgraded and serviced to further increase their range for early detection of alien ships heading for Tzurac in deep space. Underground bunkers had been checked for safety and restocked with provisions to last for a month. The citizens of Khazor had been alerted to the possible threat on the horizon. They had been advised to be prepared to evacuate their homes and take shelter in the bunkers if the alarm was sounded.

Commodore Markaz had been instructed to prepare the air fleet and arm the Advanced Destroyers with Xytrinium warheads. Every available pilot was to be on standby and ready to act at a moment's notice. For the next two days, the Citadel and the Airfield were hives of activity. Sentinel troops were positioned, and spacecraft engines serviced and tested, and then loaded with stocks of munitions and Xytrinium crystals. All spacecrafts were being removed from the open fields and readied under the protection of Khazor's huge, shielded hangars.

Dakhar needed to touch base with Engineer Grant Thompson to check on his progress in resurrecting the Diutrons. He activated his Pledge ring and sent his hologram to Planet Iota.

Captain Shardok, the Sentinel soldier in charge of Iota's Military and overseer of the mining operations for the last seven years, was in the maintenance sheds when Dakhar's hologram materialised from his Pledge ring. He was surprised to see Dakhar as he was rarely contacted by the CCMO. Standing at attention, he gave an arm salute and stood resolute, his face taut.

'Greetings, Captain, stand easy.'

'Greetings, sir,' Shardok nervously replied with his arm still raised.

'You may lower your arm, Captain.'

'Yes, sir,' Shardok snapped back, still apprehensive.

'I need to talk with Engineer Thompson. Is he there with you?'

'He's about twenty feet away, sir. I'll just call him over.'

Shardok swivelled his head to the right and yelled above the background noise. 'Grant, come over here!'

The redhead looked up from what he was working on and spotted Dakhar's hologram. He downed tools and walked over briskly while wringing his hands on an oil-stained rag. 'How'd ya' be, General?' he asked in his strong Irish accent.

Dakhar replied, mimicking the accent. 'I'd be wantin' to know if our Diunon robots are up and runnin' yet, Grant?'

'Yep, one t'ousand five hundred of 'em on Terra Major and five hundred here on Iota.' Grant was clearly pleased with the progress he'd made.

Dakhar reverted to his normal voice. 'Well done, Grant, I knew I could rely on you. I'll be sending a Transport craft to Iota to pick them up. It should arrive in the next three days. I'll ask General Zawkon to send the remaining fifteen hundred Diutrons from Terra Major to Tzurac. And Grant, seeing as you know best how they work and the controls to operate them, I'd like you to come to Tzurac with them.'

'I'd be delighted, sir. But what happens if the Treldarians come to Iota? We won't 'ave the protection of the robots to defend ourselves, and there's not enough Sentinels here to hold 'em off. Can't we keep at least five of 'em here?'

Dakhar took a moment to respond before speaking firmly. 'I believe Tykran Vark and his soldiers won't be coming anywhere near Planet Iota. He's set on taking his vengeance out on Tzurac and he doesn't have the military might to attempt a diversion. In any case, Iota is close enough to Terra Major to ensure it won't be caught unprepared – troops can be sent at short notice. And if there's a threat, I'll return the Diutrons from Tzurac with an armada of ships. I wouldn't put you in harm's way, Grant. You have my word.'

The usually jovial Thompson almost glared at Dakhar. 'Alright, General, I'll place me trust in ya' judgement. But if ya' wrong, I'll be out for blood, if I'm still breathin' that is.'

Dakhar accepted the strong words without flinching. 'Farewell for now, Grant, and may the Ancient spirits protect and guide you.'

Dakhar's hologram faded, leaving Thompson rubbing the top of his head briskly, while screwing up his face and tightly closing his eyes. 'That bleedin' soldya' will be the death of me, to be sure, to be sure!' he said, quietly cursing and muttering under his breath.

Dakhar was unfazed and was straight back to business. It was late afternoon and time was crucial. He pressed the intercom to his orderly. 'Contact Senator Volhardtz and ask him to attend my office immediately!

'Yes, sir!'

Fifteen minutes later Senator Volhardtz was seated comfortably in one of the big, brown-leather armchairs in Dakhar's office. It had been five years since Dakhar had seen the Senator and Volhardtz hadn't changed much in appearance or mannerisms. Wearing his crimson robe, representative of the legal fraternity, he was still noticeably slim and his azure-blue eyes were still bright and alert in keeping with his agile mind. However, his trimmed hair and beard had turned from grey to white and a few more subtle creases had appeared on his wizened face.

'Greetings, Senator. It's good to see you again, and I appreciate you coming at such short notice. The matter is pressing.'

'Greetings, General Dakhar,' said Volhardtz in his mellow voice. 'It's good to see you too after all this time. Please tell me how I can be of help.'

While sipping his cup of tea, Volhardtz listened intently to the General, as he unfolded the events of the last few days. 'The Council of Elders has approved an emissary to Urgellan requesting an audience with Queen Tarune. The aim is to ask for her help again to quell Tykran Vark's army and forewarn her that, unless the enemy is defeated, the Treldarians might launch an attack on her planet after attacking Tzurac. Can I rely on you as I did last time?'

'This certainly is a grave situation,' said Volhardtz without hesitation. 'I'll arrange to leave for Urgellan straight away and request another audience with Queen Tarune.'

'Thank you, Senator. I know Queen Tarune places great trust in you, and I hope her people join us again in our struggle. Use one of the Sentinels' Pledge rings if you need to contact me.'

'Yes, of course. I'll keep you and the Senate informed of my progress through the ship's commander. General, can you authorise a craft for me with a Sentinel escort as soon as possible?'

'Yes, but you'll need two Advanced Destroyer II Carriers as well if Queen Tarune agrees to help us with her five thousand infused soldiers. They'll need to mobilise here on Tzurac.'

'Agreed. I'll take my leave now.'

The Senator rose and strode briskly towards the door as Dakhar called after him. 'May the spirits of the Ancients protect you.'

As soon as the door closed, Dakhar directed Commodore Markaz to request a Destroyer Carrier and two Advanced Destroyer II Carriers be made ready for Senator Volhardtz's departure to Urgellan first thing in the morning. They were to be stocked with ample food supplies for a unit of Sentinels and for five thousand Urgellan soldiers who'd hopefully be accompanying the Senator on his return trip.

Dakhar sat for a while at his desk contemplating the strategies he'd initiated. *Had he covered every situation? Were all the main players in place and ready for the unexpected?*

He reflected on other approaches he might have taken. *Should he have sent his fleet to attack Orkharn and stop Tykran in his tracks, before he had time to raise his army? Or would this have risked the lives of his two pilots and Bhalar, sacrificing three innocent lives for the greater good? No, he would have carried a restless conscience for the rest of his life if he had their blood on his hands.*

He tried to anticipate what Vark was up to. *Where would Tykran raise an army large enough and strong enough to defeat the Tzuracians and the Urgellans? The armies of General Vark and General Rokan had been killed or captured six years ago, and their space crafts destroyed. Did Tykran have other options?*

Again, he contemplated the strategies he'd initiated. *His armies were prepared and the Federation fleets of both Tzurac and Terra Major were in defence mode.* With all contingencies in place, he resolved it would be a waiting game.

Finally, he contacted Kal Zawkon to request the now-active Diutrons to be transported to Tzurac and check everything was in place in preparation for a possible Treldarian assault.

'Yes, sir,' said Zawkon in response to Dakhar's questions emanating from the now clearly visible hologram. 'All the Diutrons are activated and are boarding the Destroyer Carriers as we speak. All going well, they should arrive on Tzurac in the next two days. General Blake has the fleet on standby including the jet fighters. We've also alerted Lauren Blake at MERIC. They've deployed their Security forces and raised their defences. Now, Ehrane, all we can do is await your orders.'

'Very good, Kal. Keep me updated if you hear anything. Dakhar out!'

A SURPRISE ENCOUNTER

YARRON had been following the heat sink trail for four days at hyperspeed and was taking a short nap when he was shaken awake by a pulsating, low-pitched, monotone signal. At first he was partially disorientated, wondering where he was, but then his senses began to kick in. He could now clearly hear the computer's simulated, crackling metallic voice repeating, 'Approaching Planet Orkharn! Approaching Planet Orkharn.'

His first reflex action was a quick command. 'Computer! Shut down to Level two hyperspeed and give me visuals on the screen.'

The display showed a huge, iridescent, purple nebula of swirling gases against a dark space void, sprinkled with small, bright specks. It was amazing.

'Computer, magnify one hundred times and raise shields to full capacity.'

'Affirmative.'

On closer examination Yarron could see the planet surrounded by an asteroid belt, a white heat sink trail snaking through it. His heart was now beating faster knowing he was getting closer to rescuing Bhalar.

'Computer, switch to stealth mode with shields to seventy percent and continue on course at cruise speed!'

As the craft neared the asteroid belt, Yarron's mind worked overtime. He was venturing into dangerous, unknown territory. He knew he had to disguise himself and blend in with the population if he were to find out where Bhalar was being held. He still had stowed on board the clothes and hair dye he'd used in disguising himself as an Urgellan when hunting the Bladers on Planet Krima. *That's it*, he thought.

Leaving the controls on autopilot, he made his way to the cabins at the rear of the craft where, after frantically searching storage trunks, he finally found what he needed and began his transformation. The beard had to go. So did his long, straw-blonde ponytail. After dying his hair and eyebrows jet-black, he donned the forest-green, suede outfit with matching knee-high, suede boots. Then he removed his Pledge ring and hid it in one of the small secret compartments in his jacket. Looking at his reflection in the mirror, Yarron hardly recognised himself.

He would be unable to use his Sentinel weapons, so he found and readied the Urgellan weapons he'd acquired before his last encounter on Krima – a laser pistol in a holster, and two short double-edged blades in leather sheaths. He attached them all to his wide, deep brown leather utility belt, the green jacket being just long enough to discreetly cover the weapons.

Seated back in the pilot's seat, Yarron monitored the screen. It showed he was now fifty miles away from the planet's surface.

Then, suddenly, without warning, the craft was struck by what he thought was one of the floating asteroids. It exploded with a powerful blast, the impact almost sending the ship off course. 'Computer, analyse what that explosion was and report damage!'

There was a brief moment before the metallic crackling voice acknowledged. 'It was not the usual composition of an asteroid and not composed of organic rock. Residual chemical analysis shows traces of Xytrinium and alloy metals. No damage was incurred on the structure. Shields are down to fifty percent.'

Yarron raised his voice in shock. 'Damn! That was an explosive mine, and we're in a minefield! Computer, set your sensors to detect more of these mines and stay on a narrow path closely following the heat sink source.'

'Affirmative.'

After travelling for another hour through the pastel-coloured haze without further incident, the screen showed a clear view of an ash-coloured planet. The wide urban sprawl of a congested city reached to the base of a high, smoky-blue mountain range in the distance. Some of the buildings had tall chimney stacks with grey smoke belching from them and polluting the atmosphere.

He hovered over the planet looking for a suitable area to land close to the city, until he spied a patch of forest surrounded by a vast expanse of desert and sand dunes some miles from the capital, Bharkaz.

But before landing, he wanted to know more about the residents and industry of this planet. He interrogated the computer archives, without success.

'I have no information on record,' came the metallic response from the computer.

'Great. I'm totally in the dark, and flying blind,' said Yarron, shrugging his shoulders and holding his arms out with palms up. 'I'll just have to take it as it comes and hope for the best.'

Yarron's past experience had proved the best way to extract information in a foreign location was to frequent the local taverns. The inebriated would usually talk freely before they collapsed on the floor in a totally drunken state or slumped asleep in a chair, though sometimes he'd had to fight his way out of the bar when they became aggressive. He knew he had to keep a low profile and avoid drawing attention to himself. *But where would he find Orkharn currency to pay for the drinks …?*

'Take the ship down,' he ordered.

After landing safely, Yarron quickly shut down the engines and disembarked, leaving the cloaked ship in place and activating the security locking program. After calculating the direction and distance on his wrist pad, which looked very much like a leather wrist guard for an archer, the small, computerised digital screen lit up showing the way.

Although his breathing was slightly heavier than usual due to the partially polluted atmosphere, he made good time. After forty minutes walking at a Sentinel's pace, he reached the outskirts of the city confirmed by the noise of machinery and chattering. He slowed his pace as he neared the main thoroughfare. Either side of the wide cobbled road were clutters of market stalls in diverse colours and sizes, displaying food, clothing, jewellery, pottery and all sorts of paraphernalia. There were even animal corrals. Unusual, aromatic fragrances mixed with pungent odours permeated the electric atmosphere. The combined cacophony of smells, noises and colours stimulated all the senses.

Yarron headed to one of the stalls bartering weapons and tools, aware that other stall holders were watching him as a stranger dressed in unusual clothes. The Treldarian owner was overfed with shifty eyes and the look of a hungry predator. Yarron spoke to him in fluent Treldarian. 'Good day, my good sir. How's business?'

'Business would be better if you'd like to purchase an item or trade something,' the stall owner said in a raspy tone wringing his sweaty hands in anticipation of a sale.

'I have something of sentimental value you may be interested in, for cash,' Yarron replied.

'Show me what you have stranger, and I might consider your offer.'

With impressive dexterity Yarron removed one of the short blades from its sheath in a single, smooth action and handed it to the owner, whose gleeful eyes widened. The stall owner showed a keen interest in the item and began carefully studying its intricate design and strange markings, while the surrounding stall holders returned to business as usual and their goal of attracting other buyers.

Then, with lightning speed, the predatory owner tightly clutched the handle of the blade, grabbed Yarron by the collar of his jacket and thrust the sharp point towards his throat. But with his own lightning speed and super reflexes, Yarron grasped the stall holder's wrist, tightening his hold with a vice-like grip to prevent the point of the blade making contact. The Treldarian squealed in agony as Yarron produced a laser pistol from nowhere with his other hand and placed the barrel on the owner's forehead.

'Don't shoot!' begged the stall owner, trembling in fear, his face turning white and covered in sweat. 'I'll give you anything you want. Name your price.'

Without flinching, Yarron quickly surveyed the crowded table of items marked with their prices. One particular piece was a sabre blade marked with the highest amount of three hundred krads. Casting his piercing blue eyes back at the owner, he snapped, 'Four hundred krads!'

'Sold!' the terrified owner instantly uttered in a high-pitched squeal, releasing the blade.

As Yarron lowered his weapon, the owner hurriedly reached for his cash box and counted out the amount in coins of different denominations with shaky hands.

After Yarron pocketed the money and holstered his weapon, he turned to the stall owner as if nothing had happened. 'Thank you, sir,' he said, smiling. 'You certainly know how to reach a great bargain. Good doing business with you.'

The overfed owner stood in shock as he watched the stranger casually flip his jacket collar up and walk on. The event had happened so quickly, the surrounding stall holders were oblivious to it all.

What Yarron needed now was a light cloth robe which blended in with the local colours and patterns. He headed across the road to a clothing stall run by a salacious-looking female with a coffee-toned face and long, jet-black, plaited hair. She was adorned head to foot with heavy, gold-coloured jewellery, and her eyes and lips were painted with bright, exotic colours. The sight reminded Yarron of the brilliant rainbow feathers found on the tropical native birds on Mankro.

There he spotted a long, unbuttoned robe hanging on one of the racks. It was about his size, and in wide coloured stripes of rust and beige, with a hood. The price tag showed thirty krads. He smiled and tried it on. *Perfect*, he thought.

The now smiling female sensed a sale. She approached him with gleaming, hazel eyes, her palm outstretched. He paid without bartering, thanked her in Treldarian, and went in search of a tavern.

Feeling better disguised and more confident with cash in his pocket, Yarron could now focus fully on his mission to rescue Bhalar. He walked at a steady pace, pleased his efforts to disguise himself were working effectively and the villagers were no longer scrutinising him. He was also relieved he'd not seen any Sentinel patrols on the streets, though this was a surprise considering the last he heard, Orkharn was under martial law.

After several minutes, he came across a tavern. Standing in the shadows across the road from it, Yarron was able to observe without being seen. About twenty Treldarian soldiers were either seated or staggering around with goblets in hand, waving arms and talking in high volume. They were in the company of several scantily clad females, who were laughing and giggling, and being fondled while they teased the drunken soldiers.

Many thoughts ran through his mind. *If these were some of Tykran's crew from the* Piken, *where were the rest of his one hundred and twenty? If Bhalar was still alive, where were they holding her? And what had happened to the company of Sentinels left in charge to impose martial law on Orkharn?*

Yarron needed answers. His mind was racing and his pulse was quickening with every minute spent thinking of a way to extract the information he needed without being exposed. Concentrating on the problem and focusing his hearing and eyesight on the rabble across the street, he hadn't noticed a figure approaching quietly behind him …

Suddenly he felt a hand on his right shoulder. With lightning reflexes, he spun around to his left, at the same time unholstering his pistol with his right hand, grabbing and twisting the wrist of his assailant with his left hand, forcing the figure to yield, while dropping to the ground on their knees. He was pointing his pistol at the head of a young, and very beautiful female with soft, pouting lips and subtle dimples in her high-boned cheeks. And, although she was in pain, she signalled Yarron to remain silent by pressing a finger vertically across her lips.

Pulling her to her feet, but still pointing his pistol at her head, he whispered, 'Who in the Gods' names are you? I nearly blew your head off.'

'You're hurting my wrist. Let me go,' she demanded in Treldarian, trying to tug herself free. 'I could have stabbed you in the back if I wanted you dead.'

Yarron lowered and holstered his pistol but kept hold of her wrist to prevent her bolting across the road to the Treldarian soldiers.

'Come with me and I'll tell you who I am, and why I think I can help you and you can help me,' she said.

The mysterious female quickly led him through narrow back streets full of tightly packed, old, rundown and decaying rock and timber buildings. Strange, pungent odours from cooking food and burning wood-smoke emanated from them. After trapsing around two blocks, hidden in the shadows, they entered the side door of a large, white, marble building, filled with steam and sweet-smelling, herbal liniment. Finally, they reached a small room draped in sheer, pink-coloured curtains. Incense and perfume lingered strongly in the air, and several candles of varied sizes and shades burned with low, flickering flames.

'Take a seat while I get you a drink,' the mysterious female said in a soft, silky-smooth voice. 'You must be thirsty.'

Yarron watched her as she reached for a tall, purple-coloured, glass carafe from a lowset, wooden cabinet, and picked up two bronze goblets, placing all the vessels on a small, wooden table beside two large, scarlet-cushioned, rattan chairs. She was dressed in similar, skimpy clothes to the females at the tavern, showing off her lithe, curved and well-endowed copper-toned body. Her frizzy black hair was teased to emphasise her stunning facial features.

After sitting next to Yarron on the wide seat, she poured a ruby-tinted liquid in both goblets. Cautiously and discreetly, he waited for her to take a sip first, just to be sure the liquid wasn't drugged. Then, after taking a sip himself, he placed his goblet on the table. The vintage wine tasted sweet and was smooth on the palette.

'So, who are you? And why are we here?' he asked in a low voice, his face remaining serious, as he leant back, folding his arms across his chest.

'I'm on your side. Please, let me explain,' she pleaded, taking another sip before continuing. 'My name is Shanowah and I'm the proprietor of this establishment. I know you're not Treldarian, even though you're fluent in their language. I shadowed you as you strolled through the markets. You have the walk and peculiarities of a soldier but you aren't familiar with the environment or our customs. You're a stranger in a strange land.'

'I was that obvious?' asked Yarron who was becoming more curious.

'Yes, you were. But alert with an enquiring mind. I've been in this business a long time, and I can read instantly the profiles of most, if not all, males.'

Yarron intervened. 'And what exactly is this business you've been in?

She smiled seductively and spoke in a smooth and silky voice. 'I'm in the business of entertaining. Soldiers come here to indulge in the healing hot baths, enjoy the soothing massages and partake in pleasures of the flesh. They like to escape from their daily drudgery and be pampered by our seductive magic. We are Ludaxian women and mistresses in the art of seduction from which we derive a profitable living.'

'I hope you're not intending to seduce *me* out of my money with your wayward, wily charms?'

'No, I wouldn't do that to a happily married soldier.'

Yarron was momentarily shocked and almost lost for words. His eyes widened. He grabbed Shanowah tightly by the arm and looked her in the face with steely-cold eyes. 'How do you know I'm married? Who have you been talking to? And don't lie to me if you value your life!'

Shanowah remained calm and replied with confidence. 'Let go of my arm and I'll tell you all I know.'

Reluctantly, Yarron released his grip. 'Alright, I'm listening.'

Shanowah handed him his goblet. 'Please, drink while I tell you the whole, long story.'

She explained how several hundred years ago the Treldarians had invaded their planet Ludax, enslaved the females and brought them back to Orkharn to use for their pleasure, while forcing the males to continue producing food for their army. The Treldarians continuously kept replacing the females when they'd outlived their use. So, to make the most of their bad situation, the women started to demand payment, making the Treldarian soldiers compete for the affections of the particular females they wanted.

Yarron was becoming irritated. 'What's this got to do with you knowing all about me?'

'Patience,' Shanowah counselled. 'In their relaxed euphoria, the Treldarian soldiers would sometimes unintentionally divulge valuable secrets, not only about military plans and strategies, but also about other soldiers and their secrets. The Ludaxian ladies would use this information to earn more krads, or money, in your language, through blackmailing. And, they'd store this extra money as a group hoping one day to have saved enough to pay someone or some kind visitor to Orkharn, to help them escape from this planet.'

'So?'

'Patience, Yarron. Now, let me tell you what has happened in the last five days …' Shanowah paused to take another sip of wine before continuing.

'After an absence of six years, Lieutenant Vark, now self-promoted to the rank of Captain, suddenly arrived back on Orkharn in a Tzuracian Destroyer with his army of about a hundred soldiers. We'd heard rumours that all the Treldarians had either been killed or imprisoned in the great battle with the Tzuracians so we were all shocked he'd returned. We were happily enjoying our freedom, even under the authority of the Sentinels. General Vark's soldiers were total brutes who treated us as their personal sex slaves, often beating us in their drunken stupors. At least the Sentinels treat the Ludaxian females with respect and dignity.'

She stopped to take another sip and wipe her lips with the back of her hand. She was not going to be rushed. 'On their first day here, after killing the unit of Sentinels, the sex-starved soldiers overran the taverns and the health spas like animals hunting in packs to devour their prey. I was the host for Captain Vark and in his semi-delirious, euphoric state, he told me of his escape. He described how he had attacked the village on Mankro and taken your wife Bhalar hostage. He said he was out for revenge, because it was Bhalar who helped you escape from the Treldarians, and *you* who exposed the Treldarians' plans to invade Tzurac and Terra Major. He wants to execute you and Bhalar like the Tzuracians who executed his father.'

Shanowah could see Yarron becoming more anxious, sensing a mixture of hate and fear. His blue eyes turned to cold steel and he clenched his jaws. 'Where is Bhalar?' he demanded. 'Is she here? And is she still alive?'

Raising her arms and outstretching them with her palms facing Yarron as a gesture for him to settle, she spoke to calm him. 'I can see how *very* upset you are, and I understand how you feel, but all is not lost. Bhalar is safely locked up in the cells.'

'Thank the Gods!' Yarron breathed a sigh of relief.

'Tykran's intention was to lure you to Orkharn using her as bait. And I was ordered to seduce you and drug you when you arrived, making it easy for you to be carried to the cells.'

Yarron looked suspiciously at the goblet of wine he was holding, and then looked back at Shanowah questioningly.

'No, Yarron, the wine is *not* drugged,' she said convincingly. 'But Vark would kill me without hesitation if he knew I was about to betray him. You see, I've no intention of following Tykran's orders. No, I want you to save Bhalar and then help the Ludaxian women escape with both of you. We despise these Treldarians!'

Yarron nodded to show he understood. 'So where is Bhalar being held? And where is Tykran? I want to kill him!'

'I can show you the way to Bhalar's cell and we need to move fast. But you'll have to hold off killing Tykran because he's not here.'

'Not here?' Yarron was visibly annoyed.

'Tykran left with most of his soldiers about two days ago in search of a race he said lived on a planet far beyond a boundary line drawn up over four hundred years ago. He's hoping to persuade this alien race to join him in defeating the Sentinels. He left the rest of his army to guard Bhalar and help capture you.'

'What about the two Tzuracian pilots who were with him? What's happened to them?'

'They're the pilots flying him in the Tzuracian ship to this unknown planet.'

'Okay, Shanowah. Show me the layout of the cells where Bhalar is located and tell me how many soldiers are guarding her. If I can save her, then we have a deal.'

DARK ALLIANCE

TRAVELLING at Level eight hyperdrive speed with one hundred of Tykran's soldiers on board, the *Piken* was making good headway into the uncharted void of the far-reaching Eastern Quadrant.

As they examined the parchment chart on a round table in the space behind the pilot's cockpit, Lieutenant Krag expressed some doubt. 'Sir?' he asked Tykran. 'How do you know we're travelling to the right planet, considering it's been over four hundred years since the Treldarians last had contact with these Rozakians?'

'Well, Lieutenant, I don't know for certain it's the right planet, but it's the only clue we have to follow. And we can't waste our fuel and our precious time searching the whole eastern quadrant the other side of this boundary.'

Tykran called out to the Tzuracian pilot under his guard. 'Captain Jharryn! How long before we reach Planet Rozak?'

'Two days, Captain Vark!' she said promptly.

Vark's men had been restless from the outset and having two good-looking females for pilots on board hadn't helped. The first night onboard while the others were bedded down in the cargo hold, Captain Jharryn had been confronted in her quarters by three mean-looking, lustful soldiers. Her martial arts skills totally surprised her attackers who ended up with bruises, lacerations and a few broken fingers. But now, after three days in flight, Vark's soldiers were becoming very irritable and beginning to fight amongst themselves. They needed to be disciplined.

Tykran turned to Krag to resolve the problem. 'Lieutenant, I want you to control the soldiers and start getting them into shape. When confronting our new allies, we need to appear as a well-trained, well-ordered, tough military force to be reckoned with.'

'Aye, sir. I'll see to it immediately.'

So, for the next two days the soldiers underwent gruelling hand-to-hand combat training, weapons handling and physical exercise. Their aggression was appropriately channelled and soon they were ready to fight together as a disciplined team.

In the early hours of the morning on the fifth day the ship was shaken by a violent blast to the hull, which tossed the sleeping soldiers out of their hammocks. The engines shut down bringing the *Piken* to an instant standstill.

Tykran, who was lying on the floor of his cabin, dazed after being woken abruptly, was alerted by the strained voice of Sub-Lieutenant Rhamak on the intercom.

'Captain!' she yelled in a shrill voice. 'We have visitors, and they are hostile. You must come to the cockpit at once.'

Tykran jumped to his feet, threw his boots and jacket on, and hastily dived out the cabin.

Standing at the cockpit and looking out he was confronted by three strange, dark-coloured and menacing spacecraft.

Rhamak was receiving a transmission on her headset. 'We're being hailed, Captain.'

'Put it on loudspeaker and screen, Lieutenant, and raise the shields to full capacity.'

'Yes, sir.'

Vark knew if he armed the weapons on the ship, it could be interpreted as a sign of aggression. But save for their shields, they were totally at the mercy of their visitors, whoever they may be.

The screen lit up with a single image of a figure from the waist up. He was wearing a tight-fitting, dark-grey, shiny, metallic uniform. His face was unusual, with pastel grey skin, a square jawline, dark, sunken round eyes with straight thin slivers for eyebrows, black short-cropped hair and round, pinned back ears. The figure began to speak through his pencil-thin mouth in a strange unintelligible language. He spoke in a low-pitched monotone voice for a short burst only, and then went silent.

Tykran stared for an instant, mesmerised by the figure, and feeling intimidated. He had no idea what the Rozakians looked like, or if this was one of them. He spoke, not knowing whether the aliens would understand his language. 'We are Treldarians, and we come in peace. Why did you fire on our ship?'

He stood silent not knowing what to expect and watched as the grey figure moved his arms to the lower part of the screen and began to communicate to his surprise, in Treldarian.

'We are Rozakians and you Treldarians are trespassing in our territory. You have breached the pact you had with us! Never cross over the boundary!' His voice became louder and more threatening. 'I did not fire on your ship, but you're being held by a tractor beam which has disabled your weaponry system. I suggest you turn back before we change our mind and destroy your ship, which does not look like a Treldarian craft.'

'You know our language?' Tykran asked cautiously.

'We have records of your language from four hundred years ago and I'm using a translating device. So, you understand my warning?'

'Yes,' Tykran responded quickly. 'I know of your race and I say again, we come in peace. In fact, we desperately need your help. We're in a stolen Tzuracian Destroyer but I'll explain everything to you if you permit an audience in person.'

There was a momentary pause while the figure stared at the screen. Then the loudspeaker came to life. 'I will send a small craft to bring you to my ship – *just you*. And leave your weapons behind.'

The screen went blank.

'Wow!' said Krag. 'Our first encounter with Rozakians! They look deadly mean and imposing! We sure need them on our side.'

Tykran nodded heartily.

'Lieutenant Krag, take six of the soldiers to the Cargo Bay and have them stand in formation to greet our new potential allies. I'll join you shortly. I'll leave you in command. If anything happens to me, I want you to return to Orkharn, execute Bhalar and Yarron if he's there, and find sanctuary with the soldiers on one of our known hideouts. The battalion and you may end up like General Dranz's Bladers, turning to piracy if our plan fails.'

'I can come with you, sir, as security for your safety.'

'No, Lieutenant. You heard what he said, and I need you to stay and lead the soldiers.'

No sooner had they finished their conversation, than Lieutenant Rhamak called out from the cockpit. 'Captain, your ride is here.' A small craft had landed in the cargo bay.

Tykran made his way to the small, unusually shaped, silver craft feeling apprehensive. On arrival he was searched roughly for weapons by one of the Rozakian pilots and then secured in a seat with his hands cuffed. The Rozakians were taking no chances with this alien intruder. The side door closed, the small craft exited the cargo hatch and, two minutes later, it was back inside the Rozakian mother ship.

After disembarking the craft with his hands still cuffed, Tykran was escorted by seven very large, grey-suited soldiers, all eight feet tall, with similar features to the figure seen on the screen of the *Piken*. They were heavily armed with unique weapons. Around their necks hung small, metallic silver discs and around their waists they wore a kind of utility belt with various metal objects attached. No words were exchanged as they marched Tykran through a maze of narrow, drab, grey coloured passageways, illuminated by pale, glowing panels on the walls and ceiling.

Several minutes passed, before the lead soldier in front turned and held his arm up as a gesture to stop. His hand was wide and webbed like an aquatic creature with elongated fingers. The soldiers came to a halt and the leader stamped his finger on a small, green, illuminated keypad on the wall to his left, activating one of the large panels which slid sideways rapidly in silence. The lead soldier stepped through the opening, the others following, still surrounding Tykran.

On entering the large room and coming to a halt, Tykran was confronted by the figure he'd met on the screen. He was seated behind a long and wide metal table, surrounded by six grey metallic chairs. The room was spartan in appearance. It had drab grey walls and there was a square electronic device with small flashing lights on the table in front of the figure who was also wearing a metallic silver disc around his neck. Two of the soldiers grabbed Tykran by the arms and forced him into the chair opposite the figure.

'I am Commander Nukwar,' the figure said, the dialogue coming in electronic, synthesised Treldarian from the square box on the table. 'I'm the captain of this vessel and responsible for our planet's security,' he declared in a terse voice. 'Who are you? And what do you want?'

Tykran felt very vulnerable at this moment. The Commander was even more intimidating in person and the tone of his voice more threatening. Tykran felt that to gain this military commander's respect, he needed to project an aura of fearlessness and authority. It was a soldier's code of honour to show strength, not weakness.

'I'm Captain Tykran Vark, leader of the Treldarian Second Legion,' he proclaimed proudly. 'And I didn't appreciate the manner in which you intercepted my ship. I came in search of an ally who could not only help in my quest but be rewarded for their support. Now I'm not sure if I made the right decision to seek you out.'

Commander Nukwar sat in silence mulling over the Treldarian's words. 'Alright, Captain Tykran Vark, you have my attention. Explain your dilemma.'

Tykran now felt more confident to present his case. He explained the ongoing battle for the powerful, blue crystal Xytrinium; the defeat of the Treldarians by the Sentinels six years ago; his father's execution; and his own army's imprisonment and their escape.

'I want to exact revenge on the Federation for what they did to the Treldarians and my father. I want to annihilate the Tzuracian Federation and reclaim control of the Xytrinium reserves. To do this, I need a powerful ally, an ally with superior weaponry and the military might to overpower them!'

Commander Nukwar spoke forcefully. 'So, if we decide to help you, and risk our ships and our lives, what do you offer in return? What's in it for us?'

'You will share in the rewards. Your race will receive half of the valuable resource of Xytrinium crystals already in reserve, with regular shipments each month to replenish your stocks. And you will be able to receive these shipments without the interference of the Sentinels and their Federation of Planets.'

'But what good is the Xytrinium to us? I don't see it.'

'Xytrinium is a volatile substance which can be used to power spacecraft and make very powerful weapons. The Sentinels have also mastered how to utilise the crystals in medical equipment and other machinery.' Tykran deliberately stopped short of mentioning the powers of Xytrinium infusion. He didn't want the Rozakians to have more power than the Treldarians.

Nukwar appeared more interested. He knew the energy source Rozenium, currently used by the Rozakians to power their ships and weapons was almost depleted. *Here is an opportunity worth pursuing*, he thought.

Tykran sensed the Commander's mind churning over and saw a gleam in his eyes.

'Alright, Captain, you've stirred my interest. But I'll need to present your proposal to a higher authority, and they'll decide. We'll return you to your ship, and you can follow us to my planet. Now go!'

* * *

'So, what happened?' Krag asked anxiously when Tykran returned to the *Piken*.

'Good news. They seem interested in our deal. But we need to follow them to their planet. Keep your fingers crossed.'

After following the Rozakian ship for two hours, they eventually came in sight of Planet Rozak, a large, pale grey sphere, encircled with wispy white cloud. As they entered the atmosphere at low level cruising speed, the surface revealed high and rugged purplish mountains descending to alluvial plains of grey sands, sparse vegetation and wide dark rivers with numerous small tributaries.

Within minutes the landscape changed, revealing a large city overshadowed with numerous tall towers. The triangular buildings of ultra-modern architecture were constructed from a bluish metal which reflected faint rainbow colours, with a similar effect as when oil floats on water.

Over the intercom near where Tykran was standing came Captain Jharryn's voice. 'Captain, the atmosphere is breathable and similar to Orkharn's with seventy-seven percent nitrogen, twenty-two percent oxygen and other small amounts of gases such as carbon dioxide.'

'Thank you, Captain.'

Tykran's gaze was interrupted again by noise from the loudspeaker. 'Captain Tykran Vark,' sounded Nukwar's monotone, low-pitched voice, 'your ship will berth at the landing bay jutting out from the tall tower displayed on your screen. Head for this and a tractor beam will guide you in after you've shut down your engines.'

'Affirmative, Captain Nukwar.'

'Did you get that direction, Captain Jharryn?' Tykran called out to the pilots.

'Yes, hard *not to hear* over the loudspeaker.' She was more sarcastic than usual, covering her anxiety about their arrival on a strange planet with potentially aggressive aliens.

Tykran turned to Krag. 'I want you to come with me when we're escorted to their Commanding Officer. This time, safety in numbers.'

'Aye, sir.'

The tractor beam latched on just as the vessel cut its engines and the *Piken* was pulled slowly into the huge landing bay and lowered onto the smooth, shiny floor. The side door retracted and Tykran and his Lieutenant stepped out, only to be surrounded by a unit of metallic grey uniformed Rozakian soldiers, well-armed with stoned-faced expressions. Captain Nukwar stood in front of the welcoming committee, aiming an odd-looking weapon in their direction. He paced towards them and handed them each a small device, signalling to place it in their ear.

Tykran looked inquisitively at Krag, but both did as they were asked.

'These devices are translators so we can now understand each other,' Nukwar explained and both Treldarians nodded. 'But you'll need to be searched for weapons before we take you to our Supreme Leader.'

Nukwar directed two of his soldiers to undertake the task. Convinced the visitors were carrying no weapons, Nukwar replaced his weapon into his shoulder holster, giving a hand signal for Tykran and Krag to follow him. The Rozakian soldiers surrounded them, and they all began to march after Nukwar.

Like the Rozakian spaceship, the building they were in was devoid of colour and just as spartan. However, the passageway was far wider and there were many more soldiers moving hurriedly in all directions, whilst staring at the alien newcomers.

Within minutes they had all arrived outside a glass encased structure with metal frames holding large panels of opaque glass neatly in place. Nukwar waved his hand over a small, round, black dome on the wall and one of the glass panels slid silently open. He gave an order for the six soldiers to remain outside, then ordered Tykran and Krag to step inside. Nukwar followed in behind them before the sliding door sealed itself.

Standing before them was another tall soldier dressed slightly differently in a dark grey uniform with silver metal bars for epaulets and a thin mandarin collar. The long sleeves of the uniform had narrow silver bands on the cuffs and the tight-fitting trousers had two thin silver bands running down the side seams of the legs. The trousers were met by black, solid-heeled boots.

Nukwar gave the introductions. 'Captain Vark, this is our commanding chief, Supreme Leader Wazine.'

Tykran could see Wazine was wearing a translator device in his ear to interpret Treldarian language. 'Greetings, sir. This is my Second-in-Command, Lieutenant Krag,' Tykran said, waving his hand in Krag's direction. 'We've travelled a long way to meet you, and hopefully become allies in the war against the Tzuracians.'

Wazine stood motionless, staring into the eyes of his captives. 'Captain Nukwar has informed me who you are and what you have proposed. As much as the Rozakians wanted to remain distanced from the Treldarians and any other races, for that matter, it may be that you have arrived at just the right time.'

Tykran looked sideways at Krag who had raised his eyebrows in surprise. *What was Wazine thinking? Why was this the right time?*

They didn't have to wait long for an answer.

'Our empire has remained supreme in this quadrant for over three thousand years due to our advanced weaponry and spacecrafts. This has been made possible because we've been able to derive our own power source. Our planet consists largely of a metallic ore called braktite, which in your language is a magnetic alloy. We have mastered its unique and very powerful qualities to produce devastating weapons which emit high concentrated magnetic waves that can shatter anything they strike. Our blood and DNA is based on this alloy and therefore we are required to shield ourselves from these destructive, powerful waves by wearing a protective armour. Our uniforms repel the magnetic fields especially when we activate the silver disc around our necks or in our armoured breast plates.'

Tykran was curious. 'So, if you have such a powerful resource at your disposal, why are you interested in Xytrinium?'

'Here lies the dilemma. Unfortunately, our resource is almost depleted, and we have searched the Eastern quadrant for over a hundred years with no success to locate more braktite. If these

Xytrinium crystals are as powerful as you profess them to be, then we need this resource not only as an energy resource to survive, but also to power our spacecrafts and weapons.'

Tykran and Krag exchanged a satisfied glance. *How lucky could their timing have been?*

'So, Captain Vark, we're willing to help you in your cause, provided we share equally in the Xytrinium reserves and provided you show us how to use this resource in all its forms. If you agree, then we will be your allies.'

'Thank you. I agree in principle,' replied Tykran, looking at Krag who was nodding his head in silent excitement. 'However, I need to tell you that all our Treldarian vessels were destroyed by the Tzuracians in the last battle, and we need ships to mount this assault. Can you supply these?'

'How many ships do we need to defeat your enemy? And how many soldiers?' asked the Supreme Leader.

Tykran did a quick rough calculation. 'I think we need a thousand ships and five thousand soldiers.' He feared this might deter the Rozakians and was surprised and elated by the quick and decisive response.

'Done.'

DARING RESCUE

BACK on Planet Orkharn, Yarron and Shanowah began planning Bhalar's rescue from the prison cells and an escape with the Ludaxian beauties.

'The best time to go for Bhalar is after sunset when the Treldarian soldiers have only two guards on duty,' Shanowah said.

'Okay. That's in about two hours' time. Meanwhile you can show me the layout and I can work out a plan of attack.'

Shanowah nodded in agreement. 'I can come with you to distract the guards.'

'No, Shanowah, thank you, but you've done enough already to help me. You need to pack everything you need and tell the other Ludaxians to do the same without alerting the Treldarians of our intentions. How many of you are there?'

'There are fifteen of us. Do you think you can carry all of us in your ship?'

'Yes, there's enough room.'

By the time the sun had set, Yarron knew where the cells were located and the best route to get there. He had arranged for the Ludaxians to drug the Treldarian soldiers at the taverns and hot baths and then meet him at an agreed rendezvous on the outskirts of town.

Heading down the dark streets to the cell block, Yarron stayed alert, checking behind him as he went. Luckily the cloud had covered the full moon, allowing him to blend into the shadows. He moved swiftly but quietly, like a hungry fox on the prowl.

As he passed the tavern, he noticed the soldiers slumped in their seats or lying on the ground unconscious. *The plan's working, the Ludaxians have done their job.*

Finally, he reached the heavy iron gates of the cell block, which carelessly had been left unlocked. *Too easy. The Gods are smiling on me. So far, so good.*

But, although he carefully swung the gates open, they squealed in a high pitch. *Damn!* Instantly he unholstered his laser pistol in expectation of being accosted by the guards. He waited for a moment, straining his acute hearing and listening for any unusual movements. There was no response and he breathed a sigh of relief.

Inside the building, he continued cautiously down the dark, long passageway checking every sunken cavity and corner in the shadows. In the distance he could make out two Treldarian soldiers, blades strapped to their backs, and long-barrelled guns held against their chests. They were standing about five feet apart, parallel with and facing the wall opposite. The lamps above their heads lit up their semi-awake faces. They were unprepared for an encounter, oblivious to the fact all their comrades had just been drugged.

Creeping closer without a sound, Yarron was soon about twenty feet away pointing the pistol in their direction, when out of nowhere a furry little creature jumped out in front of him from an overhanging ledge making a loud, screeching noise. The guards, suddenly startled, snapped their guns into firing position straining to see down the dark passageway. Luckily Yarron had the advantage. He fired his laser pistol twice, the guards slumping to the ground with smouldering holes in their chests.

Yarron raced to where the guards lay motionless, his pulse racing and his heart thumping. They had been guarding a cell with an invisible forcefield. Inside the cell he was relieved to see his beloved Bhalar who, in spite of smudged dirt stains on her face, looked as beautiful as ever to him.

'Yarron!' she exclaimed with relief. She was overcome with joy, and tears rolled down her cheeks. 'You came for me. I can't believe you found me. It's *so* good to see you.'

'It's great to see you too, and *of course* I found you – I'd have tracked you down to the end of the universe. Now let's get out of here.'

The moment Yarron shut down the forcefield, Bhalar threw her arms around him squeezing him hard, and kissing him with passion. 'I love you,' she whispered in his ear.

'I love you too and I'm so happy to see you're unharmed.'

Yarron held Bhalar's hand and guided her to the exit. They made their way quickly undercover to the rendezvous where Shanowah was waiting with the other Ludaxians.

'All good?' Shanowah asked as they approached.

'All good. Bhalar, this is Shanowah, the Ludaxian who saved me and helped me find you,' Yarron said. 'She told me what Tykran Vark has planned. In exchange, I've agreed to take her and her friends back to their own planet to escape from their Treldarian captors.'

The two women exchanged looks of gratitude.

'Now if you'll all follow me, I'll take you to my ship.'

With Yarron carefully retracing his steps back to his craft, they arrived about an hour later.

When they were all aboard and comfortably seated on the bench seats on each side of the hull with Bhalar in the co-pilot's chair, Yarron activated the engines. 'Where exactly is your planet, Shanowah?' he asked.

From her small carry-bag Shanowah produced a compact shiny metal disc that fitted onto her palm. She pressed a tiny button on the side of the disc, the lid sprang open, and a green holographic image appeared showing the coordinates of Planet Ludax.

With no further questions asked, Yarron instantly punched the information into the console and commanded, 'Computer, set navigation program for Ludax, and set hyperdrive to maximum. What's the estimated arrival time?'

The response came back in that familiar, tinny, crackling voice, 'At Level 10 hyperspeed the ship should arrive in two days' time.'

'Computer, cast off!'

Breaking free of the planet's gravity, Yarron switched to autopilot and then turned to Bhalar. 'I need to explain. Dakhar contacted me by Pledge ring as soon as he found out that Tykran Vark and his soldiers had escaped. Unfortunately, this was several days after the event, and too late for me to get back to the village before they attacked Mankro. I'm sorry I wasn't there with you and the children. I was devastated when I returned to the village and learned of your fate. I thought I'd lost you.'

Bhalar could see the hurt on Yarron's face and realised how he must have felt. She gently placed her soft hand on his cheek and brushed a fallen tear away, then stroked his black hair. 'Yarron, it wasn't your fault,' she said in a quiet, reassuring voice. 'You weren't to know.'

She sighed. 'I'm just thankful I wasn't hurt, and the children were kept safe. We tried to fight Tykran's soldiers off, but we were overpowered. Some of the villagers were killed or wounded. Tykran knew I was the one who helped you escape from my father after he captured you. Before he was executed, my father told him we had returned together to Mankro. Holding me hostage was a way of trapping you, knowing you would come after me.' She stared into his eyes for some time before she spoke again. 'Thank you for saving me.'

They leaned over and kissed long and passionately.

Shanowah lent her head towards her fellow Ludaxians, who were experts in seduction. They were sighing while watching the two pilots embracing. 'Now that's what you call *true* love.'

* * *

Two days passed without interruption and soon Yarron's ship was on the surface of the planet Ludax. As they were disembarking, Shanowah turned to Yarron and held out a small leather purse. 'Here's the money we saved as a reward for helping us escape.'

Yarron raised both hands gently pushing Shanowah's hand away and smiled sincerely. 'I want you to keep that money. I'm just so grateful to you in helping me save my wife. And it was my pleasure to rescue you from those drunken soldiers.'

Shanowah returned a broad smile. 'In that case, to show our appreciation, I'd like you and Bhalar to remain for a while on Ludax as our special guests, to rest and rejuvenate in our beautiful, tropical climate.'

Yarron beamed. 'Well, *I* can't refuse an offer like that from a beautiful woman. How about you, Bhalar? Grenham is looking after the children until we return and we could both do with a couple of days together to refresh and regroup.'

'Yes, I agree, as long as the children are safe.'

* * *

Three days passed quickly in the blissful paradise. Yarron washed the black dye from his hair and grew a blonde stubble, looking more like his old self each day.

Soon it was time to go and just before he and Bhalar departed, he sent a hologram to Dakhar explaining events over the last seven days and forewarning him of the army Tykran was trying to recruit from the outer regions of the Eastern Quadrant.

'I'm heading back to Mankro with Bhalar to reunite with our children and help restore the damage Tykran and his army caused. Let me know if you need my help in stopping the alien army. Tykran is out for revenge and has nothing to lose. If I hear anything more, I'll let you know. Yarron, out.'

CUT AND RUN

AFTER arranging to meet back at Planet Orkharn in ten days' time, Tykran and his soldiers left the Rozakian Supreme Leader to organise his fleet and prepare for the long journey ahead. On Orkharn, strategic plans would be detailed, and battle assaults mapped out with more precision, using the charts his father had drawn up when executing the Treldarians' last invasion of Tzurac. But this time, Tykran intended to avoid the fatal errors made by his father. This time, the attacking forces would not be divided to attack on two fronts, a major flaw which exposed them and ended in their defeat.

Three days later, the *Piken* touched down on Tykran's home planet. Trekking from the landing bay to the capital Bharkaz with the two Tzuracian pilots under guard, Tykran sensed something was wrong. He turned to Krag, 'It's too quiet, wouldn't you agree, Lieutenant?'

'I agree, sir. There's no sounds of music and laughter coming from the taverns or the health baths, and I don't see any Ludaxian females prancing around.'

As they approached one of the main taverns, Tykran could see some of his soldiers outside, drinking quietly. *Most unusual*, he thought.

One of the soldiers sighted Tykran and his crew, and immediately stood to attention. The others seeing the reason for his action, did the same.

Tykran questioned one of the soldiers, 'Where's Sergeant Jhakmar?'

'Inside the tavern, sir!' he replied obediently, saluting his Captain.

'Go get him soldier and bring him here!'

'Yes, sir.'

The soldier soon reappeared with Jhakmar at his side. Jhakmar saluted and stood at attention.

'What's going on, Sergeant?' Tykran demanded with an inquisitive look.

'I have some very bad news, sir.'

'Don't tell me, the tavern's run out of brew,' Tykran said sarcastically.

'No, sir. Bhalar has escaped with Shanowah and the other Ludaxians.'

Tykran's facial expression instantly changed from a wry smile to a mixture of shock and infuriation. Shaking his clenched fist at Jhakmar he burst out yelling, 'How the hell did this happen? You better have a good explanation, Sergeant, if you value your life!'

Trembling slightly, and with beads of sweat appearing on his forehead and moisture dampening his collar, Jhakmar began to explain. 'A day after you left for your journey to the outer reaches of the Quadrant, one of the soldiers caught sight of a stranger wandering through the market stalls. What caught his attention was the unusual clothing the stranger was wearing and his uncertainty about the place. The soldier informed me of his suspicions but before we could question him, he was befriended by Shanowah, who led him away to the baths.'

'That must have been Yarron,' said Tykran, interrupting. 'Go on. What happened next?'

'Yes, it must have been Yarron. And we assumed Shanowah would be entertaining him in her boudoir as planned, so we continued drinking into the night.'

'Yes, that was the plan. Shanowah was to drug him so you could capture him and lock him up. So, what went wrong?'

'Well, *we* were drugged instead of *him*. The following morning, all of us who'd been at the tavern drinking with the Ludaxians woke with massive headaches feeling disorientated, and it was no ordinary hangover. The changing of the guards at the prison cells for the night shift hadn't been carried out by the replacement guards as they were also drugged. So, I immediately went with four of the soldiers to the cells, only to discover the two guards had been killed with a laser pistol and Bhalar was gone. So was Shanowah and the other Ludaxians. They all escaped with Yarron.'

Tykran wiped his hands down his face to restrain his anger, blurting out, 'That double-crossing bitch has betrayed me. When I catch up with her, she'll wish she were dead and so will the other treacherous Ludaxians who helped her. And if Yarron and Bhalar now think *they're* safe, they're under an illusion! Their fate will be in my hands if it's the last thing I do.'

Krag placed a hand on Tykran's shoulder to settle him. 'Well, sir, we can catch them later. Our only option now is to focus on our immediate priorities. The Rozakians.'

Tykran knew his Lieutenant was right. 'Sergeant Jhakmar, I want you to sober up your soldiers and start gathering provisions and munitions in preparation for a major war. Our alien army will be arriving in a few days, and we don't have much time. Report back to Lieutenant Krag when you've completed the task. Dismissed!'

'Yes, sir!' said Jhakmar as he saluted, about faced and began yelling orders to his soldiers.

'And you, Lieutenant Krag, escort these Tzuracian pilots back to their cells, and then report back to my office. We have plans to make.'

'Aye, Captain,' replied Krag, saluting.

They had no idea the two pilots had also made plans of their own …

* * *

On the *Piken*'s return flight from Planet Rozak, Captain Jharryn had overheard some of the soldiers talking amongst themselves. They confirmed something big was being orchestrated with a powerful alien force. Jharryn decided she could no longer remain passive as Tykran's pilot. She needed not only to contact General Dakhar to warn him what might be coming but also to take action. She needed more detailed information and the only ones who knew exactly what was happening were Tykran and Lieutenant Krag. Although it was extremely dangerous, she had to formulate a plan to capture the Lieutenant. Tzurac's future depended on it.

While sitting at the console one night, when the soldier guarding her was temporarily distracted, she seized the opportunity to begin typing a plan into a private file marked innocuously 'Gas levels'. She whispered the filename to her co-pilot while they were in their cabin changing shift and over the next couple of shifts the two pilots secretly exchanged notes in the file in readiness to take action.

Their bold plan was to kidnap Krag, reclaim the *Piken* and take him back to Tzurac where the TSF could interrogate him using mind probes. And they agreed the best time to do this was when they first landed back on the surface of Orkharn. Then, most of the soldiers would be tired and weary from the long trip and their minds would be fixated on the Ludaxian females and the euphoric health baths for rejuvenation and recreation.

* * *

As the two pilots were being marched back to their cells by Krag and two of his soldiers, they sensed things were turning in their favour. Their escort had left them uncuffed; Tykran's soldiers on Orkharn were still recovering from the after-effects of being drugged by the Ludaxians; and the soldiers from the *Piken* were tired and heading off to the taverns and healing baths before being involved in preparing provisions for the war to come.

Halfway to the cells and well distanced from the other soldiers, Jharryn and Rhamak nodded to each other. Now was the time to make their move. Simultaneously they lashed out with a side kick to the knees of the soldiers on each side, whipping the pistols from the soldiers' holsters. Jharryn moved with amazing speed and whacked the butt of the pistol with a blunt force on the back of Krag's neck, while Rhamak blasted the two soldiers. The three soldiers collapsed to the ground at the same time. Krag was unconscious, the other soldiers dead. After checking to see that all was clear, they dragged the two dead Treldarians out of sight. Then Rhamak, using super Sentinel strength, heaved Krag over her shoulder.

As they rushed to the *Piken*, Rhamak panicked for a moment, calling to Jharryn, 'You don't have the remote to unlock the ship!'

'But I know the manual codes,' she replied, calmly, 'so don't worry. Just concentrate on getting Krag there.'

After reaching the ship, Jharryn quickly accessed the side door and once they were inside, locked it behind them. While Rhamak bundled Krag into one of the seats in the cargo hold, shackled his wrists and ankles, and locked the shackles to the floor of the hull, Jharryn jumped into the pilot's seat and activated the engines. As she clicked the relevant controls, the console came to life with different coloured lights flickering across the panel.

Rhamak jumped into the co-pilot's seat and strapped herself in as Jharryn gave a command, 'Computer, set the coordinates for Planet Tzurac and blast off.' Their pulses were thumping and hearts pumping rapidly as they turned to face each other with a grin, 'Well done, Lieutenant. So far, so good,' said Jharryn.

Tykran who was heading for the Administration Building, heard the engines start up. Coming to a standstill, he turned his head in the direction of the sound, only to see the *Piken* disappearing rapidly into the outer atmosphere. He feared the worst as he ran back to the tavern to find his Sergeant looking up in the direction of the fading, wispy white trail left by the spaceship.

'What in the Gods' names is going on, Sergeant?' Tykran demanded.

'I don't know, sir, but I'll try and find Lieutenant Krag and report back to you.' Taking a small unit of soldiers with him, Jhakmar and the unit jogged towards the cells.

Returning within minutes puffing and panting, Jhakmar nervously reported his find. 'Sir, the guards are dead from laser blasts to their bodies, and there's no sign of Lieutenant Krag or the Tzuracian pilots.'

Vark seethed, realising Krag had been captured and knowing he had no craft at all to chase them. *He would probably never see his faithful Lieutenant and friend again.*

Jhakmar watched as his Captain's immense anger came to the boil, like a miniature volcano erupting. Tykran's face turned blood red, his eyes bulged and his mouth curled back to reveal a row of tightly clenched teeth. In a rage, Tykran swooped up a half-filled metal goblet with his right hand from the table beside him and heaved it with all his might towards the bar, smashing and shattering several of the glass bottles on the shelves behind it. Jhakmar managed to duck just in time, while the other soldiers stepped backwards in fear of being in the line of fire.

After taking control of his emotional outburst and slowing down his rapid breathing, Tykran slowly turned to his Sergeant. 'Take your soldiers and start preparing for our long journey to Tzurac. We'll need food supplies for two weeks, and munitions for a full-scale battle. Store them in the hangars near the docking bays in preparation to load them on board the Rozakian ships when they arrive. Dismissed!'

Jhakmar saluted, turned on his heels and started shouting orders to the rest of his soldiers. Within, minutes the tavern was deserted, leaving Tykran to process the inevitable. *The pilots had captured Krag and were taking him to Tzurac where the Sentinels would no doubt torture the truth out of him, exposing the secret alliance with the powerful, alien Rozakian force and their plans to invade Tzurac. His attack would no longer be a surprise and the Tzuracians would be at the ready.* And, with Lieutenant Krag gone, Tykran had no other soldier with the same experience to consult on his war strategies. He was devastated and momentarily at a loss.

But then Tykran steeled his thoughts. He was not done. After just recruiting a powerful new army, this was not going to deter him from seeking his revenge. He resolved to be more determined than ever. He'd wait for the Rozakians to arrive and formulate his strategies with the Supreme Leader. And he'd keep Krag's kidnapping under wraps because nothing must interfere with his planned vengeance. They could win the war with or without a surprise element.

* * *

On the *Piken*, now travelling at Level 10 hyperspeed, Captain Jharryn located her Pledge ring and sent a hologram to General Dakhar telling him they had managed to escape in the *Piken* with Tykran's Second-in-command, Lieutenant Krag as hostage. 'All going well, sir, our estimated time of arrival is in three days' time.'

'Great news, Captain. You've done well, and I'm relieved you and Sub-Lieutenant Rhamak came to no harm. Krag's information will be vital and give us the advantage we need. We heard from the exiled Sentinel Yarron Blandhar two days ago that Tykran Vark is gathering a large, powerful army of an alien race.'

'Yes, sir. I can tell you this is true and the alien race from Planet Rozak have powerful weapons. You'll learn more once you've fully interrogated our Treldarian captive.'

'Thank you, Captain. Stay safe and may the Ancient Spirits protect and guide you.'

'Thank you, sir. Over and out.'

The hologram closed down just as Krag was starting to rouse himself. Rhamak saw and heard him at the back of the ship, trying to break free from his shackles. She jumped out of her seat and went to check on him. Like many Tzuracian pilots she had studied several languages at the Academy and was fluent in the Treldarian dialect.

'So, you're awake and wondering where you are.' She grinned. 'No use trying to break those shackles – they're made from Xytrinium.'

'Where are we, you Tzuracian trash?' cursed Krag in a hateful, gravelly voice. 'When Captain Tykran catches up with you, he's going to tear your limbs off and throw you to the dogs.'

'Well, he has to find a ship first and then he has to catch us.'

Krag fell silent, not wanting to divulge any information by telling them about the alien weaponry and their superior battle crafts.

He could feel a large and very painful lump on his head. 'What did you hit me with, bitch?' As blood dripped on the floor he added, 'I've got a cracked skull. It's giving me a lot of pain and I'm bleeding.'

'Well, that's the least of your worries,' said Rhamak. 'You just sit tight and keep quiet, or we'll have to gag you.'

Krag shrugged his shoulders in frustration, knowing he was beaten.

Rhamak returned to her co-pilot's seat and strapped herself in again. 'How's our fuel reserves, Captain?' she asked knowing the ship had covered a lot of space and they'd had no time to refuel during their rushed escape.

'According to the energy readout on the console screen, we may have to refuel at one of the depots on the way. But what about our food supplies Sharne? Do we have enough to last the trip?'

'I took a quick inventory check when I was passing the kitchen and we have plenty, even with an extra mouth to feed.'

'Good. Best you catch up on some sleep while I take the first ten-hour shift. I'll keep an eye on our prisoner and wake you when it's your turn.'

* * *

After three days with no interruptions and a refuel at one of the depots, the *Piken* landed safely on their home planet, Tzurac. Jharryn and Rhamak were welcomed personally by General Dakhar who commended them for their brave efforts in risking their lives to escape, bringing with them a valuable asset. 'I'll be recommending you both for a medal,' he said, with great pride.

Lieutenant Krag was escorted under protest by Security from the Airfield direct to the Citadel, where he was placed in a high security holding cell awaiting interrogation by the TSF. He sat forlornly in his cell, realising he was implicated in killing innocent Tzuracian staff on Planet Lokar, and knowing he would soon be helplessly divulging Captain Vark's secret plans with their invincible mind probing techniques. Whatever the Tzuracians did with him – whether it would end with life imprisonment or execution – he would suffer guilt until his death as the one who betrayed Tykran and undermined the planned assault. *How could he let himself be captured so easily and become the weak link?*

PREPARE FOR WAR

WITHIN twenty-four hours of their arrival, the Security Forces had completed their mind probing interrogation of Lieutenant Krag and presented the vital information to General Dakhar.

Dakhar was very surprised to learn that Tykran had raised so quickly an alien army of five thousand soldiers and one thousand ships. And he was even more concerned these aliens had advanced weapons that used a strange ore called braktite and harnessed its powerful magnetic properties. According to Krag's confession, they had designed suits made from this substance to protect themselves 'against high concentrated magnetic waves that can shatter anything it strikes.'

After shutting down the report on the small screen on his desk, Dakhar sat silent for a long interval stroking his neatly trimmed, blonde beard with his right hand. Deciding if the robotic Diutrons in their current form would be defenceless against these advanced weapons. He activated the intercom to his orderly, 'Corporal Markhaz! Get hold of Grant Thompson and have him come to my office at once.'

'Yes, sir.'

The Irish engineer was still activating the two thousand Diutrons in the Airfield hangars when the call came through. He had arrived from Planet Iota only two days ago and was feverishly trying to meet the deadline for the robots to be ready. The Flight Sergeant who called him over could hear Thompson's Irish swearing from a distance as he approached.

'Mr Thompson, sir, you've been summoned to General Dakhar's office, and he wants you there now.'

'Och, can't a lad get any work done 'round 'ere without bein' interrupted all the time,' he cursed in his Irish temper. 'Alright, I'm comin!' he said, as he angrily slammed down the heavy metal tool he'd been using, grabbed a grease-stained rag from the back pocket of his overalls, wiped his hands on it, and swaggered out the main door.

Minutes later he was seated in one of the large leather chairs in Dakhar's office leaning back in comfort with an inquisitive look on his face.

'Sorry to keep you from your work, Grant. I'm aware of the time pressure you're under, but this is extremely important and confidential.'

Thompson, seated on the leather couch, leant forward, resting his chin on his clenched right fist with his elbow on the arm of the couch. He looked worried. 'You've got me attention, sir. I'm all ears.'

'I have a challenge for you,' said Dakhar seriously, engaging Grant's eyes. 'I've just learned who our enemies are and heard about the advanced weaponry they'll be using.'

The Irish engineer listened carefully while Dakhar elaborated. Every so often he nodded and sometimes shook his head in bewilderment. By the time Dakhar had finished, Grant was almost tearing his red hair out by the roots.

'Holy Mother of Jesus,' he blurted out loudly in his strong Irish tongue. 'You're sayin' you want *me* to design and make some kind of anti-magnetic shield for both the Diutrons and your soldiers that'ill deflect a concentrated powerful magnetic wave? And like ya wanted it yesterday? What am I? Some kind of miracle maker? You must be daft lad.'

'Grant, I know it sounds as though I'm asking the impossible, but I believe in you, and I know how brilliant you can be when you put your mind to it. If you like, I can ask Kyron Tyros – or Shield to you – to help with this critical task. He's a brilliant engineer as you know, and two heads are better than one. I'll also have our scientists join in. What do you say?'

Grant and Kyron went back a long time. They'd met when both were working for MERIC, Kyron Shield having come to Iota when Xytrinium was first discovered there in a massive explosion in the mines Grant was overseeing. After uncovering an internal conspiracy in the mining company, Kyron had gone on to take charge of MERIC and become Grant's boss and Grant had watched with admiration as Kyron prospered, leading the company, marrying the company's top computer engineer, Torri Madison and mentoring both Torri and the company's Executive Officer, Lauren Blake, to take over as directors from him. He was exceptionally talented and Grant could think of no-one better to work with.

Grant knew the Federation was facing another life and death situation. He would do his utmost to protect and save the Tzuracians and stop any other races from being annihilated by this dark, destructive force. 'Well, I'll do it,' he said, 'but only with Kyron. And it's goin' to cost yer a carton of top-quality, single malt Irish whisky.'

'You have a deal, Grant,' said Dakhar, smiling and offering his hand to shake. Grant was a character unlike any other he'd met before.

Thompson rose and shook the General's hand, saying 'I'll get started immediately' as he walked out the door.

Dakhar buzzed Corporal Markhaz again. He spoke with urgency in his voice, saying, 'Contact Kyron Tyros and tell him I need to see him as soon as possible.' He pressed the off switch before his orderly could reply.

Fifteen minutes later, Kyron, a tall, well-built Sentinel with short-cropped, fair hair and steel-blue eyes, appeared at Dakhar's office door. In public, protocol required salutes and ranks to be acknowledged, but in private, the close friends called each other by first names.

'Come in Kyron and take a seat.'

Kyron closed the door behind him as he walked to the large leather chairs and seated himself.

'How have you been? I haven't seen you for quite a while. I hope all is well with you and Torri, and the children?'

* * *

Dakhar and Kyron also had a history. It had been the discovery of Kyron's Sentinel heritage that first brought Dakhar to Terra Major with a fleet of Tzuracians to help with the discovery of Xytrinium and the conspiracy within MERIC by Director Samuel Jensen's son, Jackson. Dakhar and Kyron shared a close bond just as their Sentinel fathers had before them and they had developed a strong friendship over the years as they restored calm and established relationships between their planets.

As CCMO on Terra Major, Dakhar had mentored Kyron and had been proud to see him graduate as Lieutenant and First Officer Kyron Tyros after successfully completing his cadetship with the Officer's Training Academy in the new Earth-based Tzuracian military citadel. Kyron had graduated in the first round of officer graduates trained there.

And in the last six years since then, the two families had spent much time together on Terra Major. Tajhira and Torri shared everything with each other and, as doting mothers, discussed everything in raising their children. When not with the children, they would be out shopping, socialising or at the gymnasium, Torri delegating Lauren Blake to run the day-to-day administration of MERIC in her absence.

Kyron had been promoted to the rank of Captain and held the responsible position as Senior Instructor at the Officers Training Academy in the Citadel on Terra Major. The cadets were usually mentored by Tzuracian instructors with qualifications in their fields of expertise. However, in the teaching of martial arts, a subject in which Kyron excelled, Kyron was the mentor chosen by Ehrane Dakhar to instruct the would-be junior officers. It not only maintained his skill set, but also let him pass on the refined knowledge and proficiencies he had learned from his father, Captain Ahrmon Tyros. And Kyron would often accompany Kal Zawkon on interplanetary flights when instructing the cadets in battle simulations, weaponry tactics, navigation and field evasions aboard a variety of fleet ships.

Kyron and Torri had always intended to move to Tzurac at some stage, ideally when their children reached their mid-teens. But the move had happened earlier than expected. When Dakhar was recalled from Terra Major six months ago he had arranged for Kyron to relocate there too with his family as Captain in the Regiment on Tzurac.

There, Kyron and his family had been given the Tyros estate which his father once owned, and which had been preserved. Similar in architecture to Ehrane Dakhar's old-world mansion, it was also located at the base of the foothills where a river flowed on the western boundary and an orchard bearing citrus fruits, benefitted from the natural irrigation. Kyron much preferred this to being accommodated on the military base near the Citadel, and he spent most of his leisure time introducing his family to his Tzuracian relatives.

Kyron and his family felt at home on Tzurac. Torri had initially been apprehensive about leaving her home planet, her position at MERIC and her English parents, though Kyron reassured her they would have regular visits to Earth to see her parents, as well as Lauren Blake, to check on MERIC's progress. And their two children, Zuri, now thirteen, and his sister Ehrana, eleven, had assimilated well into the Sentinel Junior Cadet Academy together with Dakhar's son, Kyrah, and were making new friends. Torri was now convinced they had made the right choice.

And there was something else Torri was ecstatic about. Three years ago, the Tzuracian alchemists had discovered the protective gene which prevented a Xytrinium infusion from causing rapid ageing in humans. Using a sample of the gene taken from the only survivor among Jackson Jensen's mercenaries, and with genetic engineering, infusion with modified Xytrinium was now safe for humans – the double helix in humans remaining unaffected. In sanctioning the breakthrough procedure, the Tzuracian Senate decreed only those humans married to Sentinels would be permitted to use this modified infusion method and only on approval granted by the Senate. Torri had been granted approval and was delighted about living a long life and growing old with Kyron. Kal Zawkon and Lauren Blake too were elated when they learned the Senate had also approved this procedure for Lauren. They couldn't have asked for more.

* * *

'Yes, thanks Ehrane. I'm thoroughly enjoying my position and Torri is fitting in well with the community and socialising more with her newfound friends. Zuri and Ehrana are receiving excellent grades in the Junior Cadet Academy and are soon to graduate into the Officers Academy.'

'I'm pleased to hear everything is turning out well and you now consider Tzurac as your true home.'

'Yes, it's a good feeling. And how are Tajhira and the children?'

'Tajhira is well and is hinting about having another child to keep Terrazah company. Kyrah is so involved in his cadet training, he doesn't have time to play with his little sister.'

Kyron sat listening and nodding with keen interest, enjoying the company of his best friend, but he was aware this was not just a social meeting. So, he responded by changing the subject. 'We must all get together again for dinner soon, but what's the real reason you summoned me here? It must be serious, though I thought the Red Alert was over.'

'I'm afraid it is serious.' Dakhar told Kyron the events of the last eight days and finished by saying, 'In preparation to combat this powerful, alien army, I need you, as an immediate priority, and being an exceptional engineer, to assist Grant Thompson to manufacture devices to repel the enemy's magnetic weapons. We need these for our soldiers, as well as for our spacecrafts and the Diutrons. Without them, I fear we won't survive an attack.'

Kyron was now seriously focused on the issue, the concern showing on his face. 'What time frame are we looking at?'

'Yesterday,' Dakhar said only half joking. 'It was only by chance, and the bravery of the captured Sentinel pilots, that they managed to smuggle out Tykran's second in command, Lieutenant Krag, from Planet Orkharn. You remember him, don't you? They arrived here just over twenty-four hours ago and under interrogation, Krag divulged who the alien forces are and the type of weapons they possess. He also said they're already on the move.'

'Okay,' said Kyron. 'I'll let Torri know I'll be working late for the next two days on a special confidential project. I'll go to the workshops now if that's where Grant is working.'

'Thanks. I'll let him know you're on your way,' replied Dakhar. 'Oh, and I've also arranged to have some of our technical scientists help you both. May the Ancient spirits guide you.'

Soon after Kyron left, Dakhar buzzed his orderly again. 'I want you to set up a meeting with the Senate as soon as possible. Let me know when this has been arranged.' Again, Dakhar cut off the intercom before waiting for the corporal to acknowledge. He was in a hurry. It was late in the afternoon on Tzurac, but early morning on Terra Major and he still had time to send a hologram.

General Kal Zawkon was in his office at the Citadel on Terra Major when the image started to appear. It soon materialised into a familiar figure. 'Greetings, Ehrane.'

'Greetings, Kal. I'm contacting you to inform you of recent developments.' He had Zawkon's full attention.

After providing a condensed version of events, he said, 'Grant Thompson and Kyron Tyros are working feverously to develop a weapon to counteract an expected arsenal of alien, magnetic weapons. I think the alien force will concentrate their attack specifically on Tzurac, and therefore I need all the firepower mobilised around Tzurac. I'm asking you if you can send half of Terra Major's fleet to Tzurac with you at the helm of the Flagship. I need you, Kal, because you have the experience and proven capabilities in battle strategies to help thwart this one thousand fleet armada. What say you?'

'Of course, you'll have my support as always, no further debate needed. I'll make the necessary arrangements and should be there within two days.'

'Thank you, Kal. Over and out.'

Dakhar was startled when the intercom sounded. 'Sir, you have an audience with the Senate this evening at nineteen hundred hours.'

'Thank you, Corporal.'

Dakhar had one last task to perform before attending the audience. He contacted the Control Centre using the internal line system. 'Control Centre, this is General Dakhar. I need to speak with your Communications Officer.'

'Yes, sir, this is Lance Corporal Bhranik and I'm the Communications Officer for the late shift.'

'Okay, Corporal, I need the status on the location of the Urgellan Army which is being transported to Tzurac.' Dakhar was optimistic Queen Tarune had offered her five thousand strong army in support of the coming war, as she had done in the past. He was hoping Senator Volhardtz had been convincing enough to persuade her of the possible disastrous outcome if Tzurac failed to defeat the powerful alien force.

'Sir, Senator Volhardtz is on board the Destroyer *Ishwark* leading two Advanced Destroyer Carriers with five thousand Urgellan soldiers. They will be docking in five hours.'

'Thank you, Lance Corporal. Out!' Dakhar breathed a sigh of relief. *We have numbers.*

* * *

Dakhar stood before the Council of Elders who appeared slightly inconvenienced by the urgent late sitting. After they had settled in their respective chairs, Senior Senator Ghalbrak asked Dakhar to speak.

'Senators, please forgive me for the late sitting. I wouldn't have called this meeting if it wasn't urgent.' Dakhar began from the last report concerning Tykran's escape and the events leading to the current situation. 'After discovering details about the alien force's lethal weapons from Lieutenant Krag's confession, I have commissioned engineer Grant Thompson and Captain Kyron Tyros, together with some of our highly technically skilled scientists, to develop a defensive weapon against their powerful and destructive magnetic weaponry. We've only a narrow window of time, but I'm confident this team will successfully create a device to repel and destroy this powerful force.'

The senators shuffled in their seats. Some were sceptical.

'I've also ordered all the Diutrons to be resurrected and brought to Tzurac and requested General Zawkon to send half his fleet here from Terra Major. I believe the alien forces will focus their invasion on Tzurac believing that if they can annihilate us and our Sentinels, there'll be nothing to prevent them from totally decimating the Federation of Planets. Queen Tarune has offered her support by sending an army of five thousand soldiers from Urgellan and they'll be arriving on Tzurac in five hours.'

Ghalbrak waved his hand to interrupt Dakhar. 'Why do you think these aliens will concentrate their forces on Tzurac?' The other senators nodded their heads and muttered amongst themselves. It was only when Dakhar started to reply that the senators quietened.

'Because Senator, Tykran Vark is determined to seek his revenge on those who executed his father here on Tzurac. And they're after our Xytrinium. He's offered these aliens a bounty of Xytrinium for their alliance and the Rozakians desperately need another energy source because their own natural resource, braktite, is rapidly depleting.'

'And what are the alternatives if we're unable to invent defensive weapons in time?' Senator Ghalbrak asked. Again, the Elders began to mutter and shake their heads.

'We have two alternatives, Senator. We can fight the enemy with what we have, though I don't like our chances of surviving. Or we can evacuate Tzurac and try to find a safe haven knowing they won't stop hunting us.'

There was dead silence in the room.

* * *

Back at the workshop, Grant Thompson and Kyron Tyros were working frantically on a solution to develop and manufacture devices to counteract the destructive magnetic force the aliens used in their weaponry. Scratching his ginger scalp hoping ideas would come to the surface, like rubbing an oil lamp to summon a genie, Grant presented to Kyron on a blank 3D hologram, some hypothetical ideas based on the scientific principles of magnetism as a basis to work from.

'You an' I know lad,' he said speaking in his thick, lyrical accent, 'repulsion is based on same polarities, and attraction by opposite poles. We also know that magnetic waves can be destroyed by two main methods, excessive heat and a strong alternating current. So, here are some suggested options to discuss before we rush into a minefield. First option in a defence situation is to create somethin' which can absorb the energy waves and neutralise 'em or ricochet the waves like a force field. Second option relates to an assault weapon using high voltage with an intensified alternating current, which would totally disrupt and shatter their own protective magnetic field.'

Kyron listened intently, the wheels of his mind working overtime processing alternatives before he spoke. 'Grant, here's a thought. Regarding an assault weapon, we could make a modified version of our laser guns using the principles of alternating current which at the same time would also create extreme heat – like harnessing a lightning bolt and releasing it at will. This would shatter their magnetic shields and disable their weapons.

'As for protecting our soldiers, the ships and the Diutrons, maybe we could produce an anti-magnetic shield. Something portable a soldier could wear and activate on command, which surrounds the body, and we could amplify this application for our Destroyers and Diutrons.'

They both knew they had long hours of work under pressure ahead of them …

BATTLE TACTICS

TYKRAN was frantically pacing the floor of his office with a half-filled goblet of fermented wine in his hand. He hadn't slept well for the last two nights because of a troubled mind. His soldiers were almost finished gathering supplies and armaments, but the Rozakian armada was nowhere in sight. The arrangement had been for them to mobilise on Planet Orkharn ten days after Tykran departed from their planet. Eleven days had now passed and Tykran was beginning to have doubts. Having lost his Lieutenant, and having no spacecraft of his own, he was feeling isolated and vulnerable as well as frustrated.

His mind raced. *Had the Rozakians decided not to join forces with him after all? Or had they run into trouble in their journey? Perhaps they had decided to invade Tzurac themselves and keep all the Xytrinium? After all, he had little to offer them and they knew that Treldarian weapons were inferior to Rozakian weaponry.*

Then his mind turned to Lieutenant Krag. *How much information had the Tzuracians extracted from his loyal and trusted Lieutenant? He'd heard the TSF had methods of interrogation which rendered the tortured mind vulnerable and without resistance. If Krag had divulged everything, he would have told them about the Rozakian fleet of a thousand ships rendezvousing at Orkharn.*

Suddenly an idea came to mind. *Perhaps knowledge of this might stop the Tzuracians from attempting to attack Orkharn to recapture him and his soldiers. And assuming it did, maybe he could temporarily delay the assault on Tzurac while the Rozakians were here and ask for two of the Rozakians' ships to gather more warriors from elsewhere.*

A loud knock on his office door startled Tykran back to reality. 'Yes! Come in.'

The door opened. It was one of the administration staff, a pretty young female with long, jet-black hair pulled back into a ponytail. She had sparkling eyes and a slim figure.

'Sir,' she said nervously, sensing Tykran's mood. 'Sorry to disturb you. I just wanted to inform you the Rozakian ships have been identified on our radar and are requesting permission to land a shuttle.'

Tykran's fears and anxiety suddenly dissipated. He was relieved and excited at the same time but kept his cool. 'Thank you,' he said in a reserved manner. 'Give them permission to land. Then contact Sergeant Jhakmar and have him organise a unit of soldiers to greet our new allies at one of the landing bays and escort them to the War Room. And arrange to have some refreshments laid out on one of the tables there. I'm not familiar with what type of food or drink Rozakians like, so I'll leave this to your discretion.'

'Yes, sir,' she replied, closing the door behind her.

Tykran checked his reflection in one of the mirrors in the room to assure himself he was presentable to meet the Rozakian Supreme Leader. His long, straight, black hair was pulled back neatly in a ponytail, and with his thick, closely trimmed, black beard, he thought he looked the part of a true leader, especially in his new Treldarian black and red woven military uniform with polished, knee-high boots. Satisfied with his appearance and in a better frame of mind with the aliens' arrival, he turned on his heels and headed out the door.

Tykran arrived at the large War Room several minutes before the newcomers and sat at the head of the table in the stately chair where his father had once overseen strategic operations in consultation with his War Council. The feeling of inheriting the General's authority was overwhelming, and his emotions started to resurface for the father he loved and missed. But now was not the time to reminisce. He needed to focus fully on the coming battle, and plan in detail the most effective and efficient way of destroying his enemy. He was determined to have his vengeance.

The Supreme Leader Wazine and his Commander, Captain Nukwar, entered the War Room under escort, both with stern looks on their faces. Sergeant Jhakmar ordered the escort unit to halt.

'Greetings, Supreme Leader and Captain Nukwar. Welcome to Orkharn. Please be seated. Sergeant Jhakmar, take the unit outside and await further orders.' Jhakmar saluted, about faced and marched his soldiers outside the room, closing the door behind him.

Once the door was shut and Tykran placed the translator in his ear, Wazine began the conversation. 'I must apologise for the late arrival,' he said. 'Some of my fleet were further afield than I expected and it took extra time for them to be recalled.'

'No need to apologise. It allowed me extra time to prepare the soldiers and organise our provisions.' Tykran smiled while mentally cursing for the anxiety the delay had caused him. 'Please help yourselves to some wine and food, while I present my thoughts on how to plan our attack on the Tzuracians.'

'Go ahead,' said Wazine in a commanding voice. 'We're keen to hear.'

'As you may be aware, I was with my father, General Vark, the last time the Treldarians invaded Tzurac. I have a good recollection of the war strategies the Tzuracians used to defeat our ships in the space battles and our troops on the ground.'

Tykran poured himself a wine in one of the goblets and took a few sips before continuing. Pointing to some charts on the table he said, 'If you take a close look at these maps, you can see the planet Tzurac surrounded by three moons. The Tzuracians mobilised their ships behind one of these moons, Kelzhar. As our fleet passed this moon, half of the Tzuracian destroyers came from behind, while the other half confronted us in front. We were caught by surprise, trapped between the two. They obviously had long range sonar detectors on the moons and knew which direction we were approaching from and at what speed.

'My father, being a seasoned war veteran, was quick to execute a tactical diversion. He gave the order to deploy all the scout ships to attack the Tzuracian Destroyers. While their ships were preoccupied fending off the swarm of scout ships, our ships cloaked and headed for Tzurac. We blasted the protective dome with a Xytrinium torpedo, allowing our fleet to land and commence a ground attack. But our ground forces were defeated by the Sentinels and an allied race, combined with giant robots using laser cannons. We were unprepared and outmanoeuvred.'

He paused. 'Knowing what to expect, we will be better prepared this time. *We'll* have a superior strategy and we'll be strengthened by *your* advanced weapons.'

Supreme Leader Wazine studied the charts intently with Captain Nukwar while contemplating an answer. After some time, he sat back in his chair and gulped a couple of mouthfuls from his wine goblet. 'I have some ideas on how to defeat your enemy,' he said speaking with supreme confidence. 'First, we must knock out the detectors on the three moons so the Tzuracians will have no warning of our approach or the speed at which we're advancing.'

'And how do you propose to do that without creating loud explosions that will be detected on Tzurac and alert them?' Tykran interjected.

'There'll be no explosions. We can send long range probes which emit extremely strong magnetic waves to interfere with and distort the signals of the detectors. We've done this in the past and found it to be very effective.'

Tykran was reassured and nodded. 'Well,' he replied, 'I agree with your suggestion. When we near the Grekadian Star System we should send probes to each of the moons to try and knock out their transmissions to Tzurac and prevent them from giving away our position.'

Wazine continued. 'Using the moons to our advantage in screening our approach, we can use a three-pronged attack. We send in a third of the fleet first, delay before sending in the second group, and then wait for the right moment to dispatch the last group. This way, their fleet will be in disarray, not knowing which way to defend themselves.' He laughed out loud.

'Once our ships have annihilated the Tzuracian fleet and destroyed their protective dome, we descend on the planet to wage a ground battle. We must keep their city intact to use as a base and we need to capture their leaders to find out where they store their reserves of this powerful blue crystal, Xytrinium. What are your thoughts, Captain Tykran?'

Tykran thought for a moment. 'Your proposed strategy might just work. But the last time we employed Xytrinium warheads on our torpedoes to decimate their protective dome they were all used up unfortunately.'

Wazine burst into loud laughter again. 'We don't need Xytrinium warheads,' he said with a look of disdain. 'Our powerful braktite magnetic missiles will do more damage!'

Tykran raised an eyebrow. The Supreme Leader was nothing if not confident.

'Now tell me about these other Tzuracian allies you mentioned,' Wazine continued.

'It turned out these allies were from Planet Urgellan. They were forest dwellers skilled in archery and swordsmanship. They went almost undetected, blending into the greenery in camouflaged green outfits. As my soldiers and I stalked through the bushland toward the Tzuracian capital, Khazor, we were repeatedly ambushed. We were unable to match their stealth and speed.'

Wazine was dismissive. 'These Urgellans may not be there this time. But if they are, they won't stand a chance against our superior trained soldiers.' He continued to probe. 'And what about the robots?'

'They're eight feet tall with laser cannons on their arms. They're remotely controlled and can't be beaten.'

Again, Wazine was dismissive. 'Well, we'll be prepared in case the Tzuracians decide to recruit them again. I don't believe they can't be beaten. If they have electronics in them, a powerful magnetic wave will dismantle them. Now, Captain Tykran, is there anything else you want to discuss before we make our final plans for the assault?'

'Yes, there's one other request I have,' Tykran said confidently. 'One of our allies who supported the Treldarians in the last battle are the Kyroni. They are fierce warriors in hand-to-hand combat and have no fear when committed to the cause. Many of them were killed, and the leaders were sentenced to prison on Planet Lokar, but most of the survivors were imprisoned back on their own planet under Sentinel guard. I'd like to free those on Kyronis and ask them to join us, which I've no doubt they will. They'll want revenge for their fallen warriors. I need two of your vessels with some of your soldiers as planet Kyronis is currently under martial law.'

Captain Nukwar was initially unsure. 'How many warriors are there?'

'Between five hundred and a thousand.'

'And how long will it take to collect them?' asked the Supreme Leader, slightly annoyed at the suggestion of more delays.

'I should be there and back within four days, giving you and Captain Nukwar more time to streamline our war strategies and load our provisions. We can leave as soon as I return.'

'Alright,' said Wazine. 'But if we're doing this, I suggest you leave today. Captain Nukwar will fly you in the shuttle to the two ships and you can take more of your soldiers with you if you wish.'

'Thank you, Supreme Leader,' Tykran said. 'Please make yourselves at home.' He called out to Sergeant Jhakmar who reacted immediately and entered the War Room. 'Sergeant, please escort our guests to administration and request they find suitable accommodation. They'll be staying for a few days.'

Wazine interrupted, 'I'll be returning to Rozak and leaving Captain Nukwar in charge. He'll keep me informed of developments.'

'Very well,' said Vark.

Vark turned again to Jhakmar. 'Select a unit of soldiers to accompany me for a journey to Planet Kyronis. You'll be in charge while I'm away for four days. Captain Nukwar will direct you to one of his ships where you and the other soldiers will load the supplies and munitions for our attack on Tzurac. I'm entrusting you, Sergeant, to do the right thing. Now go.'

Saluting Tykran, Jhakmar about faced and asked the Rozakians to follow him out the door. He was right in the midst of things and enjoying his new status as Tykran's right-hand man.

As soon as they all left, Tykran pulled out the co-ordinates for Planet Kyronis, then went to his sleeping quarters to prepare for the trip and collect a portable transponder-interpreter to communicate with. An hour later, he was on board the shuttle heading for one of the Rozakian Destroyers. He was hoping the Kyroni were still on friendly terms and would allow him to gather as many of their warriors as he could.

DEFENCE STRATEGY

UNDER tight time pressure and with the assistance of Tzuracian scientists, Grant Thompson and Kyron believed they had found solutions to the two-part weaponry challenge. Working feverishly for the last three days and into the late hours of the nights, the Irishman had applied his experience and know-how to personal defence shields that could be quickly manufactured. Kyron had concentrated on weapons which could fire a massive, alternating current over a considerable distance, similar to a lightning bolt. This lightning bolt could be adapted to a hand-held pistol or magnified to use as a cannon either on board a Destroyer or on land.

On the fourth day, they presented their prototypes to General Dakhar and gave a practical demonstration on the parade ground.

'Alright, gentlemen, show me what you've come up with,' Dakhar said eagerly.

Grant was the first to show off what he thought was a brilliant idea. He handed Dakhar a wide leather utility belt, which was light in weight and adjustable like most buckled belts. Attached to it was a small black box the size of a hand-held communicator and made of hard moulded material. It had two coloured press buttons, one green the other red.

'Okay, Grant. Show me what it does.'

'I'd be delighted,' said the red-haired engineer in his strong accent with an excited gleam in his eye. He was like a boy with a new toy. He strapped the belt around his waist and turned to Dakhar. 'I've asked one of the scientists to power up an electromagnetic generator which gives off an intense magnetic wave too powerful to walk through without serious injury or death. When I activate the device I'm wearing it'll encase the whole of me body in an invisible protective shield without interferin' with me movements or preventing me from firing a laser pistol or wielding a blade.'

Grant ordered one of the scientists to switch on the generator and stand well back. After activating the device which gave off a soft hum, Grant grabbed a large spanner from a nearby bench and tossed it towards the generator. When the spanner entered the magnetic waves it blew into thousands of small pieces of shrapnel, forcing Dakhar and Kyron to use their cloak shields to protect themselves from the flying debris. With raised eyebrows and a shocked look on their faces, they turned back to watch Grant stroll confidently through the magnetic field. To their amazement there was no reaction, even though the generator was still churning out the lethal magnetic waves.

'Alright, ye can turn off the generator,' Grant yelled to the scientist before strolling back to Dakhar and Kyron with a huge smile on his face. 'Well, what do ya' think of that, lads?'

Dakhar was incredulous. 'I think you've done a great job, Grant and in such a short time. I'm very impressed. How does it work?'

'Well, thank you, sir,' responded the Irishman proudly. 'It works on the principle of demagnetising or neutralising the magnetic waves. Reversing the incoming polarities simultaneously with the outgoing magnetic waves, cancels out the effect. The small black box contains a computer circuit which is programmed to receive and read in nanoseconds the frequency and polarity, responding accordingly.'

'Amazing, Grant. How soon can you manufacture these in quantity for eight thousand soldiers? And can this be adapted on a larger scale to shield our warships and destroyers?'

Thompson scratched his wiry, rusty mop with his head down and a squint on his face. 'If we 'ave all hands on deck and we bust our butts, we could 'ave it done within t'ree days. In the same time, ya technicians should also be able to integrate this reverse polarisation program into the existin' defence systems on ya battleships and destroyers. Keepin' in mind though, your ships will still have to decloak and temporarily lower their shields before firing. If they don't, the fired missiles will hit the electro anti-magnetic shield and backfire on the ships.'

'Great,' said Dakhar. 'I'll ensure the Admiral passes this vital instruction onto the commanders. And what about the Diutrons?'

Grant was quick to answer. 'They'll also 'ave these wee devices hooked up to their circuitry which'll be activated by remote.'

Dakhar smiled. 'I'll give the order to commence manufacturing the devices immediately.'

He turned to Kyron with a look of anticipation. 'And what have you come up with for an assault weapon, Captain?'

'Sir, I've designed a system which generates a massive alternating current, very similar to a bolt of lightning. It can be directed over long distances using a hand-held pistol similar in size to our laser pistols. The small generator can also be used in a long-barrelled gun, as well as adapted to the cannons on our Destroyers and also attached to the arms of the Diutrons. I'm unsure how effective our existing laser weapons will be against this alien force, but I'm confident this new electrical weapon will be lethal and dispose of our foe. And it'll take the same amount of time to manufacture as Grant's device.'

'Can you demonstrate?'

Kyron thought for a minute then called out to the technicians to start up the electromagnetic generator and take cover. Picking up the prototype pistol from the table, he aimed and fired the weapon. A stream of bright flashing light bolted out of the muzzle accompanied by a low humming sound, striking the generator. The machine instantly exploded, shattering into thousands of tiny pieces of shrapnel. The onlookers gaped in amazement at the devastating results.

'Very impressive,' said Dakhar, the expression on his face reinforcing his comment.

'And I only had the weapon on the lowest setting,' Kyron said modestly.

'Excellent,' exclaimed Dakhar. 'You've both done very well. We'll commence production immediately.'

After dismissing his two prize engineers Dakhar returned to his office. Sitting at his desk he started to map out a plan of defence for the two war zones, land and air. He decided the strategy for land defence would be similar to the tactics he employed last time Khazor came under attack. It had proved successful with the supporting Urgellan forces. Unfortunately, Tykran Vark was aware of the manoeuvre from the last encounter, but it would still be very effective even without the element of surprise.

Before he settled on the air strategy, Dakhar requested his orderly to invite Commodore Tarhdok to his office as soon as possible. The Commodore arrived within the hour and the two commanders were soon in heavy discussion concerning mobilisation of the fleet.

'Here's what I propose,' said Dakhar. 'In the last invasion the fleet was mobilised behind one of our moons, Kelzhar. As the Treldarian armada passed by this moon, our fleet divided and surrounded their ships in front and behind. Unfortunately, the Treldarians deployed their scout ships *en masse* and while our fleet of warships and Advanced Destroyers were occupied fending off these annoying gnats, most of the Treldarian armada cloaked themselves, escaping to land on Tzurac.'

'So, what do you have in mind this time, Ehrane?'

'Well, because our enemies may be expecting us to execute the same tactics as last time, I suggest we divide our fleet into three, mobilising a third of the fleet on the dark side of each moon. No matter which direction they approach from, we'll still be able to ambush them by bringing forth all the segmented fleet and surrounding their armada.'

'Sounds good,' remarked Tarhdok as he stared at the chart. 'This means there'll always be a third of our fleet at the ready whichever moon the enemy approaches. But, would the two thirds of our fleet behind the other two moons be able to cover the distance required in time to help them surround the enemy?'

Dakhar smiled. 'Yes. I've calculated the distances and if our divided fleet times it right, they could all meet at the same time, undetected with their cloaking. Once the battleships arrive at the scene, we can deploy smaller fighter crafts from these if needed. You must prepare and brief your commanders, emphasising the need for them to only communicate using their Pledge rings.'

Tarhdok nodded in agreement. 'I think this strategy might just work. I'll start preparations immediately, time being crucial for our success.'

After rising from their chairs, they exchanged the Sentinel handshake and Tarhdok departed.

'Corporal Markhaz!' shouted Dakhar over the intercom. 'Arrange to have all the Urgellan soldiers assembled in the courtyard in one hour's time and have Grant Thompson and Kyron Tyros come to my office again, as soon as possible.'

'Yes, sir,' replied Markhaz.

Within twenty minutes, both engineers were in Dakhar's office. 'Thanks for coming so soon,' he said. 'I've arranged for the Urgellan soldiers to assemble in the courtyard this afternoon to inform them of our strategy. When I've finished, I want you two to tell them about the new inventions you've developed and show them how they're to be used.'

Grant and Kyron looked at each other with raised eyebrows, without speaking.

Dakhar continued, 'Am I correct in assuming these devices will be ready?' The engineers nodded in unison; their fingers crossed behind their backs. 'Alright then, go and collect the prototypes and meet me in the courtyard.'

As soon as they left, Dakhar ordered Corporal Markhaz to request the Senate Council attend the gathering in the courtyard and have the communication technicians set up the public address system.

It was late afternoon by the time everyone had assembled with the senators seated in a half circle at the back of the stage together with Grant and Kyron. The senators were draped in their assigned coloured robes depicting their fraternities, a mixture of reds, purples, yellows and blues. Standing at attention, either side of the courtyard were the Tzuracian Sentinels dressed smartly in their maroon uniforms.

Dakhar had a feeling of déjà vu as he approached the dais and saw a sea of green stretched out before him. The Urgellan army of five thousand, dressed in their forest-green suede outfits, with their clan tartan caps, armed with their weapons of choice, bows and blades, filled the courtyard to the brim. As he reached for the microphone on the dais, the chattering of the huge crowd dwindled to a dead silence.

'Urgellans and Senators, may I have your attention!' Dakhar took a deep breath before continuing. 'I have gathered all of you here today to inform you of an enemy which is approaching our planet with the sole purpose of annihilating the Tzuracians.'

A whispered chatter surged across the crowd.

'This warmongering army comes from the other side of the Universe. They have been persuaded by the escaped Treldarian prisoner, Tykran Vark, the son of the deceased General Khuram Vark, to take possession of our powerful Xytrinium. They must be stopped here on Tzurac to prevent them from destroying other races in the Federation of Planets and commandeering Xytrinium for their own selfish gains. I've been informed this dark force uses weaponry which none of us have encountered before and they've never been defeated.'

Aloran, the Chieftain Leader of the Urgellans, now looking a little older, interrupted Dakhar calling out, 'So, how are we supposed to stop them with our inferior weapons?'

Dakhar pointed to Kyron and Grant, who held up the small, magnetic protective device and pulsating, magnetic laser weapon for all to see. He responded quickly before the clans became agitated, saying, 'We've devised defence and attack mechanisms in the form of personal protective shields to neutralise the enemy's powerful magnetic rays and modified laser blasters to not only penetrate their protective armour but also wound them badly, if not fatally. These items will be issued to all of you within the next three days. Your arrows will still be of good use after the arrow heads have been fitted with anti-magnetic Xytrinium tips.

'I'll speak with Aloran after this assembly to discuss where to deploy the clans in our strategic defence. Keep in mind that the Rozakians' DNA has not been infused with Xytrinium, so we still have superior strength and enhancements when it comes to physical confrontations, except for the one hundred or so Treldarian soldiers in Vark's army. I believe with your stealth and surprise tactics we'll have a successful outcome, as we've had in the past. So go now with your courageous hearts and strong determination to do battle and may the spirits of the Ancients protect and guide you to victory.'

With great vigour and renewed confidence, the Urgellan clans burst into their gallant war cry, raising their shields and weapons in the air, screaming and shrieking, the amplified racket reverberating around the walls of the Citadel. After the noise had finally subsided, Aloran strode towards Dakhar to discuss their war strategy. The senators rose from their seats and were led by Ghalbrak to the Council Chambers.

GATHERING ALLIANCES

ON the other side of the galaxy, Tykran Vark had captained the borrowed Destroyer escorted by a crew of twenty Rozakian soldiers and had arrived at his destination in stealth mode. The Destroyer was now hovering in the outer orbit of planet Kyronis.

'Lieutenant Bakrar,' Tykran called out using his portable interpreter, 'we need to discuss tactics to wipe out the Tzuracian Sentinels who are lording over the Kyroni using martial law protocol and stop them sending word back to Tzurac!'

The Lieutenant was a perfect example of his Rozakian race and rank. He was eight-feet tall with straight, short-cropped, black hair, and he wore a tight-fitting, metallic grey uniform. He was mean-looking, threatening and humourless. It was obvious he was not impressed with the Treldarians and intolerant of their primitive behaviour and inferior weaponry.

'We can send a powerful magnetic pulse blast to knock out their communications,' he replied in his accented native tongue. 'Then descend in our shuttles while the Sentinels are in a state of chaos and take down these Tzuracian soldiers.'

'Good plan,' said Tykran, acknowledging him through his interpreting earpiece. 'Only one problem. The Sentinels can communicate through their Pledge rings and the magnetic pulse may have no effect on these signals. I don't want to risk the possibility of them alerting Headquarters on Tzurac. I want to maintain the element of surprise on all battle fronts.

'So, I propose we land this craft in stealth mode in a remote area a short distance from their Capital, Vexar, and silently storm their fortress at night. Having our craft in close proximity will make it easier to bring the Kyroni onboard, as I'm unsure how many Kyroni warriors there'll be. It won't be dark for another two hours giving us time to prepare your soldiers and their weapons for assault.'

Lieutenant Bakrar stood silent, mulling over Tykran's plan of attack, his head tilted slightly upward to the left, his eyes fixed as if searching his mind for an imaginary enactment. Then he broke his trance. 'Very good, Captain,' he said in his rough baritone voice, 'we'll follow your lead as you've had more experience with these Tzuracians.'

Two hours later the Rozakian craft had silently and invisibly touched down in a clearing shielded by a thick forest of tall trees, half a mile from the capital. The climatic conditions on this planet were erratic, changing daily from blistering heat to grey overcast conditions scattered with intermittent downpours of drenching rain. It was ideal for the invaders to undertake a stealth attack at night with the cloud cover blotting out the moonlight.

Armed with their magnetic-configured weapons they stalked towards Vexar's citadel in single file, led by Tykran, his drawn blade in hand. Stopping within one hundred yards of the fortress and giving a hand signal for the brigade to halt behind him, Tykran scanned the perimeter with his powerful night-vision magscope.

After some minutes, the alien Lieutenant could not contain his impatience and placed his hand menacingly on Tykran's shoulder. 'What do you see?' Bakrar whispered.

'Two Sentinels guarding the high wooden gates to the Citadel, two more on the terraced wall above and one in each tower on the east and west corners.' Tykran passed the magscope to the Lieutenant. 'Take a look yourself and see if you can make out anything I might have missed.'

Bakrar grabbed the device and placed the lenses on his eyes, tracking the magscope from far left to far right. He held the device for some time before removing it and speaking quietly. 'There are two patrols of six sentinels marching around the perimeter – I saw them before they disappeared around the corner. If we wait a while, we'll be able to time their routine. That way, we can knock out the other Sentinel guards before they appear again at the front of the gates.'

Tykran nodded. 'Good strategy, Lieutenant. I suggest you have your soldiers ready themselves. Once we've eliminated the Sentinel guards at the gates and on the terrace, we can penetrate the interior of the Citadel and locate their command centre to find out where they're holding the Kyroni warriors. I'd prefer not to kill any of the Sentinels, just capture and secure them.'

Bakrar raised his weapon to chest level and pulled a lever on his magnetic weapon, activating a luminous red glow from the thin slots each side of the device. With an indignant look, he declared, 'This is war! We do not let our enemies live. Only if we need them as slaves.'

But Tykran held his ground. 'Well, this is *my* command, and I'm only concerned with killing those responsible for the death of my father. We do it my way or you will answer to your Supreme Leader. Do I make myself clear! Inform your soldiers of the order.'

Bakrar nodded his head in reluctant agreement, maintaining a stone-cold glare.

An hour passed before the Sentinel patrols reappeared in front of the gates and another minute passed before they were out of sight again.

Tykran signalled to the Lieutenant to come closer, 'Can you stun the Sentinel guards from this distance with accuracy?'

'I am the best shooter in our ranks,' he said with pride. 'I'll have no trouble knocking them out.'

'Great,' said Tykran. 'Do it now so we can charge to the Citadel gates.'

Bakrar knelt down and lined up the targets. Within two minutes all the Sentinel guards were stunned including those in the near towers, by a red electrical pulse, with little more than a soft hum coming from Bakrar's weapon. Then Tykran hand-waved the command to advance. Approaching the Citadel cautiously, they discovered the heavy and tall wooden gates were attached by strong metal hinges to the grey stone walls. The gates were locked from the inside and the only way into the solid building was to blast the wooden gates or scale them. Tykran wanted to maintain silence and take the fortress by stealth. Time was of the essence and a quick decision had to be made. So, they formed a human ladder allowing a Rozakian soldier to scale over the top.

Checking his timepiece, Tykran alerted Bakrar they only had thirty minutes before the Sentinel patrol returned. Just as he finished telling him, the gates suddenly sprung open with the muffled sound of clunking metal. The soldier had done his job.

'Grab those two unconscious Sentinels and carry them inside. Tie them up and make sure they're also gagged including the stunned Sentinels in the two towers,' ordered Tykran in a loud whisper, 'and confiscate their Sentinel rings. Lock the gates as soon as we're all behind them.'

The citadel grounds were illuminated by bright, glaring floodlights housed in the tall wooden towers on the corners of the complex, their powerful wide beams traversing the expansive courtyard. Either side of the huge stone-cobbled square were rows of small semi-detached buildings constructed of stone and wood and fitted with doors and windows.

There were no Sentinels to be seen, but there was noise coming from one of the buildings halfway along the left side of the citadel. They could hear loud, raucous chatter and laughter accompanied by strange music. *Must be their drinking tavern,* thought Tykran. The invaders knew they had to move fast before the alarm was raised.

Tykran turned to Bakrar before advancing. 'My father, General Vark, visited this planet and the Kyroni complex when he was recruiting for the last battle, but I haven't seen this citadel before. So, we need to proceed with care and be alert for anything that comes at us.'

Bakrar nodded an acknowledgement and spoke quietly, 'Why don't you take half my soldiers and check out the buildings on the right side? I'll take the rest to search on the left. What are we looking for?'

'The Sentinels must have a central headquarters. When we find this, we'll be able to determine where they're keeping the Kyroni prisoners. If you find their headquarters first, don't kill any of the Sentinels, just stun them, alright?'

The Lieutenant nodded and signalled his soldiers to fix their weapons on stun and then to divide and advance. They set off, weapons at the ready, creeping slowly past each dwelling, eyes and ears sharp. It was obvious to Tykran that a curfew had been enforced as the Citadel was devoid of civilians.

On reaching the brightly lit tavern, Tykran burst through the double doors with the Rozakians, weapons raised and aimed at the crowd of Sentinels. Above the noisy music, he shouted out in Tzuracian, 'Raise your arms and don't do anything stupid if you want to live!'

While the surprised Sentinels were caught off guard and followed his orders, the bartender drew an old-fashioned rifle from under the counter and fired towards the intruders. The noise was deafening and the projectile struck one of the Rozakians in the shoulder. Tykran's speed reflex kicked in automatically. He fired his laser pistol and hit the large bartender squarely between his eyes. But Tykran hadn't set his pistol to stun and the smouldering hole in the bartender's head oozed blood as he collapsed dead on the bar. The Sentinels raised their arms even higher in fear, offering complete surrender.

Hearing the loud noise, Lieutenant Bakrar and his soldiers stopped in their tracks, and raced across the courtyard to the tavern, wary of who else the noise might have attracted. By the time they arrived, the music had been turned off and the Sentinel soldiers had been herded into a corner, their weapons confiscated along with their Sentinel Pledge rings.

As he entered the room Bakrar spied the dead barman bleeding on the bar. 'What happened, Tykran?' he asked.

'They were asked to raise their arms, but the barman decided to play the hero and foolishly raised his weapon. I had no choice but to take him out!'

'What happened to 'don't kill any of the Sentinels, just stun them, alright?'

'The barman wasn't a Sentinel, Bakrar. He was a Kyroni, and he wounded one of your soldiers. Besides, it let the Sentinels know we mean business.' Tykran walked over to the group of Sentinels with his laser in hand and demanded loudly in Tzuracian, 'Who's in charge?'

One of the Sentinels spoke up in a confident voice, 'I'm Lieutenant Horanz of the sixth battalion, and I command this unit.'

'Good,' said Tykran, pointing his laser pistol directly at the Sentinel's head. 'Are there any more of your Sentinels I should know about? And don't lie to me as your lives are at stake!'

'No,' replied the Lieutenant, 'we're all here except those on patrol duties.'

'Okay. I want you to take me to your headquarters *now*. Bakrar, have your soldiers round this lot up and follow me.'

After arriving at a stone building some fifty yards away from the tavern, they all entered through a wide wooden door.

'Now, said Tykran to Horanz, 'where are the prison cells where the Kyroni are locked up?'

Horanz pointed to the floor. 'They're kept in the basement.'

'Right,' said Tykran, 'then we'll follow you there. Start moving!'

On sighting Vark and his alien acquaintances, the Kyroni started rattling their cages in a frenzy and calling out in their native tongues. Tykran fired his pistol in the air and the rabble fell instantly silent.

'I'm Captain Tykran Vark, son of the late General Khuram Vark,' he said, speaking in the Kyroni dialogue through his translator, 'and I've come to set you free on the condition you join my army to fight the Sentinels. If you decline the invitation, you're welcome to stay in your cells.' Bakrar listened carefully to every word Tykran said through his interpreter earpiece.

One of the Kyroni in the first cell spoke out. He was clad only in well-worn, chestnut brown leather pants, tucked into knee-high leather boots with tattoos on his bare chest and unkempt, long, jet-black hair tied back in a traditional Kyroni ponytail from the centre of his bald head. He spoke in Treldarian in a raspy, accented voice.

'Captain Vark, my name is Zamir and I'm the leader of the Kyroni. We recognise you from the battle we fought with you and your father. We thought you were killed in battle but we're happy to see you survived. I speak for all my people, when I say we would be honoured to fight alongside you again to avenge our fallen brothers. The Sentinels are our sworn enemy!'

There was a roar from the prisoners and more clashing of plates and cups on iron bars. Tykran waited for the noise to subside. 'When I unlock these antiquated prison cells you are to follow our new ally, Bakrar, and his company of soldiers and assemble at the Sentinel headquarters.'

He pointed to the captured Sentinels the Rozakians had herded behind him. 'These lucky Sentinels will be taking your place in the cells. But they're to remain unharmed. Do not attack them. Do I make myself clear? Now, let's move!'

Once assembled in the Sentinel headquarters, Tykran raised his arms high in a gesture to quieten the excited Kyroni. The noise subsided and he began to address the crowd. 'Friends, thank you for agreeing to my terms. You are about to enlist in the greatest army the Tzuracians have ever encountered. These alien soldiers you see before you are a very advanced race and they've agreed to join forces with the Treldarians and the Kyroni to finally thwart the Tzuracians and share in the rewards, particularly the Xytrinium reserves. You've been given a second chance to avenge your enemy and you'll be given better weapons and armour by the Rozakians with which to fight the Sentinels.'

The freed Kyroni roared enthusiastically and began doing a war dance, chanting and waving their arms in the air with clenched fists.

Tykran shouted over the noise, 'Silence! We will now board the Rozakian warship and head back to my planet, Orkharn, to make plans for the invasion. Grab your weapons and everything you need.'

The Kyronis' weapons had been confiscated by the Sentinels and locked in the armoury but within the hour, they had forced the doors open and gathered their sabres and axes. *How primitive,* Bakrar thought to himself. *They'd be useless in our army without our weapons.*

Tykran was aware that the Sentinel patrol was still circling the fort. He quelled the noise of the rabble and waited patiently for the patrol to disappear around the side of the fort before herding the Kyroni quietly towards the spacecraft. He counted at least a thousand as they entered the craft.

The warship was soon underway, heading back to planet Orkharn and Tykran soon realised the Kyronis' super-strength and aggressive behaviour had returned. *Just as I expected, the antidote has worn off them as well,* he thought. *They'll be invaluable to us. But we'll need to keep them in check so we don't have war with the Rozakians before the battle begins.* So, he directed the Kyroni leader, Zamir, to keep his soldiers restrained while on board the craft and avoid altercations by not provoking their new allies.

* * *

It was not until twelve hours later that the Sentinels patrolling outside the fortress on Kyronis, finished their night shift and discovered the locked-up Sentinels in place of the Kyroni in the cells. They were amazed they had not detected the break-out and immediately contacted the Control Room on Tzurac to inform General Dakhar of the assault and the rescue of the one thousand Kyroni by Tykran Vark and his strange looking allies.

Dakhar grimaced at first when he heard the news and realised the efforts Vark was putting in to recruit a massive army to try and annihilate the Sentinels. However, he was still quietly confident Tzurac was well prepared to combat this dark force in spite of its huge numbers.

OLD ENEMIES

BACK on Mankro, Yarron and Bhalar were busy repairing the damage done to the Treldarian civilians and the war-torn village. Their children, Jelkah and Zentar, were thrilled to have their mother and father back home and all the family was safe and unharmed. However, Bhalar sensed something was bothering Yarron. He was distant in his thoughts and he'd lost his appetite since returning.

One night after dinner when the children were safely tucked in their beds, Bhalar could no longer restrain herself. 'Yarron, aren't you feeling well? You've gone off your food and you're dwelling on something serious. Is it something I've done? Please tell me, my love, and I'll see if I can mend your troubles.'

'It's nothing you've done, Bhalar. You're perfect in every way. But there is something on my mind and I'm afraid you won't like what I'm contemplating ...'

'Tell me about it. I'm worried about you and we've always shared our troubles and resolved them together as a team.'

Bhalar waited patiently, staring at Yarron and feeling his anguish. Yarron placed his face in cupped hands and then wiped his hands slowly over his cheeks as if trying to gather his thoughts and catch them in a face cloth. He looked at Bhalar and took a deep breath before speaking.

'I'm sorry for bringing this disaster to you and your village and for endangering our children, not to mention the villagers. Because of me, Tykran Vark is seeking vengeance for his father's execution and is out to kill me. He knows I was the one who forewarned Dakhar of the Treldarians' plans to attack Tzurac and he knows you helped me. It's all my fault.'

Bhalar smiled sympathetically and reached out to hold Yarron's hand tightly. 'You mustn't feel guilty. I saved your life once, but *you* saved mine. If you hadn't come here when you did, I would have lived a life of slavery, and the Federation of Planets would have been destroyed. We would not have our two beautiful children and a home to call our own. You're a brave and compassionate person, and I'm so thankful to be with you.'

'Thank you, my love. I'm also very thankful to be with you and the children. But I'm concerned for our safety. Vark will be furious I rescued you from right under his nose and he may come back to Mankro, chasing us.

'And Shanowah explained why there were very few Treldarian soldiers around on Orkharn when I rescued you. Vark had taken most of his soldiers to the far side of the Eastern Quadrant in search of another army. He intends to persuade them to join forces with him for another attempt to destroy Tzurac, to avenge what they did to his father and to take control of the Xytrinium reserves. If his army is successful, it's clear he'll continue to annihilate the other planets of the Federation and attack us again.'

Bhalar shook her head in despair. 'So, what do you have in mind?'

'I must contact Dakhar to let him know Vark's plan. He needs to know, although I've rescued you, I'm concerned about our safety and the children's safety if Vark decides to pursue us to Mankro again.'

Bhalar cut in. 'What could Dakhar do about our safety? After all, you're no longer a Sentinel soldier and you've been banned from Tzurac.'

'I was thinking of asking him if I could take you and the children to Terra Major for sanctuary. And, in return, I could offer to help stop Vark if he attempts to invade Tzurac as his first priority.'

'I don't like your chances, Yarron, but Dakhar may be in need of all the help he can get. I guess it's worth a try, as long as Mankro isn't left exposed.'

Yarron reassured her. 'I'd return to Mankro immediately if our moon came under attack. So, I'll holograph Dakhar now as time is crucial.'

It was late in the evening when Dakhar was surprised by the appearance of a foggy apparition forming in his study via his holograph ring. The apparition began to take the more solid form of a familiar figure. 'Yarron, why are you contacting me? And why this late? I said we'd contact you if we needed you.'

'General Dakhar, I wanted to let you know I succeeded in rescuing Bhalar safely from Orkharn. Vark kidnapped her hoping I would come looking for her. Fortunately for me, when I arrived Vark was away in the Eastern Quadrant searching for a new army to join his quest, which I assume is to destroy the Federation and those who executed his father.'

'You assumed right, Yarron. We're thankful to the Tzuracian pilots who escaped from him after capturing his Lieutenant, Krag. The TSF extracted vital information from Krag and we now know Vark has recruited an advanced and sophisticated alien race to his army. Their superior weaponry and armour would definitely annihilate us. But Grant Thompson and Kyron have developed some sophisticated hardware to counteract this new and unseen armament. I think we've got it under control. So, is there anything else, Yarron?'

Yarron took a deep breath and spoke slowly. 'It's more like a request. With Vark out for vengeance and commanding an even bigger and more advanced army, Bhalar and the children do not feel safe here on Mankro. I'd like your permission for them to stay on Terra Major until this whole situation is resolved.

'In return, I'd like to offer my services in helping fight with you. I was also thinking of approaching the Nujharenes to see if they'd swap allegiances and join us. Last time the Treldarians sent the Nujharene warriors like lambs to the slaughter without modern military training and with inferior weapons. I'm not sure how many young warriors they have now, but it might be worth a try. We could train them this time and equip them with your new advanced defence hardware. In exchange for their support, I could offer to supply them with Xytrinium and show them how to use this resource to better their advancement in medicine, agriculture and spacecraft.'

Dakhar thought quickly. 'It wouldn't be an issue for your family to retreat to Terra Major, Yarron. And in my view, we need all the resources at our disposal to combat the deadliest force in the Universe, including your offer to fight again with the Sentinels. But I'd need to consult with the Senate about this and about the Nujharenes. Leave it with me and I'll get back to you as soon as possible. Thank you, Yarron, for volunteering yourself for the cause. Until tomorrow, I bid you goodnight.'

'Thank you, sir, and good night.'

* * *

Dakhar spent the rest of the night tossing and turning, mulling over in his mind what Yarron had proposed. He was

172

already awake by the time the golden streaks of the sun seeped through the narrow gaps of the wooden shutters. He spoke softly to Tajhira telling her he had to leave early to organise an urgent meeting with the Senate. Tajhira sighed. *This was another downside of being married to the most senior Sentinel officer on Tzurac.*

After quickly dressing into his maroon military uniform, he kissed Tajhira on the cheek, saying, 'Kiss the young ones good morning for me and I hope everyone's day runs smoothly.'

Back at the Citadel, Dakhar was soon busy setting up a consultation with the Senate members and checking for any messages or reports which had come in overnight. Two reports had been sent to his office.

One, from Grant Thompson, he read with keen interest. Thompson reported that all the protective magnetic devices had been completed, tested and fitted to utility belts ready for distribution to the Sentinels, the Urgellan soldiers and the Diutrons. But Grant was still working with the other scientists to modify the armoury for the cannons on the fleet of destroyers and warships. The other report was from Kyron, with more good news. The magnetic pulsating laser pistols were ready for issue to all the troops.

Dakhar was in the middle of reading these reports when he was interrupted by his orderly, Corporal Markhaz. 'Sir, your appointment with the Senate is set for 1000 hours.'

'Thank you, Corporal. Contact Grant Thompson and Captain Tyros and ask them to meet me in my office at 0900 hours. That'll be all.'

The Corporal saluted, turned on his heels and strolled out of the office, closing the door behind him.

An hour later, there was a message on his intercom, 'Yes, what is it, Corporal?'

'Captain Tyros and Engineer Grant Thompson are here to see you, sir.'

Dakhar glanced at the timepiece on the wall. He couldn't believe how fast the time had passed. 'Send them in.'

The intercom went dead and in strolled the two engineers. Dakhar and Kyron exchanged Sentinel salutes and Thompson casually waved his hand before taking a seat on one of the leather lounge chairs. The Sentinels took the other available lounge chairs as Dakhar said, 'I called you both here because I want you two to attend a Senate committee meeting in an hour.'

'Shite!' the Irishman cut in. 'I'm on a very tight schedule 'ere and I don't need to waste me time talking to a bunch of stuff shirts when there's a war about to happen' and I'm bustin' me ass to meet deadlines!'

'Calm down, my friend' said Dakhar in a mild voice, waving his hands in a slow downward motion. 'The Senate has been concerned about the resources we're using to develop something that might not be capable of fending off the invaders. I need you and Kyron at this meeting to convince them what you're doing is vital to the preservation of not only the Sentinels, but also the Federation of Planets. The weaponry you and Kyron have invented is the only thing, I believe, will save us all. The Senate needs to know how valuable you are, Grant, and how much importance is placed upon this being a successful endeavour.'

Thompson raised his head and spoke confidently. 'Well, General, when you put it like that … I'll be glad to tell the Senate just how valuable this work is and make them appreciate the effort me and Kyron 'ere have put in to save their naive butts.' Grant always spoke his mind.

'I'm convinced they'll see your reasons for wanting more time and resources when I tell them of the pressure we've all been under to produce these weapons. The senators don't fully realise what is involved to combat this enemy and that's why I need you there to explain the time constraints and what is needed to defeat this superior dark force from the other side of the Eastern Quadrant.'

Kyron sat silently, nodding his head in agreement.

'Well, enough said.' Dakhar rose from his seat and the others followed his lead.

By the time the three arrived exactly on time at the Council Chambers, the senators had already seated themselves on the podium around the curved marble bench.

'Be seated soldiers, and you as well, Grant Thompson,' directed Ghalbrak in a serious tone. 'Why have you summoned us, General Dakhar?'

Dakhar rose, bowed his head respectfully and cleared his throat before answering. 'Senators, thank you for coming this morning. There are a few urgent matters I need to raise regarding the coming enemy attack.' Dakhar paused to take a deep breath and have a sip of water, while Kyron and Grant sat silently nodding.

'In regard to the weaponry we intend using to combat the enemy, I'd like these engineers to enlighten you on how this will work and the reason it has taken some time and a lot of resources to achieve the almost impossible …'

An hour later the senators were convinced by the two engineers of the effort needed to produce something so essential to swaying the battle in Tzurac's favour.

'Alright, General,' remarked Ghalbrak, 'the Senate now has a comprehensive understanding of the situation and the need for extra resources. We thank the engineers for their extra effort and long hours labouring through this tight schedule.'

Thompson signalled a 'thumbs up' and nodded his head. 'So you bloody well should!' he muttered under his breath.

'Is there anything else you'd like to tell us, General?' the senior Senator asked.

'Yes, there's another matter of concern. Late yesterday evening I received a transmission from the banished Sentinel, Yarron Blandhar, on Mankro. After fleeing from prison, Vark recently attacked Mankro to replenish his depleting Xytrinium fuel. His band of rebels killed and injured some of the villagers, and kidnapped Yarron's wife, Bhalar. Yarron sought my permission to bring his family from Mankro to Terra Major for security, as he fears Tykran Vark may try again.

'In return for his family's sanctuary, Yarron has offered to try and recruit our old enemy, the Nujharenes and join us in the fight against this dark force. If the Tzuracians supply them with the new weapons Kyron and Grant have developed, he will train their warriors how to use them. And in order to persuade them to fight with us and not against us this time, he would offer them Xytrinium to improve their living conditions and way of life.

'Senators, we need more troops, including Yarron, with his military and pilot skills, to combat this six-thousand-strong advancing army, now with the Kyroni included.'

Kyron and Thompson both turned their heads with surprised looks on their faces. It was the first they'd heard about this.

The senators now appeared more disturbed and started mumbling amongst themselves. Ghalbrak raised his hand to silence the noise and then spoke to Dakhar. 'We're indebted to Bhalar and Yarron for forewarning us prior to the last invasion, and the Senate would gladly offer sanctuary to Yarron's family on Terra Major for their safety and wellbeing during this time of uncertainty. However, we need to discuss further, the recruitment of our former enemy, the Nujharenes, and Yarron Blandhar's offer to fight alongside the Sentinels. After all, he *is* a former traitor. We'll adjourn to the other room while you three wait here.'

Within thirty minutes, the senators returned to deliver their decision. Once seated, Ghalbrak spoke on behalf of the other senators, 'General, you may inform Yarron of our decision. We'll accept his offer of volunteering and in trying to recruit and train the Nujharenes, and we'll give them the new armaments they'll need. However, he has less than two weeks to transport them here and train them. So, start making arrangements immediately as time is running out.'

'Thank you, Senators,' said Dakhar as he rose from his chair, bowing his head, the others following his lead. 'You won't regret this.'

As soon as they left the Council Chambers for Dakhar's office, Thompson couldn't contain himself. 'Did me ears deceive me in there? Did you say six t'ousand strong!'

'You heard right, Grant. Vark recently invaded Planet Kyronis and released the one thousand prisoners being held captive there.'

'Holy Mother of Jesus!' exclaimed Grant, holding his outstretched arms up to the heavens, 'I don't like our chances.'

Kyron was quick to intervene. 'Ah, that's a defeatist attitude, Grant. We have our secret surprise weapons not to mention our resurrected robotic Diutron army. And, in the hands of our elite Sentinels, we have a strong fighting chance of defeating this alien army, particularly on home ground. We still have a few tricks up our sleeve.'

'I suppose ya right, Kyron,' said Grant, nodding his head sheepishly.

Back in his office, Dakhar immediately contacted Yarron through holographic transmission to inform him of the Senate's decision and alert him to the time constraints he was under. 'I'll contact Brigadier Zawkon to request help in transporting the Nujharenes back to Tzurac if you're successful in persuading them to join us.'

* * *

'Ehrane, what's happening?' Zawkon said in surprise on seeing Dakhar's hologram suddenly appear in his office.

'Good to see you too, Kal,' said Dakhar light-heartedly, surprised by the abrupt opening.

Dakhar relayed Yarron's request as well as the Senate's approval and asked Zawkon if he could assist Yarron in his quest to transport the Nujharenes to Tzurac from their home planet, Nujhar. 'There may be at least one thousand of them, but I'll leave it to your discretion to arrange what ships are needed. I'm asking you because Terra Major is closer to Nujhar.'

'If you're sure the dark force won't attack Terra Major first, then I can help out. I'll make the arrangements with Yarron as soon as you finish this transmission.'

'Thank you, Kal, and may the Ancient spirits protect you.'

Zawkon watched the holograph fade and then contacted Yarron straight away, knowing time was of the essence.

DANGEROUS LIAISONS

IT was late afternoon when Yarron received a transmission from General Zawkon via his Sentinel ring. He was with Bhalar in their study researching dusty, old, charted maps of the Clavistoq system, looking specifically to find the chart for Nujhar.

'Greetings, Yarron,' sprang the words from Zawkon's image. 'I hope I'm not disturbing you and Bhalar at this time?'

'No, Commander. General Dakhar contacted me just moments ago. He informed me I have approval from the Senate for my family to be given sanctuary on Terra Major and to pursue my quest in persuading our old enemy, the Nujharenes, in becoming our allies to join forces against the dark force which is rapidly approaching. Bhalar and I were just searching for Planet Nujhar on the map.'

'That's what I want to discuss with you,' said Zawkon. 'If you're successful in recruiting the Nujharenes, General Dakhar has asked me to arrange transporting them to Tzurac. I need to know how many ships would be needed for this exercise.'

Yarron paused for a moment mentally tallying numbers to ships. 'At this stage I'd advise one warship, if it can carry up to a thousand, just to be optimistic.'

'Okay. I'll commission a warship to go to Nujhar immediately. It should arrive in the Clavistoq system in three days' time. Will this give you enough time?'

'That should be enough time … if I come out alive, knowing they were our enemies in the last war.'

'Alright, Yarron. Good luck and may the Ancients protect and guide you.'

Yarron gave Zawkon the coordinates he and Bhalar had just found and the image faded within seconds.

'I can come with you, if you want some back up,' Bhalar offered.

But Yarron shook his head. 'I appreciate your offer, and I know how concerned you are about my safety, but if anything should happen to me, you'll be here to take care of the children.'

'Promise me you'll come back safe and sound,' she said, realising just how dangerous this mission was going to be. 'And how do you propose to communicate with the Nujharenes when you don't know their language?'

'That's a good question. When I went to Nujhar with Chekhmar he was able to talk to them in their own language and he said he'd spent some time there. So, if their leader Kelfas is still alive, he may know how to speak Treldarian.'

'Well, I'll worry every minute until you return.'

An hour later, having refuelled his Destroyer for the trip, Yarron was heading to Moon Nujhar. He was well aware of the danger he could encounter and knew the Sentinels were the Nujharenes' bitter enemy. Realising they would instantly recognise him if he wore either a Sentinel uniform or an Urgellan outfit, he decided to don Treldarian civilian clothing hoping the Nujharenes had never seen it before.

A day later Yarron was suddenly awoken by the craft's intercom. 'You are approaching the Moon Nujhar. Alert, you are approaching the Moon Nujhar.'

His pulse now racing and his heart beating faster, Yarron sprang to the controls on the console, pushed the intercom and began rapidly giving commands. 'Computer, reduce to cruise speed, raise shields to full capacity and give me visuals on the main screen.'

'Affirmative.'

Instantly, the ship reduced speed from Level eight hyperdrive to cruise and the main screen came to life. Before him was a nebula of pale, swirling green gases which intermittently flashed sheet lightning. It was beautiful, yet ominous.

A smaller screen on the console gave a reading of specific details of the moon's characteristics. The atmosphere was breathable for Tzuracians, and the surface mountainous, with several active volcanoes, scattered lakes and dense forests. There were high concentrations of copper mixed with tin, manganese, zinc and aluminium and he was surprised when some deposits of Xytrinium were also detected.

'Computer, put the ship into stealth and cloak mode and magnify screen tenfold.'

'Affirmative.'

As the ship breached the wispy clouds, he could see clearly where most of the activity was. There were aircraft busily travelling in and out of a hive-like structure, carved out of a large mountain. He recognised this from his previous voyage to Nujhar with Chekhmar.

'Computer, land the ship in the forest about three miles from the mountain activity.'

'Affirmative.'

The ship slowly descended and landed softly on a large space within the forest. Yarron disembarked taking his laser pistol but leaving his Sentinel ring hidden on board.

As he stalked cautiously through the dense foliage heading towards the mountain, he listened to the strange bird calls which were so different from those on Mankro. Then, without warning, a flock of large, brightly feathered birds took flight from out of nowhere. They had been frightened by several greenish-tinted, pointed-eared Nujharenes, who had bows drawn and spears trained on the intruder. They uttered some strange words in a ferocious tone and Yarron immediately raised his arms high, palms open, as a form of surrender.

'I come in peace,' he called out in Treldarian. The natives looked at one another as if they recognised the language. One of the larger ones strutted over to Yarron, confiscated his laser pistol, grabbed his arms and twisted them behind his back, binding his wrists together with grass-knitted rope. He gave what sounded like an order in his native tongue and pushed Yarron in the back, forcing him to start moving.

After trapsing through the thick forest for about half an hour, they came across a large expanse of open ground with a wide, dirt path leading towards a kind of city. Either side of the path were acres of paddocks growing grain and fenced in corrals housing large, domesticated beasts. Yarron recognised the surrounds from before and knew the city to which they were heading.

After reaching the base of the mountain on which the city was built, they began to ascend the familiar, wide stone steps, finally reaching a levelled out paved area. When he saw the entrance with its towering rock pillars, covered with sculptured battle scenes of past battles of Nujharene warriors, it brought back the same eerie feeling Yarron had encountered on his previous trip.

Yarron was escorted into a torchlit passageway to the cave that had been converted into a throne room. Nothing had changed since his last visit. There was a bronze throne chair on a raised, circular pedestal made of highly polished, grey-streaked volcanic rock and rectangular panels on the walls and floor consisting of the same material. They were in an illuminated atmosphere created from the intense light beaming down from huge oblong panels on the high ceiling.

Yarron was forced to sit in one of twelve bronze chairs which faced the pedestal in a semicircle with escorts standing rigid behind him. Two minutes later he heard footsteps behind him and saw the aged Nujharene leader, Kelfas, in his long white robe, and now with much whiter hair, climb the pedestal very slowly with great effort and seat himself, exhausted, on the throne chair. He was still carrying his short staff with the fist-sized emerald on top of it, and he stamped it on the floor, like a judge slams a gavel on a sounding block, to gain Yarron's attention. The Nujharene leader stared intensely at the intruder. After studying Yarron for some time, he raised his shaking arm and pointed his wavering finger directly at Yarron, saying something in his native tongue.

Yarron couldn't understand him and responded in Treldarian. 'I am Yarron, and I was here last with the Treldarian Chekhmar over five years ago.'

Kelfas spoke back to him in Treldarian, his voice sounding old and feeble. 'I recognise you. We joined Chekhmar in the fight against the Tzuracians. I gave him two thousand of my best warriors on the condition he would give us Xytrinium and show us how to use it to better our living and advance our farm machinery and weapons. We've heard nothing since. Is this why you've returned? Where are my warriors? Did we defeat the Tzuracians?'

He's heard nothing in six years! Yarron was quite surprised. He needed to work out how to tell Kelfas the bad news, but convince him to join the Tzuracians, and without putting his own life in danger. *Should he pretend to be a Treldarian hunted by the Tzuracians? Or divulge his true identity as one of their archenemies, a Tzuracian?*

'Please hear me out. The truth sir is I'm a Tzuracian, but no longer attached to their army.'

The three escorts instantly stepped in and grabbed Yarron ready to stab him.

'Stop,' said Kelfas, 'let him tell us the whole story. Then we'll decide his fate. Go on, Tzuracian.'

'When I was here with Chekhmar I was, in fact, spying on the Treldarians to gather information on their military plans to invade Tzurac and destroy the Federation of Planets. I disguised myself as a fugitive Urgellan mercenary but later I was discovered and captured by Chekhmar and his soldiers on their planet, Mankro. I managed to escape and, with this information, helped save the Tzuracians from defeat.

'Unfortunately, your warriors were slaughtered in the battle. They were fighting with inferior weapons and with no real war strategy against a well-trained, well-equipped, superior army. The Treldarians knew this and used your warriors just to increase their numbers. The Treldarian Generals and Chekhmar were all executed. This is why you haven't heard from Chekhmar or your warriors all this time.'

There was a deathly silence in the room.

After a long five minutes, Kelfas finally spoke. 'So why are you here, Tzuracian? You are either very courageous or very stupid for coming here, knowing your life is in danger.'

Yarron composed himself before answering. 'I come of my own doing to ask you for help. After the last war, General Vark's son Tykran was imprisoned for life on Planet Lokar, but he recently managed to escape with the remaining Treldarian soldiers. He seeks vengeance for his father's execution at the hands of the Tzuracian Senate. He's gathering a massive army of five thousand soldiers and one thousand warships from beyond the Eastern Quadrant. It is an army so superior and so advanced it could destroy the Federation of Planets and allow Vark to take control of the valuable resource Xytrinium.'

Kelfas interrupted. 'So, what has this got to do with our moon and the Nujharenes? We're not a member of your Federation of Planets, and we don't possess any Xytrinium.'

'This massive army will not stop at invading the Federation of Planets, Kelfas. They plan to conquer every planet in the Universe, take the resources and enslave the inhabitants in order to feed their army. And on entry to your planet, my ship detected deposits of Xytrinium on Nujhar. So, you have Xytrinium and Nujhar is vulnerable.'

Yarron paused for effect. 'This dark force is already on the move and there's only a small window of time to organise ourselves. When you last spoke to Chekhmar, you told him you were using fossilised fuels for your energy supply and this will eventually dry up. If you join forces with the Tzuracians to help stop this warmongering army, I will supply you with Xytrinium and show you the incredible wonders it can achieve. I'll also help you to extract the deposits you have on Nujhar with the advanced machinery the Tzuracians use.'

Kelfas sat quietly contemplating Yarron's words. 'Why should I trust you? And why should I trust the Tzuracians after they slaughtered my army?'

'I wouldn't have risked my life to come here unless I was sure I had a good deal for you. Even though I'm a free agent no longer attached to the Tzuracian army, I trust the Tzuracians and you can too. They only want peace and shared use of the Xytrinium among the planets in the Universe.'

Finally, after what seemed like an eternity, Kelfas agreed. 'I am persuaded by your words. You are correct in saying our natural fossil fuels will soon be depleted and I do have concerns about this advanced war machine invading our moon. But if I decide to contribute to this war effort, I do not want our moon to be under the control of the Tzuracians and I can only offer a thousand young warriors if that is what you need.'

'Thank you, Kelfas. Yes, we need your warriors, and I'll ensure they're properly trained and equipped with the advanced weaponry the Tzuracians have recently developed. You have my word. I'm pleased you have confidence in me and trust me with your warriors and I'll honour my promises.'

'I'm curious though,' queried Kelfas. 'How do you propose to transport our warriors to Tzurac? We haven't seen your ship and you said we don't have much time.'

Looking a little guilty, Yarron cleared his throat. 'I was optimistic and hoped you would offer your warriors for the cause. So, I prearranged a Tzuracian warship to rendezvous here at Nujhar within three days. It should be arriving in the next day or so.'

Kelfas smiled. 'We Nujharenes have the ability to read the minds of others, and I know you've been telling the truth. Just bring our warriors back to us when this war is over. In the meantime, while we await the arrival of this warship, you will stay and celebrate our alliance.'

ACTION STATIONS

BACK on Tzurac, Dakhar was busy working out his war strategy with the leader of the Urgellans, Aloran, Fleet Commander Admiral Okerahm and Grant Thompson. A 3D holographic image was projected in the centre of the room showing the outlay of the capital, Khazor, with the Citadel in the middle of the holograph. Several concentric circles had been drawn around the capital, each circle in a different colour.

'I see you've been very busy, General,' said Okerahm.

'Yes, of course. We need to outsmart the enemy using a carefully thought-out strategy with all the resources we have at our disposal.'

'What the hell am *I* doin' 'ere then?' Grant quipped with his cantankerous lilt.

'You, my friend, are going to play a very important role. You see that yellow-coloured circle on the outside of the image,' said Dakhar pointing to the map, 'this is where the minefield will be buried, about a mile from the Citadel. I know you've worked very hard already, but I need you to modify the pulsating mines we used against the Diutrons in the past, into the new, high-intensity electro-magnetic repulsion system which will annihilate the enemy on contact. I can have a unit of Sentinels help distribute and bury these mines once you have them all ready. How long do you estimate it will take?'

Scratching the wild, ginger crop on top of his head, and then screwing up his face as he calculated, Grant replied, 'I reck'n about t'ree days.'

'Good,' said Dakhar. 'Now, see the red shaded circle,' again Dakhar pointed to the holograph and Grant nodded his head, 'well, that's where the Diutrons will be mobilised. When the time comes, Grant, I want you to assemble all fifteen-hundred, equidistant apart around the circle about half a mile out from the Citadel, just in front of the minefield. This way, any of the enemy who survive the minefield, will have to face the Diutrons. Again, you'll have to instruct some of the Sentinels on how to manipulate the remote controls and they'll be stationed amongst the Urgellans in the forest.'

'Okay, General, I get the idea.'

'Thanks, Grant, I knew I could rely on you. Now, I'll let you go and start your work, while I discuss the rest of the ground and air strategy with my military colleagues.'

Grant rose from the leather chair and headed for the door. He knew he was pressed for time and didn't want to waste a minute more.

As the door closed Dakhar turned his attention to the Urgellan leader. 'Aloran, you see the green circle on the image?'

Yes, General. Let me guess. This where you want my soldiers placed?'

'Yes, the same as last time. Keep them hidden in the forest, using surprise attacks on those making it past the Diutrons and then retreating back into their hiding places. This way we'll continue to reduce the enemy numbers still heading for the Citadel.'

Aloran was a little concerned. 'I know this was a successful strategy last time, but won't they be expecting this second time round?'

'The Treldarians most likely will be,' said Dakhar, 'but the other alien army won't be familiar with the tactic. And I've arranged not only to replace your traditional arrow heads with anti-magnetic Xytrinium, but also to modify your sword and dagger blades. Your troops will be armed with their new reverse-polarity body shield and reverse high-voltage electric pistols. They'll be very well equipped and protected this time. And if any of the enemy manage to escape the Urgellan net, they'll be confronted by the Sentinels as well as the Nujharenes – assuming Yarron has been successful. While they're on the run, the Urgellans can shower them with a barrage of arrows. What do you think, Aloran?'

Aloran nodded to indicate he was reassured and satisfied.

Dakhar clasped his hands together. 'And if any are still on the run, the Diutrons with the Urgellans will continue to pursue them towards the Citadel, leaving the enemy sandwiched between them and the Sentinels and Nujharenes in front of them. The aliens won't be able to retreat. The last stand is, if they reach the wall of the Citadel, the mounted wall cannons will come into play.'

Dakhar collapsed the holograph and replaced it with a 3D holograph of the orbiting moons. 'Now, Admiral Okerahm, I have a plan for our fleet. Commodore Tarhdok and I have already discussed this. Instead of concentrating our entire fleet, waiting in stealth mode behind one of our moons like last time, I propose we divide our fleet into three groups, each one allocated to one of the three moons. When the enemy armada coming from the Eastern Quadrant passes between the moons, we surround them from different directions and strike in a crossfire.'

'Yes, the Commodore told me the plan, but it's too simple and too obvious,' said the Admiral without hesitation. 'Tykran knows we tried a similar strategy last time and they'll be expecting this.'

Dakhar was a little stunned at the Admiral's abrupt response but trusted his judgment. 'So, what's the alternative? What do you have in mind?'

'They will be expecting the same battle formulas we utilized in the past against the Treldarians. They won't be expecting a different type of warfare and, if we use one, we'll catch them off guard. So, instead of having a huge space battle in one place, at one time, we could use guerilla tactics and unexpected ambushes like the Treldarian rebels used in the past when they attacked our transport freighter ships.'

'Go on,' said Dakhar listening intently, 'I'm intrigued.'

'Well, here's what I propose …'

Admiral Okerahm rose from his padded lounge chair and strolled to a large whiteboard standing the other side of Dakhar's desk. Picking up a drawing utensil, he began to sketch lines in the form of a large cross, dividing the board into quarters. 'This represents the quarters of the universe,' he said, marking them West, East, North, and South. Then he drew circles the size of a small coin in the different quarters, placing names beside them. On the North quarter he wrote the name of Tzurac, in the West quarter he wrote Terra Major and in the East quarter, he wrote Orkharn.

'Now, I know we use a strict Code of War ethics and fight an honest, fair battle, but the whole Universe is at the mercy of these cold-blooded murderers and we'll lose if we play our hand of cards at once against their one thousand warships. Using guerilla tactics, we may survive and live to fight another day. How long before you estimate they'll reach Tzurac, assuming the alien Armada is setting off from Planet Orkharn to travel from the Eastern Quadrant?'

'Approximately five, maybe six days allowing for refuelling if they don't have extra fuel on board,' said Dakhar.

'Then, here's what I propose. We direct Zawkon with some of his fleet on Terra Major to intercept them halfway to their destination. It would take Zawkon's warships and some of his destroyers about three days to intercept them. Creeping up on them in stealth mode and without warning, he will hit them hard and fast using Grant Thompson's modified reverse-polarity cannons and then rapidly retreat to Terra Major. With his attack, we could damage up to a third of their fleet and whatever number of their army is on board. I doubt they'd give chase because they won't want to deviate from their main goal.'

The Admiral continued without interruption. 'Then, as their remaining ships come within a 20-mile range of one of our three moons, we employ the same tactic with a third of our Tzuracian ships. We stay in stealth mode, then pounce on them before retreating rapidly back to that moon, repeating the same tactic with the other two moons in turn. If they give chase with some of their warships, we'll have some of our decloaked Destroyers waiting to intercept them, catching them off-guard. By the time the remaining ships in their armada have reached Tzurac, their fleet will be barely a third its original size and their army depleted to as little as two thousand.

'The remaining alien ships will try to destroy the protective dome, and when that fails, they'll try to land their ships on the outskirts of Khazor to offload their troops, if we're lucky, in the minefields. Our ships can then regroup and attack them from above while they're on the ground.'

The Admiral clapped his hands together confidently and took his seat again, waiting to hear Dakhar's thoughts on the plan's merits.

'I like the idea of using guerilla tactics but I have some concerns about the enemy's reactions. Suppose when they're first attacked by Zawkon's fleet, they do decide to send a couple of Warships in pursuit?' the General said.

The Admiral was quick to respond. 'We could have a small number of Destroyers, cloaked and waiting further down the retreating path, ready to strike. The enemy would fall into a trap. It would be the same when it came to our moon attacks – we have Destroyers ready and waiting on each of the retreating paths.'

'Then it sounds like a good plan to me,' said Dakhar, clasping his hands with confidence. 'I'll ask you, Okerahm, to start arranging this and I'll contact General Zawkon to inform him of his role. Aloran, start outfitting your soldiers, confirm their weaponry has been modified, and mobilise them in the assigned areas. Now let's get moving my friends and may the Ancient spirits be with us.'

Once the Admiral and the Urgellan leader left, Dakhar holographed Zawkon. 'Greetings, Kal,' he said when his holograph was totally formed.

'Greetings, Ehrane, a very pleasant surprise. I take it this is not a social call?'

'No, my friend, this is an urgent request. We need part of your fleet to help in fighting this new enemy.'

Dakhar went on to explain the proposed war strategy using guerilla tactics requesting Zawkon send some of his warships and Destroyers post haste to intercept the alien armada. 'I estimate the armada has already left Orkharn and it will take them close to ten days to reach Tzurac. If your ships leave in the next day or so, it will take about three days to intercept them, before hightailing it back to Terra Major. Has Grant Thompson modified your Warship cannons and the torpedoes on the Destroyers with his reverse polarity system?'

'Yes, he has. With the help of some of your scientists he sent with the specifications, this is under control.'

'Excellent! I'll leave it to you to consult with General Blake to keep him informed and arrange the ships. Keep me posted on your progress, Kal. Good luck, and may the Ancient spirits protect and guide all of you.'

Dakhar had no sooner finished his transmission when the intercom buzzed. 'Yes, Corporal, what is it?'

'Sir, I've just been informed Yarron Blandhar and the warship with the Nujharenes have docked.'

'Thank you. I'll go down and greet them. Out.'

After docking his ship, Yarron walked nervously to where the Nujharenes were disembarking. He was wearing his Urgellan apparel, but still felt uncomfortable back on Tzuracian soil where many Sentinels still considered him a traitor.

As he approached the docking station, he was met by a unit of armed Sentinels, all weapons trained in his direction. He raised his arms high above his head and froze on the spot. It was just as he feared.

There was a momentary stand-off until Dakhar arrived and came to his rescue. 'Lower your weapons!' Dakhar shouted at the escorting Unit. 'Yarron has helped persuade the Nujharenes to join our forces. He's also volunteered to help us in the impending war. He has complete immunity from the Sentinels. Understood?'

The Sentinel unit complied and Yarron lowered his arms and walked more confidently towards Dakhar, determined to carry on unfazed. 'General,' he called out, 'some of these Nujharenes can speak Treldarian so you'll be able to direct them accordingly without sign language.'

'Okay, thanks Yarron. Alright, Lieutenant Vadhim, take our new recruits to get them kitted and trained with our new equipment and then I'll direct them to where they're to be mobilised. Let me know when they're ready.'

'Yes, sir,' replied the Lieutenant as he stamped his left heel on the ground and gave a Sentinel salute. 'Let's move you lot to the armoury. Quick march!'

When they were out of earshot, Dakhar spoke in private to Yarron. 'Thank you for your courageous effort in persuading the Nujharenes to join our cause. And I'm sorry to hear about Bhalar being kidnapped and the damage done to your village, as well as the injuries Vark and his soldiers inflicted. Which reminds me, where are Bhalar and the children now?'

'I managed to collect them from Mankro on the way here and transport them safely to Terra Major before rejoining and escorting the warship to Tzurac. I've left them in General Zawkon's care.'

'Good, I'm grateful you're volunteering your service and your Destroyer to help fight this dark force, but you'll need to see Grant Thompson immediately before you go anywhere else. You'll need to be fitted with his newly- designed black box which will provide body-armour to protect against the powerful, devastating magnetic weapons the alien army possesses. You'll also need your Destroyer's shields, torpedoes and cannons modified if you're going to come in close contact with their warships.'

Before Dakhar continued, Yarron cut in. 'I want to make amends for all that's happened. If I hadn't passed on information prior to the previous attack by the Treldarians and their combined armies on Tzurac, Tykran Vark would not be out for vengeance against me, and it might not have come to this.'

'Don't blame yourself for Tykran's vengeance. He also wants to avenge the execution of his father by those who sentenced him. If it hadn't been for the help you've given us, Yarron, we wouldn't be here having this conversation. So don't punish yourself with guilt.'

'Thank you for your reassurance, General, but you must know I have a personal score to settle with Vark for kidnapping Bhalar and placing my children in mortal danger. So, when the opportunity arises, I won't hesitate to put this mangy dog down, permanently!'

'I well understand how you feel, but that's not the Sentinel way of treating war criminals.'

'I'm not a Sentinel anymore,' Yarron said defiantly. 'I'm going to see Thompson and then my mother.' He stormed off leaving Dakhar to mull over his words.

Yarron hadn't seen or contacted his mother for over five years, since his dishonourable discharge and banishment from Tzurac. She had forgiven him, as any loving mother would forgive their children's mistakes. However, Yarron still had pangs of guilt for deceiving his mother. He had stolen her Security ID card to gain access to the Science building where she worked as an alchemist developing a new formula to inject Xytrinium into Sentinel DNA. So, after being kitted out with Thompson's new protective device and Kyron's anti-magnetic laser pistol, Yarron went directly to visit her at her home on the outskirts of the city.

On the way there, he was unexpectedly confronted in an alley which he had taken as a short cut, by two darkly clad males wearing black material masks that covered their hair and the lower half of their faces. They were armed with sabres and were blocking his pathway.

'Halt!' called out the taller of the two.

'What do you want?' shouted Yarron, suspecting they were disgruntled, disguised Sentinels. 'I have money if you want it.' He knew full well they wanted his life. They wanted payback for his initial treachery in stealing the Xytrinium formula and letting it fall into the wrong hands. And payback for him getting away with his crime without imprisonment for life or execution.

Suddenly both charged at Yarron, sabres in hand, ready to cut him to pieces. Yarron drew his staff sword and snapped it open to its full length. Switching it to a blade, he leaped into the air, sailing over the top of his assailants, swinging his weapon and targeting the taller one. He twisted into a somersault and landed facing them in readiness for the next manoeuvre.

The tall one held his neck with his left hand where the severed carotid artery was gushing blood profusely. He fell to the ground writhing and gasping for air. The other assailant, seeing the fate of his partner-in-crime, dropped his sword and ran off in the opposite direction.

'Coward!' Yarron called after him.

Yarron sheathed his staff sword and went over to the wounded assailant but he was already dead.

While checking his clothes for identification, Yarron found a Sentinel ring in one of the assailant's pockets. The markings on the ring identified him as a corporal from the Forty-first Infantry Regiment. He holographed Security to explain the incident and advise them where they could locate the attacker, saying he would provide an official report in the morning. But it was a setback for Yarron. He realised he would be in danger wherever he went on Tzurac.

He walked hurriedly following the familiar path to his mother's house, and then nervously knocked on her front door. He avoided using the electronic buzzer, which automatically activated the surveillance cameras, as he wanted it to be a surprise.

His mother slowly and hesitantly prised the door open to a narrow gap. Then, recognising him, she suddenly flung the door wide open. Tears rushed to her wrinkled, blue eyes as she exclaimed, 'Yarron, my son, is it really you?'

He lunged forward and wrapped his arms tightly around her not letting her go for at least five minutes. 'I've missed you *so* much, Mum.'

Yarron spent the rest of the afternoon telling her about his blessed life on Mankro with his wife Bhalar, and showed her holographs of their beautiful twins, his son Zentar and his daughter Jelkah, who were now three years old. 'Yes, mum, you're a grandmother.' Yarron's mother smiled with joy.

'I'll holograph General Dakhar and ask him to have them copied for you to a 3D picture frame.'

'That would be absolutely wonderful, Yarron, thank you very much. I'll cherish it.'

When it was time to go, Yarron kissed his mother on the cheek assuring her this would not be the last time he would visit. And he left with his spirits lifted by the long overdue family catch-up.

The following morning, Yarron was called to Dakhar's office to give an account of the attack on him the previous day in the alley. After explaining the event in detail, Yarron handed Dakhar the Sentinel signet ring he'd taken front the dead assailant's pocket. Dakhar examined the ring noting the name and regiment.

'Thanks, Yarron. There are no witnesses other than the other assailant who ran off. But I believe you, and I know you would only kill a Sentinel when defending your life. I'm sure we'll track down the other attacker soon. You may go.'

'Thank you, General, for having faith in me yet again.'

After Yarron left, Dakhar started consolidating his plans in readiness for the oncoming war.

'Corporal,' he called to his orderly on the intercom, 'Set up a meeting with Senator Ghalbrak this afternoon, and get a line to Grant Thompson at the workshops as soon as possible.'

'Aye, sir.'

While Dakhar was waiting for his orderly to get back to him, he was taken unawares by a holograph from Zawkon. 'Greetings, Ehrane. Hope I caught you at the right time.'

'Perfect timing, my friend.'

'Several of our warships and Destroyers have already made it to the arranged rendezvous point and are waiting in stealth mode for the armada to arrive.'

'Very good, but remember to tell your commander, *not to hang around* to fight any battles after the initial assault. The warships are to head home straight away and let the Destroyers finish off any enemy warships foolish enough to chase your ships towards Terra Major.'

'I understand. Over and out.'

The intercom buzzed on Dakhar's desk and Dakhar pressed the receiver button.

'Sir, Grant Thomson's on the line, and your meeting with Senator Ghalbrak is at 1500 hours in his office.'

'Very good, Corporal,' said Dakhar hitting the off button and then picking up the communications line. 'Grant, have you seen Yarron Blandhar yet?'

'Aye, we've met, an' he's makin' all these demands.'

'I've given him permission to get kitted-out with all our new equipment and have his Destroyer's shields fitted out with the new anti-magnetic protection, and his torpedo cannons modified. Can you oblige him?'

'It'll cost ya' another bottle of the good stuff.'

'Okay, you have my word. As soon as he's done, can you tell Yarron to meet me in Senator Ghalbrak's office at 1500 hours.'

'Alright, General, will do.' The line went dead.

Dakhar contacted the Supply Depot on the communication line.

'Sergeant Nomhar speaking!' came a snappy voice over the com-line.

'This is General Dakhar. Can you tell me if the Nujharenes have all been kitted out with our new equipment?'

'Yes sir, only one or two more to go.'

'Is Lieutenant Vadhim, still with them? If he is, can you put him on?'

'I'll get him.'

The line went silent for a couple of minutes, then a different voice spoke. 'Lieutenant Vadhim here.'

'General Dakhar speaking. Now that you have them all kitted out, I want you to deploy the Nujharenes around the Citadel walls and wait for the two battalions of Sentinels to join you.'

'Aye, aye, sir, will get them there immediately. Out, sir.'

At 1500 hours Dakhar and Yarron were seated in Senator Ghalbrak's office to update him.

'Why is this banished, discharged Sentinel in my presence?' questioned Ghalbrak in a raised voice. 'We gave permission for him to assist us, but I thought we'd seen the last of him here on Tzurac. And I hear he's killed a Sentinel.'

Yarron bristled and almost retaliated before Dakhar intervened. 'Sir, please let me explain,' Dakhar said. 'Yarron has persuaded almost a thousand Nujharenes to join forces with us and they've now landed here on Tzurac. And if we're successful in this war, he's agreed to work with the Tzuracians to show the Nujharenes how to use Xytrinium to better their world. It's more than we could ever have achieved without him.

'Since landing on Tzurac, Yarron was attacked by two disguised and hostile Sentinels. Unable to accept his genuine motives, they were out to kill him. He only killed one of them in self-defence and we're still looking for the other one. Yarron has my complete trust. He has a key role to play in our war strategy and I ask you to accept this.'

The Senator looked Yarron and then Dakhar in the eye and then nodded, accepting Dakhar's word. 'So, tell me about your war strategy …'

WAR BEGINS

THE alien armada was halfway on their voyage to Tzurac, and the mixture of Rozakian, Treldarian and Kyroni soldiers on board were feeling confident and convinced they had already won the war.

They had just deployed long range probes to destroy the Tzuracian beacons on the three moons in the Grekadian Star System when all of a sudden, without warning, a massive blast hit one of the ships. A barrage of missiles followed, bombarding more of the armada. There was chaos. Some ships were decimated, others severely damaged or disabled. Smoke billowed from several and their movements slowed or came to a standstill. They were being ambushed.

'Where's this coming from?' yelled Commander Nukwar in his native tongue on board the flagship. Vark, standing beside him, was also in shock. He could hear the shrill voice coming through the transceiver in his ear.

'Raise shields to maximum! All soldiers to your battle stations!' came the orders through the intercom system above the high-pitched sounds of the security warning system. Lighting in the ship dimmed instantly to a pale green luminosity and figures scurried in all directions.

Nukwar turned to Vark and began firing questions at him. 'Who do you think they are? Where are they from? What weaponry do they possess that is powerful enough to breach our magnetic shields? And how did they know we were coming?'

'I don't know! I'm just as bewildered as you are.'

But then, Nukwar and Vark witnessed on the main screen, the decloaking ships responsible, making their retreat.

'They're bloody Tzuracians!' Vark shouted angrily. 'I recognise their markings. I wasn't expecting anything like this so far away from Tzurac ... unless they were sent from Terra Major ...' His mind was working overtime. 'The Tzuracians must have extracted the information from my Lieutenant.'

Nukwar was baffled. 'From your Lieutenant? The one who was present at our initial meeting with our Supreme Leader?'

'I'm afraid so, Commander.'

'How? When did this happen? Was he captured? Or did he defect?'

'He was captured by surprise on the day we returned from your planet to Orkharn. Our two kidnapped Tzuracian pilots were being escorted back to their holding prison when they seized Krag and killed the two Sentinel escorts. They commandeered our spaceship and must have headed back to Tzurac.'

Nukwar was livid. 'You stupid fool!' he yelled. 'Why didn't you mention this when our fleet arrived on Orkharn? The Tzuracians will have interrogated Krag and will know our plans. So much for our surprise attack – we're exposed!'

Vark remained calm. 'I didn't tell you earlier because I had no evidence they made it back to Tzurac and I wasn't sure whether Lieutenant Krag might foil their plot and escape. And, if I told you, it might have changed your mind about invading Tzurac.'

There was an instant animosity and distrust between the two leaders.

'We'll deal with this later, Vark,' Nukwar said behind clenched teeth, 'but for now, we need to go after those dogs and show them our might!'

Nukwar began to issue orders sending some of his surviving warships to give chase, when Vark stopped him in his tracks. 'No, Commander, that's what they want, to start dividing up your fleet. It's the old trick of divide and conquer, to weaken the enemy.'

Still angry, Nukwar retorted, 'Keep your advice to yourself, Captain Vark, you know nothing about the way we conquer our enemies,' Nukwar sneered. *Why would he take advice from someone who'd deceived him?* 'Our ships are faster and better armed than those of the Tzuracians. The only reason they managed to inflict such damage was because we were caught unaware with our shields down to a minimum.'

With that said, Nukwar ordered ten of his warships to track down and destroy the enemy. Nukwar and Vark watched with keen interest on the flagship's screen, the ten Rozakian warships speed off at maximum velocity in pursuit of the fleeing attackers as the rest of the alien armada continued on its path towards Tzurac.

* * *

'It worked, sir!' said the young, excited Communications Officer with his eyes fixed on his communications screen on the *Predarus*.

'I knew it would,' responded Wolzhart, Captain of the lead warship sent from Terra Major. 'How many are there, Lieutenant?'

'Ten, sir, moving fast.'

'Will we make it back in time to our waiting Destroyers?'

'Yes, Captain. Only just. Their ships are much faster than ours.'

'Good! I'll holograph them to let them know we're on our way and to maintain invisibility.'

Within minutes, Wolzhart's warships safely passed the agreed rendezvous point and the Rozakian pursuit ships following closely behind them, were caught unexpectedly, like a Venus fly trap. All twenty waiting Destroyers surrounded them, dematerialized, lowered their special shields and commenced blasting with their modified cannons. The enemy stood no chance.

* * *

In his native tongue, the captain of the first pursuit ship managed to transmit a distress message back to the Rozakian flagship. 'Commander Nukwar!' he called frantically above the deafening explosions inside his ship as he watched the ships around him being fired upon with devastating impacts. 'We're under attack! They were waiting for us and we had no time to raise our shields.'

On the receiving end, the crew could hear the battle in progress over the loudspeakers. Nukwar was about to respond, but he was cut short when everything suddenly went silent.

Vark turned to Nukwar and spoke coldly. 'They didn't stand a chance. They were totally annihilated before they could fire off a shot. It took all of ten minutes to destroy your ships. I *did* advise you not to pursue the Tzuracians.'

'Okay, you've made your point,' said Nukwar, clenching both his jaws and his fists in anger, resentful at being wrong. He glared at Vark. 'So, what do you suggest next, now that you've dragged us into this war, *comrade*?'

* * *

Satisfied with the outcome, Captain Wolzhart gave the order for all his fleet including the Destroyers, to return to Terra Major. He contacted General Zawkon by holograph saying, 'Mission complete. All went according to plan.' Zawkon immediately relayed the good news to General Dakhar on Tzurac. *Admiral Okerahm's strategy was working.*

Dakhar holographed the flagship of the Tzuracian fleet now mobilised behind Moon Kelzhar. 'The Rozakian armada is on its way and should pass Kelzhar in the next two days. They had a brief encounter with our first interception from Terra Major and the new modifications worked extremely well. There were no Tzuracian casualties or damage to our ships but we put a large hole in their armada. Tell the others by holograph, including the Destroyers, to stay alert, and in stealth mode with full shields raised.'

'Aye, aye, General. Over and out.'

* * *

Two days after the initial ambush the already-scarred Rozakian armada entered the Grekadian Star System containing the three surrounding moons of Tzurac. Vark and Nukwar were still debating how best to adjust their strategy, with mutual resentment.

Nukwar called to his communications officer, 'Hanuk, display a map on the main screen which shows the moons surrounding Planet Tzurac.'

'Yes, sir.'

Within seconds, a complex three-dimensional map materialised on the main screen.

He had made a mistake in ignoring Tykran's last piece of advice, so Commander Nukwar turned to him, 'Alright, Captain Vark, what's your suggestion? What route should we take to reach our objective?'

'Well, Commander, we haven't received any feedback from the long-range probes you sent out earlier to confirm whether they successfully knocked out the Tzuracians' warning beacons. Either they were ineffective or the Tzuracians intercepted them. If so, the Tzuracians were aware of our presence as soon as we entered their star system.'

Vark moved closer to the big screen, pointing out the moons and using his index finger to trace the path to follow. 'They'll be expecting us to pass near the first moon of Kelzhar, but this is where the Tzuracians ambushed and cornered the Treldarian armada last time. So, we should give it a wide berth and head midway between the other two moons, Jorhan and Wurtah, taking a more direct path to Tzurac. Hopefully, we should reach Tzurac before they have time to mobilise their fleet of warships. Stike fast, strike hard!'

'Good,' said Nukwar, 'I'll trust in your judgement. Navigators! Chart the path and relay the coordinates to the other ships Tell them to raise their shields to full capacity and tell the crews to take their positions for battle! Advance with caution at Level five hyperdrive.'

Nukwar returned to his command chair, leaned back and focused his words on Vark. 'As for you Vark, I've not forgiven you for failing to inform me of your Lieutenant's capture and withholding this vital piece of information. When we've won this war, the Rozakians will be taking control of *all* the Xytrinium in the Federation of Planets, including the Treldarians' share.'

Vark was furious. 'If *you* do that, then *you* can figure out for yourselves how to process it and use it.'

'You can't blackmail us, Captain. We can easily capture the Tzuracian engineers and force them to show us how to utilise Xytrinium.'

Vark seethed but remained silent – he was already planning on how to deal with the Rozakians. Until the war was over, he would play along with the alien force waiting for the opportunity to make his move.

BATTLE MANOEUVRES

MEANWHILE, back on Tzurac, Dakhar was mentally taking stock of the final arrangements for the coming onslaught. *The minefield was activated and ready; the Diutrons had been strategically placed; Grant Thompson had instructed several Sentinels on how to remotely control the robots; the Urgellans had hidden themselves in the thick forest and positioned lookout stations in the tallest trees; and several brigades of Sentinels, combined with the wild Nujharene natives, had spread evenly around the outer perimeter of the Citadel walls. They were all kitted out with the new defence weaponry and protective suits of anti-magnetic armour. The Sentinels on the battlements were on alert, with cannons targeted in the directions the enemy would be approaching. The citizens of Tzurac were gathered in the underground tunnels with supplies to last for a month. The only concern now was confirmation for the placement of the Tzuracian fleet.*

The intercom buzzed on Corporal Markhaz's desk. 'Corporal, get hold of Admiral Okerahm and Yarron Blandhar and ask them to report to my office immediately.'

'Yes, sir.'

Thirty minutes later they were in the General's office seated on the leather couch, opposite Dakhar.

'Admiral, I need to confirm with you whether our fleet has been distributed in preparation against the Rozakian armada and to inform you they've already entered our star system. Communications have verified they lodged disruptive magnetic pulse probes on our moons two days ago though these were neutralized by our modified beacons. So, they're flying blind into our ambush.'

Dakhar stared at Okerahm waiting for clarification.

'As we planned, our fleet of a thousand warships has been divided into three divisions deployed around the moons. I've done the same with our one thousand Advanced Class Destroyers. I don't want any of our ships on the ground when the enemy arrive, as they would be vulnerable on the airfield and in our hangars. As the enemy ships pass by each moon, we'll implement our guerilla tactics – attack and retreat. Any of their warships that foolishly follow, will be set upon by our waiting cloaked Destroyers.'

'Excellent work, Admiral.' Dakhar smiled with satisfaction.

'So why am *I* here if I'm not being deployed with the other destroyers?' Yarron questioned curiously.

'I've chosen you for a special reason, Yarron,' replied Dakhar. 'Your Advanced Destroyer, being non-shiny black, is a great camouflage against the dark void. I know how good your skills are in outmanoeuvring your opponents in dogfights. So, I'm asking you to be a vanguard while our ships lie in wait.'

'How so?'

'I suspect the Rozakian armada will send out in advance of their convoy, a small scout ship, or several, to try and detect any sign of our Tzuracian fleet. I'd like you to destroy these scout ships before they have a chance to relay any information that could expose our trap. Your ship has been upgraded and the new technology should provide some protection for you. What do you say, Yarron? Are you up for the challenge knowing how dangerous it could be?'

'I'm at your service, General, providing I have a free hand in how I take down the reconnaissance ships.'

'Yes, you have free rein. Now go to your ship and head for Kelzhar.'

Dakhar turned again to Okerahm. 'Admiral, inform the fleet of Yarron's role in our operations, and I'll inform our Sentinels.'

'Will do, General.'

The meeting was adjourned and as soon as he was alone, Dakhar contacted his wife, Tajhira. 'Hello, my darling, how's it all going?'

'It's good to hear your voice, Ehrane. You haven't been home for the last two nights and we're all missing you. Is everything alright?'

'Yes, it's been very busy here, as you can imagine, preparing for this invasion. I miss all of you very much. Have you packed? And are you leaving for the tunnels very soon?'

'Yes, we're about to leave. I'll collect Torri and the children on the way.'

'Okay, that's good. Keep your communicator handy and I'll call you tomorrow. I love you.'

One thing Dakhar had not yet checked on was the most important to consider in the security of Khazor, the protective dome. It had been penetrated by a Xytrinium warhead in the last attack. Although he was sure the alien forces did not possess the Xytrinium technology to do the same this time, Dakhar was unsure how the Dome would withstand their magnetic firepower. He needed to be reassured the Irish engineer had reinforced it to protect it against anything the aliens had. He jumped on the intercom. 'Corporal, get hold of Grant Thompson for me, immediately!'

For ten minutes Dakhar paced nervously up and down the floor before the intercom finally came to life. He rushed to stab the switch. 'Yes, Corporal.'

'I have Grant Thompson on the line, sir.'

'Put him through.'

'Very good, sir.'

'Grant, glad to hear from you.'

'General, what can I do for ya?' Grant's Irish voice sounded so lyrical.

'I want you to tell me how well the Dome's protected.'

'Well, ya' remember the day I tested this new personal anti-electromagnetic pulsing shield, when I walked into the magnetic waves of that generator and came out without so much as scratch …'

'Yes, I do.'

'Well, I intensified the field of the power ten t'ousand times with enough anti-magnetic waves to knock out ten warships in one hit. The actual generator for this is housed inside the Dome and is shielded from the energy surge. Does this convince you, General?'

'Yes, Grant, it does, thank you. Now, you need to switch this generator on and I'll broadcast to warn the citizens to stay clear of the boundary of this shield. Then I want you to take yourself to the Communications Control centre in the Citadel, not only to protect yourself, but also in case we need your advice. I'll see you there. Over and out.'

On his list of things to do was one last item. Dakhar needed to contact his friend and confidante, Kyron Tyros. This time he used his Sentinel ring.

Kyron was in the training section of the Academy when he was surprised by the appearance of a holograph. The image became clear and spoke to him.

'Greetings, Kyron.'

'Greetings to you, Ehrane.'

'Are you alone?'

'Yes, all the cadets and the other officers have left to get to their assigned posts. I was about to go to mine in readiness for the assault.'

'Kyron, I don't want you in one of the ships. I need you *here* on the ground with me. You're more skilled in hand-to-hand combat and the invaders will be landing on our planet. Please report to the Communications Control Centre and I'll meet you there. Oh, and don't worry about Torri and your children. I've just spoken with Tajhira and she's collecting them on her way to the tunnels. She's leaving now. They'll be safe.'

'Thanks, Ehrane, I'll follow your orders.'

Just as Dakhar ceased his transmission, he received a holograph from Captain Parzhak, on the warship *Lanbrad*. 'General, we've just received a signal from the probe on Kelzhar detecting the Rozakian armada. It's 155,000 miles away, heading towards Tzurac at Level five hyperdrive speed.'

'Thank you, Captain. I'll leave it to your discretion when to surprise them and I'll notify our ground troops. Good luck!'

When the hologram faded, Dakhar holographed Lieutenant Mendhez who was already in the field with the troops to keep him posted of the developments. Then he headed for the Central Control room in anticipation of the battle.

* * *

Meanwhile, Yarron had made it to Kelzhar in his Advanced Destroyer, travelling at Level ten hyper speed, and he lay in wait, invisible with cloaking. He didn't have to wait long before seeing on his sonar screen, a signal sent from the long-range beam from Kelzhar – it had detected two scout ships from the alien armada. He was eager to test out the newly fitted, electro-anti-magnetic cannons, but he needed to wait patiently for the scout ships to encroach.

To bide his time, he decided to inspect his modified laser pistol more closely. It was slightly heavier than his original pistol with a longer, thicker barrel and added to it was a beam finder to home in on the target. It was a very fancy piece of engineering by Kyron and Yarron was impressed. However, he hadn't had the chance to test it out, which he would normally do before venturing out into the field. He just hoped it would do what Kyron said it would.

Yarron's other concern was the little black box on his new utility belt. Although about the size of a small water canteen, it had been something of an inconvenience when he strapped himself into his pilot seat. But if it was going to save his life, he knew he had to tolerate it.

His interest was suddenly disturbed when a high-pitch signal alerted him to the screen. The long-range beam on Kelzhar had intersected with the beam from Wurtah, pinpointing the exact location of scout ships. 'Right,' he said out loud, 'time for action!'

After holstering his laser pistol, he activated the Destroyer's twin engines and gave an order to the onboard computer to chart the coordinates where the beams met and to head off at level ten poste-haste.

Two hours later, he was in position, cloaked and waiting for visual contact. Again, he didn't have to wait long. First, his sonar bleeped and on screen two small red dots appeared heading in his direction approximately a mile away.

'Computer, arm missiles and lock onto target!'

'Affirmative.'

Yarron waited patiently, his pulse quickening, his hands slightly moist, his heart beating loudly and his breathing shallow. Now, with his senses fully alert, he was ready to engage.

In the vast darkness of space two alien craft suddenly appeared travelling slightly apart. They were half the size of Yarron's Destroyer, dull grey and almost impossible to make out in the void, with strange black markings on their shafts. It would take two separate missiles to take them out.

Yarron gave the order, 'Decloak and fire on the two targets!'

The Destroyer gently shuddered, and for an instant nothing seemed to happen. Then he saw the two alien crafts covered completely by a dazzling white web of highly charged electricity, like forked lightning and heard a massive explosion. He hadn't expected such incredible devastation. In his past aerial dogfights, he'd witnessed the exploding effects of space crafts in flight, but none as spectacular as these. 'Far out!' he cried. 'Unbelievable!' *Kyron would be so proud of his invention*, he thought.

* * *

Back in the Control Room on Tzurac, Kyron and the Communications Officer were standing focused on a large, bleeping red dot on the main screen when Dakhar arrived.

'Thankfully our long-range beacons on the moons were unaffected by Rozakian attempts to distort the signals,' Dakhar commented as he entered the room.

Kyron and the Communications Officer immediately stood and gave the Sentinel salute, which Dakhar returned. 'At ease, soldiers. I see their armada is still moving towards Tzurac and is soon to be surprised by our fleet hidden behind Kelzhar. But what are those two small red dots moving ahead of their armada?'

'I'd say they're scout ships,' said Kyron.

'Yes, they appear to be scout ships, sir, thirty miles in front of the armada,' the Communications Officer added.

Suddenly, another dot, in blue, appeared on the screen, moving at high speed and coming from a side direction. Suddenly, the small red dots disappeared, one after the other, in quick succession.

The two officers were mesmerised for a moment, and then turned to look at Dakhar, with surprised expressions on their faces. Before they could speak, Dakhar gloated, 'Yes! Just what I wanted. My ace up the sleeve!'

'What just happened, General? queried a shocked Kyron.

'*Yarron*, that's what happened. He's a free agent now and I've given him special permission to take out every advance scout ship before they have a chance to transmit information back to their mother ship. Hit, hit fast.'

* * *

On the flagship of the Rozakian armada Vark had noted a change in the Commander's behaviour over the last twelve hours. Nukwar appeared more agitated and short-tempered than usual. Obviously, something was bothering him.

'Something wrong, Commander?' Vark asked.

'Yes, Captain, there is,' Nukwar said sounding quite angry. 'I haven't heard from my scout ships and it's been over a day now. They were supposed to report in every two hours.'

'Maybe they encountered an asteroid field which interfered with their transmissions or damaged their ships.'

Nukwar wasn't convinced. 'Or maybe they encountered our enemy, in which case they would have relayed back to us, unless they were taken by surprise and didn't even have a chance.'

'Commander, we're too far away from any of Tzurac's moons for Tzurac to attack two small scout ships and besides, we would have detected a fleet the size of Tzurac's long before any approach to our scouts.'

'Maybe, maybe not. But we need to be on the alert.' He called to the Communications Officer, 'Hanuk, raise shields to full capacity and issue an alert to all crew to send them to their battle stations.'

'Yes, sir!'

Over the loudspeakers the order came through loud and clear in the Rozakian tongue and was repeated in Treldarian.

'Now,' said Nukwar, 'we're ready for the unexpected.'

They had no idea what they were facing.

STRATEGY IMPLEMENTED

CAPTAIN Pruzhan, a seasoned veteran commanding the Tzuracian lead ship *Ikhraz* and a fleet comprising five hundred warships cloaked and positioned behind Kelzhar, was receiving feedback from his communications officer, Lieutenant Bredzar.

'Captain, the enemy armada is now 156,000 miles east of our position, passing midway between the moons of Kelzhar and Wurtah, on track to Tzurac.'

'Thank you, Lieutenant. How soon can we be there travelling at Level eight hyperspeed?'

'We can be there in less half an hour, sir.'

Pruzhan called to the Chief Pilot sitting in front of his command chair, 'Lieutenant, enter the coordinates, power up and take her to Level eight hyperdrive.'

'Yes, sir.'

'Keep the shields at fifty percent and using your holograph notify the rest of the fleet of warships to follow suit. I'll holograph our Destroyers to position their cloaked ships in readiness for any of the enemy armada that might want to chase us back to Kelzhar after our ambush.'

'Yes, sir!'

* * *

Edging closer to Tzurac at cruising speed, the Rozakian armada was at the halfway point between Kelzhar and Wurtah, when out of nowhere, Pruzhan's fleet decloaked and began pulverising the Rozakian warships.

Although he was anticipating the unexpected, and their shields were already raised, Nukwar was still shaken by the power of the assault. He started waving his arms about, pointing to his crew and feverishly blurting orders above the loud, high-pitched warning alarm. 'Commence firing at once!'

Standing next to the Commander, Vark saw the Rozakian cannon fire was having only a mild impact on the Tzuracian warships. 'We have a problem. It seems your radar is ineffective in detecting alien ships in the area. And their shields are deflecting not only your radar signals but also your cannon fire.'

Nukwar knew Vark was right though he didn't appreciate being lectured.

After ten minutes of constant cannon fire from both sides, the Tzuracian warships rapidly retreated at hyper speed in the direction of Kelzhar. On the central screen, Commander Nukwar gazed at the carnage. His armada was in disarray. Many of his warships were torn to shreds and billowing black smoke. They had been ambushed again.

Vark was also amazed at the damage inflicted. He found it hard to believe that, in such a short time, the Tzuracian fleet had caused so much damage to the Rozakian armada.

'You can turn off the security warning signal, Lieutenant Bredzar and restore normal lighting,' ordered a deflated Nukwar. Then he composed himself in the Command Chair, closing his eyes and burying his face in his palms, while slowly nodding his head from side to side. For some time, he sat there silent as if trying to decide what to do. Then he raised his head, opened his eyes and began to take control.

'We must get to Tzurac as soon as possible and destroy their troops!' he ordered. 'We need to make this into a land battle where our superior army can annihilate them and take control of their capital. I'll heed your advice, Captain Vark – this time we're not going to follow their retreating warships and end up in another ambush.'

'Glad you're listening, Commander. So how many ships survived and how many of our soldiers are still able to fight?' asked Tykran, seriously concerned.

Nukwar called to the Communications Officer, 'Lieutenant Bredzar, give me a report on how we stand!'

'Yes, sir, coming right up. We have five hundred warships and six scout ships operational. There are twelve hundred dead. Six hundred Rozakians and Kyroni are wounded, and one hundred Treldarians on board this ship are unharmed. All up sir, we have three thousand soldiers ready to fight.'

'Okay, Lieutenant, patch me through to the surviving ships.'

'Yes, sir.' The Lieutenant instantly pressed several switches on his console and called to his Commander, 'Go ahead, sir, all channels are open.'

Nukwar cleared his throat and took a deep breath. 'Attention all Captains. I know you're as devastated as I am. We have underestimated the Tzuracians. They've had some success with their cunning guerilla tactics and reduced our fleet and our military might. But this has not deterred my mission to destroy the Tzuracians and their Federation of Planets.

'Their actions have made me even more determined. We will continue on to Tzurac and land our ships around their capital, Khazor, as we had initially planned, giving our soldiers an even chance to thwart them on their home ground. So, first of all, tend to your wounded, place the fallen soldiers in our cold chambers and take up formation in your warships. Report in when you are ready. Out.'

Half a day later, the Rozakian armada was reformed and ready to continue its voyage through the void between Moon Wurtah and the planet Tzurac. Their weapons were armed and their soldiers stationed at their posts anticipating another surprise ambush.

* * *

On the hidden side of Wurtah, the Lead Ship, *Zakhron*, commanded by Captain Omhartez, another Tzuracian veteran with thirty years' experience, lay in wait with his fleet. Yarron was waiting there too. After his success in taking out the two enemy scout ships on their approach to Kelzhar, Yarron had set a course for Wurtah anticipating the aliens might send more scout ships out as their armada moved closer and closer to Tzurac. He'd advised Captain Omhartez he would dispose of any advance ships.

But, this time, no scout ships appeared.

As the sun crept over the moon's horizon, the navigator's screen at the Communications console on the *Zakhron* began to bleep quietly.

'Captain, there's a large mass heading towards Tzurac, 125,000 miles northwest of us. It must be the enemy armada.'

'Thank you, Lieutenant. I'll holograph the other captains and tell them to prepare to move. Put me on loudspeaker now so I can notify the crew to take up their battle positions.'

'Yes, sir.'

'Lieutenant, chart the coordinates and get ready to start her up.'

'Yes, Captain.'

218

After the crew was notified and the captains of the other ships holographed, the fleet of five hundred was on the move. In just under an hour, the Wurtah fleet had reached its destination and was cloaked and silently waiting.

Soon the huge Rozakian armada came into sight. But as the Tzuracian ships started to decloak, they were suddenly fired upon by the enemy. They raised their shields at once, but it wasn't in time to prevent several sustaining serious damage, and some ships were totally destroyed.

Omhartez hit the open communications button, saying, 'Retreat! Retreat!' and the Tzuracian ships that were left intact retreated to Wurtah.

* * *

'Got them this time!' yelled Nukwar as he watched the encounter, before ordering ten of his warships to pursue the retreating Tzuracian fleet.

Vark who was standing nearby gripping the Command Chair, shouted, 'What in the God's names are you doing? I thought you learned your lesson about dividing your fleet after the last disaster!'

'This is different,' said Nukwar, confident and unfazed. 'This time we caught *them* unprepared and now they're fleeing like wounded dogs. We can catch them on the run and cut them down because our ships are much faster.'

Just as he finished speaking, the main screen displayed ships at the rear of his armada being devastated. There were explosions and electrical discharges of spectacular intense lightning around some of his ships.

'Where's this coming from? Who's attacking our ships? And where are they? Lieutenant Bredzar, raise our shields to full capacity again and pinpoint the invaders.'

'Our shields are already raised to full capacity, Commander, and are having no effect. There's only one small dot on the screen. You should be able to see it if I magnify the main screen one hundred times.'

'There!' shouted Vark. 'I see it.'

A single black Advanced Destroyer could just be seen, though it was very well camouflaged in the dark void of space.

* * *

Yarron had decided to trail behind Omhartez's Tzuracian fleet in case he was needed. Luckily, when he saw the fleet come under fire and then suddenly retreat, he knew they were in trouble.

Knowing he was outnumbered; he circled in stealth mode around the Rozakian ships and started blasting them from behind in a rearguard action. His strategy was to distract their attention while the Tzuracian fleet made their escape and destroy as many of the Rozakian ships as possible before high tailing it out of there.

'Yes!' he roared as he hit first one ship and then another. In a short space of time, he'd exhausted all his missiles and destroyed at least ten enemy warships.

Before the Rozakian ships could return fire, he cloaked and sped off towards Tzurac to replenish his ammunition, refuel and report to General Dakhar. He knew he was lucky to have escaped unscathed.

* * *

Meanwhile, Captain Omhartez and his remaining fleet made it back to the shadow of Wurtah without further incident. There he rendezvoused, as planned, with the Tzuracian Destroyers and prepared to ambush any pursuing enemy ships.

As he anticipated, ten Rozakian pursuit ships soon appeared. Omhartez's fleet, together with the Destroyers, immediately opened fire. The Rozakian ships had underestimated again and had no time to retaliate. Under fire from all angles, they exploded loudly and spiralled out of control, billowing smoke. The pursuit ships were decimated.

As the Tzuracian fleet ceased firing and regrouped, Captain Omhartez requested an update. 'Lieutenant Bredzar, how many ships and crew did we lose?'

'Captain, we sustained no damage in the attack on the enemy pursuit ships, but when the armada attacked us earlier, we lost five of our ships, and two hundred of our crew.'

'Not good, Lieutenant.'

'No, sir, not good. I think they were expecting us after being ambushed by Commander Pruzhan's fleet near Kelzhar.'

'I'm going to the Council Room to inform General Dakhar. Take the Comm Chair, Lieutenant, and I'll be back soon.'

Within minutes the holograph appeared to General Dakhar in the Central Control Room. 'Tell me, Captain Omhartez. What's happening?'

'The situation is not good, General. The Rozakian fleet were expecting our ambush and we were fired upon while our shields were down. We lost five warships and two hundred crew before we retreated to Wurtah. However, ten enemy warships chased after us, and we annihilated them with the help of our Destroyers.'

'Okay Captain, I'm not happy to hear about the loss of our soldiers, but you've done well. Send me the names of the deceased and we'll notify their families and enter them on the Honour register for a formal military send off. The good news is, although the loss of warships has depleted our fleet, we were able to inflict even more damage to *their* fleet.'

'How so, sir?'

'Our young ex-Sentinel, Yarron Blandhar, attacked the armada from behind while you were retreating to Wurtah. Single-handedly, he managed to destroy ten of their ships and escape without injury to himself or his ship.'

Omhartez was amazed by the news. 'I didn't realise he'd followed our fleet. What a great asset to have back with the team.'

'I agree, Captain.'

'So, General, what will you have us do now?'

'Slight change of plan given our success so far. I've instructed Captain Pruzhan to mobilise his fleet on the dark side of Jorhan and I want you to do the same. From there, all our fleet will wait, cloaked, this time allowing the Rozakian armada to pass without interference. The enemy will reach Tzurac and attempt to destroy the Dome in an aerial assault. If Grant Thompson's powerful, anti-magnetic protection device works – and I'm confident it will – they will fail. Then the Rozakian ships will have to land on the outskirts of Khazor to unload what remains of their depleted army.

'When all their ships have landed, our fleet will move in and commence aerial attacks on both their ships and their fleeing hordes. And any Rozakian troops who escape this attack will head towards our capital where they'll encounter more surprises.'

Omhartez nodded. 'Yes, General.'

'I've already given these directions to our other fleets, and they'll be expecting you at Jorhan within the next twenty-four hours. Good luck and may the spirits of the Ancients protect all of you.'

GROUND INVASION

ORBITING more than three hundred miles from Planet Tzurac's surface and entering its thermosphere, the Rozakian armada had been reduced in size to four hundred and fifteen warships, two scout ships and two thousand five hundred fighting soldiers. Commander Nukwar was planning his attack strategy. The armada, or what was left of it, had not encountered any more surprise ambushes, which very much concerned him. His mind was churning over. *What's happened to the Tzuracian fleet? Did our ships frighten them off? Or have they returned to their home planet to set up a huge barrage or wall of resistance to protect their precious, so called, impenetrable Dome?*

Sitting deep in thought in his Command chair, he was shaken back to reality by Vark's loud voice from behind him, 'Well Commander, where to now?'

'Vark!' Nukwar shouted aggressively in his native tongue before reverting to Treldarian, 'You shouldn't sneak up on me like that if you know what's good for you.'

'And you shouldn't let yourself be taken by surprise like that, Captain.' Vark smirked. 'So, what's your plan then?'

'Well, *you* probably have some ideas to offer seeing as you've been here before,' Nukwar said, sarcastically.

'Well, you could start by having your ships concentrate on trying to smash the Dome. Then we could bombard the Tzuracians from the air and create total chaos on the ground. We could land the ships in a wide circle on the outskirts of the city and have the troops work their way in to Khazor.

'But be mindful of any hidden Urgellan soldiers as they're very good at camouflaging themselves in the forest. Although your advanced body armour should protect you against their blades and arrows, the Urgellans are silent and strike with speed. Last time the Tzuracians also used mechanical Diutrons – two tonnes of eight-foot-tall metal robots with cannons on their arms. But your superior weaponry should knock them out in no time at all.'

'Now you warn us, Vark. Full of surprises, aren't you?'

'Well, I did mention this before. Your Supreme Leader was confident they'd be no threat and dismissed my warnings. But your army shouldn't underestimate them.'

Continuing on its path towards Planet Tzurac, the alien ships progressed at Level 5 hyperdrive speed, all systems primed for a surprise ambush at any moment.

Nukwar called to the Communications Officer, 'Lieutenant Bredzar, what's our position?'

'We're three hundred miles from the city of Khazar, sir.'

On the main screen Nukwar could soon see the shape of the Dome with its blue, illuminating, pulsating opaque field. 'Notify all the warships to surround the Dome and fire one round each at the Dome at will and hold their positions while we assess the devastation.'

'Yes, sir.'

As Lieutenant Bredzar transmitted the command, Nukwar and Vark viewed on screen the space ballet of four hundred and fifteen warships take formation and release their might, anticipating the obliteration of the glowing Dome. After five minutes, the constant pounding ceased, the electrical residue subsided over the Dome and the two Captains could not believe their eyes. They looked at each other, shocked at what they beheld. There was not a scratch, not even a dent on the Dome.

'What in the Gods' names!' despaired Nukwar.

Vark too was almost lost for words. 'I don't understand, Commander. Your powerful weapons should have demolished this structure.' Vark wondered how the Tzuracians had engineered effective protection so quickly.

'Lieutenant Bredzar, connect me to the commanders of the other ships,' said Nukwar.

'Yes sir. Go ahead.'

'Attention, Captains! This is Commander Nukwar speaking. As you can see for yourselves, we've inflicted no damage to the Dome and we're sitting ducks if we stay in this holding position. So, I want you to land your crafts on the surface surrounding Khazor, on the outskirts of the forest. I'll see you down there. Order your troops to make their way to the city but be mindful of camouflaged Urgellan soldiers in the woods. Move now. Nukwar out!'

But Vark wondered what the Tzuracians had in store for them on the ground. *What weapons and protection might they now have? What was he leading his army into?*

* * *

Back on Tzurac, Yarron reported to Dakhar relaying all that had happened with his attack of the alien armada. He was standing in the Central Control Room when he, Dakhar, Kyron and the Communications Officer experienced the tremendous explosions overhead, which lasted for five minutes.

'What was *that*, General?' exclaimed Yarron, grasping one of the bolted chairs while the room shook. It was similar to the intermittent ground tremors felt on Mankro.

'Look at the main screen and you'll see what caused it.'

Yarron turned his head towards the main screen. It gave visuals of alien warships, hundreds of them, attacking the Dome. Continuous explosions accompanied by electrical webs discharged one after another. It was like watching a brilliantly lit fireworks display.

'So,' said Kyron who had been sitting silently in a chair in the corner of the room, 'they've finally arrived.'

'Yes,' said Dakhar. 'As Admiral Okerahm anticipated, about a third of the Rozakian armada has survived and reached our planet. Also, just as Grant Thompson promised, the Dome's anti-magnetic force did a great job of shielding us. They'll soon realise it's futile to persist with the bombardments, and they'll land their warships on the outskirts of the city. Then, the *real* battle will begin.'

Yarron slammed his fist on the table. 'I must join up with the Sentinels mobilised around the Citadel walls. There, I hope to come face to face with Vark and make him pay for what he did to my family!'

'If you must,' said Dakhar. 'I won't try to stop you. But remember to switch on the anti-magnetic box on your utility belt, or you won't survive if you're fired upon.'

'I should join you,' Kyron offered.

'No, Kyron!' said Dakhar fervently. 'I need you here in case the aliens breach the wall and try to take the Control Room.'

'Alright, General. If you insist.'

Kyron had second thoughts about Ehrane's motive. *Did Ehrane really need help to secure the Control Room? Or was he being overly protective of his best friend? Or, did Ehrane want his friend there to protect* him*? Dakhar had been severely wounded in close combat in the last attack and would have died if Kyron had not been there.* Both were keen to protect each other.

Yarron patted his new, anti-magnetic pistol on his utility belt and bid both farewell, as he exited the Control Room.

'May the Ancient spirits protect you, Yarron,' Dakhar called out after him.

'Same to you both,' was Yarron's distant reply.

* * *

By the time Yarron reached the Sentinels who were mobilised outside the Citadel walls, Dakhar and Kyron could hear explosions in the distance and see flashes of electric lightning bolts on the horizon shooting into the black clouded sky. The aerial view of the landscape on the main screen in the Control Room projected from cameras mounted on tall trees in the forest, showed exactly what was happening. The Rozakian warships which had landed on the outskirts of Khazor, had encountered the landmines buried just beneath the surface. The enemy troops were being slaughtered.

Dakhar holographed Captain Pruzhan on board the *Ikhraz*, which was cloaked and now silently waiting with the rest of the Tzuracian fleet on the dark side of Moon Jorhan. 'Captain Pruzhan,' said Dakhar as his translucent image came into focus, 'I want you to lead all the fleet down here towards Tzurac and, in an aerial attack, destroy the remains of the Rozakian armada and enemy soldiers which have now landed on the outskirts of Khazor!'

'Yes, General, immediately.'

* * *

As the remaining alien armada, less than half the original fleet, landed on Tzurac, Commander Nukwar was livid. Some landed directly onto land mines and he witnessed ships being blown up, one after another. The soldiers disembarking *en masse* from those ships that remained intact, were also being blown to smithereens as they trampled on hidden mines while rushing for the forest. Their grey, metallic, combat suits were useless against the landmines. Nukwar was shocked as he watched in horror their dismembered bodies being hurled into the air like *papier mâché* dolls. He'd not seen the likes before and couldn't believe their magnetic armour was offering no protection.

Standing close by, Vark yelled at Nukwar, 'Commander, what are your orders?' There was no response. Vark shook Nukwar's shoulder and repeated his question. 'Commander, what are your orders?'

Snapping out of his temporary shocked state, Nukwar began broadcasting commands over the intercom to his own crew. 'Attention crew, this is your Captain. Vacate the ship at once with your weapons, and head for the edge of the forest. I'll meet you there. Captain Vark will lead his Treldarian soldiers to the Citadel and we'll follow his lead. Go!'

Eventually, after Nukwar's crew and Vark's Treldarian soldiers had vacated the ship and made it safely through the minefield to the edge of the forest, a thunderous roar echoed above them, blocking out the sun.

'The Tzuracian fleet!' screamed Vark.

No sooner had he finished his words, than hundreds of anti-magnetic missiles came raining down on the remaining Rozakian warships, obliterating them all. Nukwar couldn't believe his eyes as he watched his remaining fleet explode in a massive fireworks display. Hundreds of lightning bolts shot out from the matrix of electrical pulses engulfing the fuselages before they all self-destructed. He was cursing himself at being so careless to have not given orders for his ships to cloak before landing.

Nukwar screamed out in his native tongue, cursing the Tzuracians. 'You've destroyed my ships! I'll kill every one of you, if it's the last thing I do!'

'Keep your voice down, Commander,' Vark warned. 'There may be enemy lurking in the forest and we don't want to alert them to where we are.'

Nukwar realised Vark was right. He also realised he and his Rozakian army had no way of escaping off planet Tzurac unless they annihilated the enemy.

After quickly coming to terms with the situation and composing himself, Nukwar communicated to his other soldiers who were scattered in a wide circle around the outer fringe of the forest, to commence forging towards Khazor. Then he gathered what was left of his own soldiers from his ship and together with Vark and his soldiers, started to advance.

But all at once, without warning, they were set upon by giant, robotic Diutrons who fired their sleeve cannons at anything and everything that moved. Injured soldiers screamed loudly as bodies were shredded to pieces and torn apart horribly like rag dolls or crushed underfoot. Blood sprayed everywhere and the smell of burnt skin fouled the air.

They drew their laser pistols and fired repeatedly at the two tonne mechanical monsters, but it had no effect on the protective anti-magnetic shields covering the robots' exoskeletons. All the soldiers could do was try to avoid being blasted or crushed while running precariously through the minefield towards the forest.

'Run! Run into the forest!' Vark yelled.

The enemy soldiers of Treldarians, Rozakians and Kyroni, now reduced considerably in number, continued deeper into the forest, temporarily escaping the war machines. And there, feeling a little safer, they regrouped.

'Take it carefully and slowly,' Vark cautioned them. 'These woods are likely to be full of hidden, well camouflaged Urgellan soldiers and they'll be armed, deadly and silent. They strike as fast as a snake with no warning. Stay alert!'

He was right. High up on some of the tallest trees, the Urgellan lookouts had spotted the enemy soldiers entering the forest. Now they sent out arrows in all directions with high-pitched whistling devices attached, to warn the waiting Urgellans of the approaching alien soldiers.

Nukwar was receiving reports from his transceiver on the losses of his army from the outskirts of the forest. Only half his armies had survived, and he was now down to about one thousand of his original five thousand fighting force.

Stalking slowly through the thick greenery, swords and laser pistols drawn in anticipation, they had so far not encountered the Urgellans. *Maybe,* thought Nukwar, *Vark was just trying to spook him and his soldiers, and there was nothing to worry about.*

The thought evaporated in an instant as hundreds of arrows came flying from nowhere and struck many of his soldiers. The rest dived behind trees, hoping not to be hit, and started blasting wildly in the direction of the incoming arrows.

Nukwar turned to Vark who was nearby and spoke angrily to him. 'Why are these arrows penetrating our powerful body armour? We've had arrows thrust on us in the past and our armour has prevented any from piercing it.'

Vark crawled over to one of the fatally wounded soldiers, withdrew the arrow and examined the hunting tip. He could see why they had pierced their armour and nodded his head knowingly.

After crawling back to his safe position, he answered the captain sarcastically. 'They're Xytrinium hunting heads but slightly different than the ones we encountered during our last invasion. By the look of them, they've been specially treated to penetrate your anti magnetic armour. I told you these Xytrinium crystals were incredible when fashioned into weapons.'

Nukwar was now even more determined to wipe out the Sentinels and take control of this precious resource.

Crawling low on their bellies, he and his army made some progress in edging closer to their target. But he was unaware that his soldiers were being silently captured, their throats slit or bodies fatally stabbed and dragged back into the cover of the underbrush. By the time his army had reached the clearing on the other side of the forest, less than half remained.

Nukwar cursed. He knew his soldiers had to keep advancing in order to escape the pursuing Diutrons and the Urgellan archers, but the vast expanse before them was open and unprotected because of the lack of trees. Looking across the barren expanse through his telescopic eyepiece, he could make out a wall of Sentinel soldiers and pale green warriors. Standing high, behind this wall of soldiers was the Citadel Vark had described.

He yelled at Vark. 'Take a look! Who are these green creatures? Is this another secret you've held back?'

Vark grabbed the telescopic eyepiece and took focus. 'I don't believe it! They're Nujharenes and they fought *with* us last time as our allies. I don't know what's going on because they're holding new weapons and wearing new armour. The Tzuracians must have somehow recruited them.'

'Damn you, Vark! And damn your surprises. You said they were wiped out in the last battle.' Nukwar cursed as Vark tried to fathom the size and strength of the army opposing them.

Nukwar had no choice but to charge into this barrage and attempt to take the Citadel by sheer brute force. 'Soldiers!' he called. 'Prepare to advance at full speed, weapons at the ready.' With his sword in one hand and his magnetic pistol in the other, he shouted, 'Charge!'

Running at full speed, the Rozakian army, together with Vark and his soldiers, were again showered by an avalanche of arrows coming from the forest as they traversed the wide-open corridor. Many of the attacking soldiers started to fall and further on, another shower of deadly feathered shafts plummeted into the running hordes. As they kept running, they frantically fired their magnetic pistols into the wall of Sentinels and Nujharenes, only to find they were useless against the protective anti-magnetic body armour.

The Sentinel Lieutenant had given the order for the Sentinels and Nujharenes to activate their antimagnetic body shields and now ordered the front row to fire with their long-barrelled anti-magnetic guns. Following frontal assault protocol, they then dropped to their knees, making a clean line-of-sight for the second row to fire. The Sentinels repeated this routine several times, each time felling many of the fast-approaching, enemy soldiers while the arrows kept showering down relentlessly on the hordes from behind.

Nukwar could see his soldiers dropping like flies all around him and Vark screamed aloud when he saw his right-hand man Sergeant Jhakmar among them. For an instant he recalled his father leading the Treldarians on the same battlefield six years ago, and he cursed. He was tormented with thoughts that the Tzuracians had outsmarted them again and his quest for vengeance for the loss of his father was doomed.

As Nukwar, Vark and the remaining enemy soldiers reached the standing line of Sentinels and Nujharenes, the Tzuracian army drew their blades and pistols ready for hand-to-hand combat and the Nujharenes unsheathed their new weapons including their ani-magnetic Xytrinium sabres, feeling totally invincible in their new armour plate and anti-magnetic body shields.

* * *

Before the Tzuracians and Nujharenes was an army of mixed soldiers. There were former enemies including shiny-headed and bare-chested Kyroni and dark-featured Treldarians in black uniforms. But most were an enemy they'd never seen before – large, eight feet tall grey aliens in shiny grey-armour heavily, armed with unique weapons. And, in their midst was Commander Nukwar issuing orders and fighting to the bitter end.

Yarron was amongst the Tzuracian soldiers as the hand-to hand combat began and froze in his tracks when he spied his personal target, the Treldarian, Tykran Vark, madly waving his sword, trying to cut down all who approached. Vark had procured a Xytrinium sword from a fallen Nujharene and he was using it on the attack.

Yarron called out loudly to get his attention. 'Vark, you snake, I'm glad you're still alive so I can take my revenge on you personally. I'm going to make you pay for what you did on Mankro.' He dashed towards Vark, slicing through the fighting enemy soldiers, then raised his sword and stood in an attacking position.

'*You*, Yarron! I've been waiting a long time to put you down, you treacherous dog. You and Bhalar betrayed the Treldarian army and cost us the last war.'

Vark charged at Yarron like a raging bull with his blade pointed at Yarron's heart. Yarron waited for just the right moment to step aside to his right, at the same time deflecting Vark's blade. Vark turned back around and swung his blade forcefully down at Yarron's head.

This time Yarron stepped to the left, rapidly raising his sword and placing the tip on Vark's neck. He could have pierced his victim's carotid artery and let him bleed out but decided to refrain. He didn't want Vark to have an easy, instant death. He wanted him to know what it was like to suffer. So instead, while withdrawing his sword, Yarron sliced through Vark's shoulder with a deep cut, sufficient to cause a sharp pain and for the bright red blood to come gushing out onto his black uniform.

Vark yelped, jumped back and placed his left hand on the wound, trying to stop the bleeding. He was livid.

Yarron realised Vark was not the superior swordsman and watched as he became more heated, his face red, his mouth closed tightly, and his pony-tailed hair in tatters.

Vark again took a wild sideways backswing to Yarron's torso. Yarron jumped back letting Vark's wide arching swing continue its momentum. Then he quickly moved in, slashing Vark's left leg above the knee with another deep slice. Blood began oozing rapidly from the deep flesh wound.

Again, Vark squealed in pain. Realising he was outclassed in swordsmanship, he dropped his sabre and snatched his magnetic pistol from its holster, firing at short range and aiming directly for Yarron's heart. Luckily, he was saved by his anti-magnetic protective shield which instantly dissipated the charge.

Vark could not believe what he was seeing. While he was temporarily dazed, Yarron swiped the gun from Vark's hand with a forward sweep of his sword and with a backward slicing action, swung his sword forcefully towards Vark's neck.

Only a hair's breadth from making contact, it was blocked abruptly with another blade, sparks igniting on impact. Yarron turned to see who had blocked his fatal blow. It wasn't one of the enemy, but instead Kyron Tyros who had appeared on the scene from nowhere.

'What in the Gods' names are you doing!' exclaimed a shocked Yarron.

'Sorry, Yarron, but Dakhar wants Vark and Commander Nukwar brought before the Senate. He sent me from the Control Room with his orders.'

Yarron was furious. 'I want my revenge! Vark deserves to die!'

But Kyron was firm. 'Stand down, Yarron.'

There was a momentary stand-off before Yarron reluctantly relented, still seething.

'Sentinels,' Kyron called to three soldiers standing close by. 'Secure Captain Vark in hand chains and take him to the Citadel to be locked up in the High Security cells.'

As the Sentinels clapped Tykran Vark in arms, Vark looked at Yarron with a nasty, nauseating grin. Although he'd been captured, he was gloating that Yarron had missed his chance for personal revenge.

Kyron turned back to the loud and bloody battle to face the enemy army. Despite their shiny armour and impressive-looking magnetic weapons, they were fast losing the battle against the Sentinels and Nujharenes. Kyron smiled to himself as he thought about Dakhar's insight and determination. *If it hadn't been for the long hours Dakhar had made he and Grant Thompson put in developing anti-magnetic protective devices and modified weapons, the outcome for Tzurac would have been very different.* He admired his CCMO and mentor and was proud to be in his service.

'Take him!' Kyron ordered his soldiers as he saw Commander Nukwar stumble and fall. 'Damn you again, Vark!' Nukwar cursed viciously, scrambling to his feet and retrieving the Nujharene sword he'd dropped and yelling 'What did you get me and the Rozakians into?'

As the Sentinels charged towards him, he swung his sword wildly trying to avoid capture, but one of the Sentinels aimed his laser pistol and fired. It was a lethal shot to the head.

Vark turned as he was being escorted away and gasped when he saw Nukwar slumped to the ground, lifeless.

Seeing the Rozakian Commander dead and the Treldarian Vark in chains, the remaining enemy soldiers dropped their weapons and surrendered. They knew they were outnumbered and realised their weapons were useless against their rivals' new protective armour. The battle was over.

The supremely confident Rozakian leader, Supreme Leader Wazine, would be left waiting impatiently on Planet Rozak for the return of his armies. He would be left deprived of ships, commanders and soldiers and of the Xytrinium to replace his diminishing stores of braktite. He would never comprehend how his invincible army had been defeated so convincingly.

AFTERMATH

BACK at the Central Control Room, Dakhar was surveying on screen, the aftermath of the battle. The battlefield was littered with dead bodies, black smoke billowed in the distance, the Nujharenes were gathering their injured outside the walls of the Citadel and the Urgellans were slowly pouring out of the forest. Grant Thompson was rounding up the Diutrons and remote marching them back to the Airfield. The Tzuracians had won the war against a powerful dark force, but at what cost?

He was caught unaware when Yarron stormed back into the Control Room. 'You said you had no qualms about me exacting my revenge by killing Vark. So why did Kyron stop me?'

'Yarron,' said Dakhar, 'I understand how you must feel, but this is a military operation and we're Tzuracian Sentinels. We must follow the rules of war and not take personal revenge on the battlefield. Vark must be tried before the Senate in a proper court of law and sentenced accordingly. Between you and me I think he'll be executed like his father and you're welcome to stay around for the trial if you wish.'

'We already know he's guilty on all counts!' said Yarron, seething with frustration. 'Why waste all this time and paperwork when he could be dealt with immediately?'

Kyron arrived to overhear Yarron's plea, and cut in. 'I know exactly what you're experiencing because I felt the same way when Jackson Jensen kidnapped my wife Torri. I wanted to kill him, personally, but I had to maintain moral standards. He ended up getting his just deserts and Vark *will* not get away with what he has done. The Universe will see to that, I assure you. Be patient.'

Yarron shook his head slowly. 'Alright, I'll do it your way for now. But if I'm not satisfied with the way it turns out, there'll be consequences.'

'In the meantime, Yarron,' said Dakhar, firmly, 'why don't you return your protective gear to Supply and contact Bhalar to tell her you're alright? She must be worried. Then prepare for the safe return of the Nujharenes while I get this place back to normal.'

Yarron stormed out of the room. He was still livid for not getting his revenge.

Dakhar turned to Kyron. 'I want you to oversee the cleanup of the battle grounds. Take the fallen Sentinels to the cryo-chambers to await their ceremonial burials and compose a list for the Honour Register. Report back to me when this is complete. And thank you for stopping Yarron just in time.'

'Just doing my job, General.'

Dakhar gave a wry smile. 'You're dismissed, Captain.'

'Yes, sir!'

Kyron saluted, turned and marched out.

Back at his office, Dakhar continued with business. 'Corporal,' he called to his orderly, 'contact Senator Ghalbrak and have him arrange for a Senate hearing to debrief them. Then get Grant Thompson on the line.'

Within minutes the intercom on Dakhar's desk buzzed. 'Yes, Corporal?'

'Your meeting with the Senate is at 1500 hours today, and Grant Thompson is on line one.'

'Thank you, Corporal.'

Dakhar picked up the intercom. 'Greetings, Grant. How are you managing after all that's happened?'

'Shite,' cursed the Irishman. 'I'm pleased it all worked, but a few of me Diutrons suffered electrical overcharge when one of your Sentinels forgot to switch on their protective anti-magnetic shields.'

'I'm glad to hear you're alright, Grant, and I want to thank you sincerely for your efforts in saving all of us and preserving the Tzuracians and our planet. We're in your debt.'

'Twas me pleasure, General.'

'After you've repaired the robots, I'd like you to march most of them to one of the docking stations. I'll let you know which one as soon as I've contacted Admiral Okerahm to organise a ship to take you and most of the Diutrons back to Iota to put into cold storage. But I want you to leave one hundred of them here on Tzurac, just in case.'

'Thank ya, General. Do I get a big shiny medal?' he chuckled, before the line went dead.

As soon as the call ended, Dakhar buzzed his orderly again. 'Corporal, get Admiral Okerahm on the line as soon as possible!'

Five minutes later he was talking to the Admiral. 'Greetings, Admiral. Your fleet of warships and Advanced Destroyers did a great job of destroying our enemy's ships. Your strategy was a great success, though I'm very sorry to hear about the loss of some of your crews and their ships. Be assured we'll give them a military funeral and compensate their families for their loss.'

'Thank you, General, much appreciated. What can I help you with now?'

'I need you to arrange some warships, serviced, fuelled, and stocked with supplies ready to take our allies back to their home planets, and keep these ships on standby. We'll need two ships for the Urgellans, two ships for the fourteen hundred Diutrons and one ship for the Nujharenes. Yarron's Advanced Destroyer also needs attention.'

'When do you need to have them ready?'

'Within the next two days, Admiral.'

'Very good. I'll let you know when they're up and running.'

As soon as he put the receiver down, Dakhar checked his timepiece. He had ten minutes to get to the Senate chambers.

When he arrived, he seated himself before the senators and waited for them to address him.

Ghalbrak took a sip of water before speaking. 'General, what do you have to report?'

Dakhar rose and tipped his head out of respect. 'We've beaten the enemy, in large part thanks to the hard work of our Irish engineer and Captain Kyron Tyros. Without their inventions of the anti-magnetic shield for our protective Dome, the shields for our armies, and the anti-magnetic pistols, as well as the modified shields for our fleet, we would have been defeated.'

There was a murmur of relief around the room with heads nodding.

'Unfortunately, we sustained some collateral damage to our fleet and some loss of lives. We had five warships destroyed and we lost five hundred crew. In the field, we lost fifty Sentinels, two Nujharenes and three Diutrons. We captured the Rozakian enemy leader along with fifty of his soldiers and recaptured Captain Tykran Vark with twenty of his Treldarian escapees and thirty Kyroni warriors.'

'Thank you, General. Good work,' responded Ghalbrak. 'We'd like to thank, personally, all those who participated in the defence of Tzurac. So, the Senate would like to hold a gathering in the main courtyard in two days' time. Can you please organise this? In regard to the captured soldiers, they will need to stand trial before the Senate. We'll organise a date for this. It will be in the very near future. That will be all for now, General.'

Dakhar headed for home, taking Kyron with him. They had both earned a well-deserved reunion with their families. Tajhira, Torri and their children were happily reunited and the Urgellan wine flowed as little Terrazah chattered about how much she was now enjoying school.

*   *   *

Two days later, after a massive clean-up, all those who had participated in and survived the battle, gathered in the huge main courtyard, which was the size of Rome's ancient colosseum. An array of various representatives and coloured flags hung from the towers of the surrounding Citadel walls and fluttered in the gentle breeze. On the podium sat all the senators in their coloured robes and at the dais stood General Dakhar. The chattering and mumbling amongst the huge crowd were almost deafening until Dakhar tapped the microphone to test it was working and the noise suddenly dissipated.

Dakhar began to broadcast to the multitudes, first in Tzuracian, and then repeating it in Treldarian for the sake of the Nujharenes. 'Soldiers, allies, friends, I'm proud of all of you for helping to defend our city and our planet against a sophisticated and deadly dark force which could have destroyed our way of life. I applaud your courage and your dedication to the cause. So, thank you, thank you all, and my condolences to the families of those who fell in battle. We will remember them for their courage and valour.'

The crowd broke out cheering and clapping, showing their appreciation for Dakhar's words of thanks for their efforts.

When the noise subsided, he spoke again, saying, 'I'll now hand over the rest to Senator Ghalbrak.' Dakhar stepped back from the dais and went to a vacant chair on the podium as Ghalbrak strolled to the dais looking every bit the oldest and wisest senator.

Grasping the microphone in his right hand and pulling it closer, he began to speak in his native tongue. Behind him on a huge screen, his words were translated instantaneously into the languages of the different races as he spoke.

'Greetings and thank you all for being here. The Senators and I, as well as the citizens of Tzurac, are indebted to you all for coming to the rescue of our planet and all the other planets in the Federation. We have been very lucky to have beaten our foe and continue peace in the Universe.'

The onlookers clapped spontaneously.

'One person in particular has played a major role in giving us the means to defeat this superior negative force.' The Senator paused for effect. 'And that person is our Irish engineer, Grant Thompson from Terra Major. Grant, please come up here on the podium.'

Grant, who was standing in the crowd with his head bowed tugging at his ginger beard, looked up in amazement when he heard his name. All eyes were looking in his direction as he meandered humbly up to the podium, dressed in his red and green tartan waistcoat with matching trousers. Ghalbrak called him to come closer to the dais.

'Grant, it gives me great honour to present this silver medal to you for your invention and its implementation that saved all of us, and for the hard work you put in labouring to complete the task on time.'

Ghalbrak handed a red velvet case to him and, as he received it, the crowd cheered and applauded loudly. Grant went red in the face and took a graceful bow. *He'd only been joking to Dakhar about a medal.*

Ghalbrak waved his hands to quieten down the raucous noise and when it subsided, he added, 'The Senate have decided to make you an Honorary Sentinel for all you have done for Tzurac and the Federation over the years.'

Grant, his green eyes now streaming with tears, clutched the microphone and spoke in his lyrical Irish accent. 'T'ank you, Senators, I really wasn't expectin' dis. I humbly accept the medal, and the honour bestowed upon me.' He bowed to the senators, before leaving the podium holding tightly onto his velvet box with a beaming wide grin on his freckled face.

Senator Ghalbrak then waved Dakhar back to the dais and returned to his seat.

'Listen up soldiers,' Dakhar began. 'We've organised transport for the Urgellans and the Nujharenes to take you back to your home planets. Please follow your leaders and make your way to the docking bays at the Airfield. Sentinels, reform into your units and return to barracks.'

The massive crowd began to file out of the Courtyard and Yarron, who was among them, headed straight for his ship. He wanted to escort the warship carrying the Nujharenes back to their planet and get back to Terra Major to be with Bhalar again, but he also wanted to see Vark's trial. He needed a plan.

As he approached his Advanced Destroyer, he met Admiral Okerahm who advised that the ship had been refuelled, re-armed and stocked for his return voyage. 'Thank you, Admiral,' he said.

'On the contrary, Yarron, it's me who should be thanking *you*, for backing up my fleet by distracting and destroying some of the Rozakian warships while my crew made their retreat from the enemy. I had no idea at the time, but I know now that your efforts were nothing short of amazing.'

'You're welcome.'

Inside his Destroyer, Yarron holographed General Zawkon.

'Greetings Yarron,' said Zawkon as Yarron's image became clear. 'I see you survived the battle.'

'Greetings, General. Good to see you too. Undoubtedly General Dakhar will fill you in with more detail at a later date.' He was his still bristling. 'I want to know if Bhalar is alright. Is it possible to bring her to the holograph so I can speak to her?'

'Yes, Yarron. She's okay and missing you very much. I'll holograph you back when I've brought her to my office.'

'Thank you, General.' With those words, Yarron's image began to fade.

While Yarron was waiting for Zawkon to get back to him and biding his time waiting for news of the scheduled trial of Vark, he worked on his plan of actions. *I need to collect Bhalar from Terra Major and see my children, and then fly on to Mankro to deliver them safely home. So, I need to ask Dakhar to supply a pilot for a warship to deliver the Nujharene warriors home without me being present, rather than keep them waiting here on Tzurac. From Mankro, I'll take off to Nujhar and rendezvous there with the warship.*

He was deep in thought, when suddenly the high-pitched security alarms resounded loudly in the Citadel. Yarron grabbed his utility belt with his sword and laser pistol still attached and dived out of his Destroyer to see what the cause might be. Units of Sentinels were running in different directions amid yelling of orders.

Yarron sprinted to Dakhar's office. Inside his building all the lighting was out, and the automatic doors wouldn't work. There was no power. To reach Dakhar's office on the first floor, the only option was to climb the emergency stairs using the dully lit stairwell.

Dakhar was sitting behind his desk issuing urgent orders. He finished and put the receiver back on its fixture. 'Come in, Yarron,' he motioned quickly with a waved hand. 'The main transformer has shut down and the backup generator is also out of commission. The holding cells no longer have a force field to prevent the prisoners escaping. I've sent several units of Sentinels over there to capture and secure the escaped prisoners, but Captain Vark and his Lieutenant Krag who were locked in the high-Security cells, overpowered the Sentinel Guards. Despite Vark's injuries to his shoulder and leg they confiscated their weapons. They haven't yet been located.'

'What the hell!' yelled Yarron. 'You must be kidding!'

Just then, Kyron also arrived at the door of Dakhar's office. 'What happened to cause the power failure, General?'

Dakhar shook his head several times. 'Apparently one of the scientists who was working with Thompson to restore our Dome back to normal shielding, triggered a switch which short circuited the grid and blew up the transformer and our reserve generator with it.'

'Was anyone killed or injured?'

'The scientist received a massive shock and severe burns. He's in a critical condition.'

'Cut the small talk!' Yarron interrupted, impatiently. 'Vark and Krag will head straight to the Airfield to hijack a ship and a pilot to fly them off this planet. I'm going there now to see if I can stop them.'

'I'll join you,' said Kyron.

They rushed from Dakhar's Office and. commandeering a vacant hover vehicle from outside the Citadel, sped to the Airfield. There they climbed a high wire fence which was no longer electrified because of the power outage and crept to one of the nearest hangars with laser pistols at the ready. Instead of passing through the front entrance, they gingerly made their way around the back of the hangar, staying on high alert.

On hearing voices coming from inside, they froze. It was an argument. They recognised a female Tzuracian voice and a male Treldarian voice.

Yarron whispered to Kyron, 'Could be one of our pilots. I think she's arguing about not having access to one of the ships.'

After making their way around to the hangar's side doors and taking a quick glimpse, Kyron recognised Vark pointing a laser pistol at the head of the Tzuracian pilot, Captain Jharryn. There was no sign of Krag.

Kyron turned to Yarron and whispered, 'I'll distract Vark by demanding he drop his pistol. If he fires at me, I have my cape to use as a shield. Watch my back in case Krag shows up.'

'Okay, let's do it.'

Kyron sprang into action, entering the side door with his laser pistol aimed towards Vark. Surprised by the intruder, Vark instantly grabbed Jharryn around the neck and pointed his pistol at her head. 'Don't shoot or she's dead!' he yelled fiercely.

Out of nowhere Krag, who'd been nearby searching the hangar, fired a shot at Kyron, which ricocheted off the cape on Kyron's left shoulder.

On hearing the noise, Yarron dived in without hesitation, and smashed the gun from Krag's hand with his sword, knocking Krag out cold with his free swinging arm.

Jharryn seized the moment, elbowing Vark in the stomach and dropping to the floor, leaving Kyron a clear shot. Kyron fired at Vark's shoulder to wound him and Vark collapsed, dropping his weapon as he fell.

As Vark reached for the pistol on the ground, Yarron dived towards him and, in a single roll, knocked the laser pistol from his reach. Then with a slick movement Yarron thrust the point of his sword against Vark's throat while pinning him down with his foot.

Kyron froze fearing Yarron would kill Vark, and there was panic and terror in Vark's eyes. Both were shocked when Yarron hesitated.

'I've changed my mind, Vark,' Yarron said calmly.

'Kill me,' Vark cried.

'No, Vark. Killing is too good for you. I hope they make you suffer in prison for the rest of your days.'

Vark was speechless as images of the dreaded Planet Lokar flashed through his mind.

Kyron rushed over and secured Vark, binding his arms behind his back with some cable, then gagging him. He then did the same to the unconscious Krag.

Breathing a sigh of relief, Captain Jharryn stood up to face Kyron and Yarron. 'Thank you both for coming to my rescue. He would have killed me if you hadn't intervened.'

'And we couldn't have saved you without your quick thinking and courage, Sentinel. Well done!'

'I can't wait to tell Sharne Rhamak about this,' she said, jovially.

Kyron contacted Dakhar with the good news. 'We've got them Ehrane. We're taking them to the infirmary and we'll report in once we've personally seen them secured in their cells again.' By the time the hover vehicle arrived at the infirmary in the Citadel, the security alarms had ceased and power was restored.

* * *

'Well, thanks to both of you for dealing with the escaped prisoners,' said Dakhar when Kyron and Yarron were settled back in his office.

The Sentinel and ex-Sentinel nodded and shrugged their shoulders as if nothing serious had happened, though Kyron was quick to add, 'And you need to thank Captain Jharryn – she's a legend!'

Dakhar smiled broadly. 'I will. She was already on my list of recommendations for a medal.'

Dakhar turned to Yarron. 'Yarron, I'm so proud of your actions. You have your revenge and a clear conscience as well. I'll be recommending Vark, Krag and the surviving Treldarians be sent back to Lokar and the key thrown away. That is, after they receive another improved injection to permanently remove any Xytrinium enhancements. They'll regret they ever dared to leave there! And it's a punishment more cruel than death.

'Now you're free to visit Terra Major to collect your family and then meet the warship returning the Nujharenes to their home planet.'

'Thanks, General. I'll take my leave from Tzurac,' said Yarron. 'But speaking of the Nujharenes, who gave their support in this war … They have deposits of Xytrinium on their planet. I told them I could show them the benefits of this valuable resource and help them extract it. And if planet Nujhar came under Tzuracian protection, the Tzuracians would benefit from having another planet to replenish their reserves. If the Nujharenes became an independent member of the Federation of Planets, they could trade their Xytrinium for modernisation. They also have other metals, like copper, tin and zinc to trade. What say you, General? Could you present this proposal to the Senate?'

'You may no longer be a Sentinel, but have you ever thought of becoming an ambassador for all new worlds?' Dakhar said warmly.

'I agree, a position like this would be ideal for you. We need someone of your calibre,' Kyron added. 'And I want to thank you for saving my life again. You're a brave and sincere soldier and to me you'll always be a Sentinel.'

'Nothing official, thanks comrades. I like being a free agent these days to do what I please with no interference, and to come and go without being ordered. I don't have to answer to anyone, except Bhalar.'

As Yarron returned to his ship at the Airfield, he reflected on events. *He had accomplished what he came for and now it was time to leave.* He gave directions to the pilot of the warship who was charged with delivering home the Nujharenes, jumped in his Destroyer and locked in the co-ordinates for Terra Major.

Three days later he was hugging Bhalar and his beautiful children. 'What would life be without you?' he said as he kissed each of them in turn. 'Now let's go home.'

He thanked General Zawkon for looking after them and then, with all his family safely on board, he blasted into the void heading for Mankro.

It was there, settled back into life in the village that Yarron received a holograph from General Dakhar. 'I wanted to tell you personally that, on the Senate's authority Vark, Krag and the surviving Treldarian and Kyroni soldiers have all been sent back to Lokar. They have all been injected with the newly developed antidote to permanently remove their Xytrinium enhancements.

'And on a lighter note, Grant Thompson has delivered the Diutrons back to Planet Iota, where they were decommissioned and placed in storage. I'm hoping he will soon have time to continue his work with you at the Xytrinium mine on Mankro and perhaps on Nujhar.'

'Good news,' said Yarron.

EXPANDING THE FEDERATION

ON Yarron's way to planet Nujhar to rendezvous with the ship returning Nujharene soldiers, a hologram of General Dakhar appeared. 'Greetings again, Yarron. The Senate has agreed to the terms you proposed and are keen to hear whether the Nujharenes accept our offer to help mine the Xytrinium on their planet in return for protection with a place in the Federation.'

After landing his black Destroyer in the same place as before, he was escorted by six armed Nujharenes to Kelfas' cave and seated before the throne, his weapons confiscated. Laid in front of him was a small feast of food which looked like native fruits and a type of baked bread. A clay jug and cup, which contained the same nectar he had tasted and very much liked the last time he was here, was also on the small wooden table.

Kelfas smiled as he spoke slowly in Treldarian, with his gravelly voice. 'I'm pleased to see you again, Yarron. I was worried things might not have gone as planned, preventing your return. Please enjoy our refreshments after your long journey.

'With the exception of only two, you have safely brought all my warriors back to me. I am sad that two fell in battle, but my warriors tell me they died with honour. They have also told me what this wonderful Xytrinium can do, particularly when used in armour and weapons. When can we start excavating the blue crystal from our deposits in the ground?'

'I'm sorry for the loss of your two soldiers but I'm grateful the others have returned with no injuries. I've discussed with our great leaders the possibility of mining your own deposits here on Nujhar, but it will take time. In the meantime, I'll donate a small amount of my Xytrinium on Mankro so you can start using this valuable resource, not just for your armour and weapons, but also for new types of farming and medical equipment, far superior to what your people are using at present.'

'This sounds wonderful, Yarron.'

'Yes, but there is a minor condition. Because of its volatile state, sophisticated equipment will be required to extract this resource on your planet. One ounce of these crystals could blow up a mountain if struck accidentally. The Tzuracians are the only ones who have this complex equipment. They can show you and your warriors how to process it and manufacture equipment and appliances, how to refine it to power your spacecraft to travel faster and further, and also give your people a source of energy which will last indefinitely, preserving your natural resources. And they have invited your planet to become a member of the Federation of Planets.'

Kelfas stamped his metal staff heavily on the ground and rose from his Throne chair. 'We do not want to be ruled by the Tzuracians,' he said angrily.

Yarron quickly and calmly, countered his words. 'No, no, Your Majesty. The Tzuracians have no intention of ruling over your planet and its people. Like the other planets of the Federation, who remain independent, without interference, your moon will also remain independent. All the Tzuracians would like to do is trade with you on some of your produce and in return they will offer military support and protection from any who threaten your way of life. Each year all they will ask for is a very small amount of Xytrinium. We on Mankro have a similar contract.' Yarron finished and waited patiently for Kelfas' response, while staring into his eyes.

Kelfas sat stroking his long white beard and reflecting on what this brash Tzuracian had to say. Yarron could hear the wheels turning in Kelfas' head as he mulled it over.

After a long interval, he finally spoke. 'I like what the Tzuracians have to offer, so I will consult with the Council of Elders. You will have your answer tomorrow.'

After a night's stay at the Nujharene village, Yarron was brought again to the Throne Room. He was again presented with fruits and bread, this time, he supposed for breakfast. But he didn't have much of an appetite and was anxious to hear the verdict.

Sitting on his throne, looking pleased, Kelfas said, 'The Council accepts the offer. When do we meet your great leaders to finalise the agreement?'

Yarron smiled widely. 'As soon as I can return to my ship and contact my superiors to inform them of your wise decision. They will make arrangements to travel to your planet and officially sanction the agreement. I'll keep you up to date by visiting you again, if that's alright, and have another taste of that delicious nectar. But with your permission, I'll leave now to travel back to my home on Mankro.'

After arriving back at his ship, Yarron holographed Dakhar to inform him of the outcome. 'Kelfas is expecting a delegation from Tzurac to bring a contract.'

'This is very good news, Yarron,' said Dakhar enthusiastically. 'You've done well in making new alliances who are happy to trade with us. I'll arrange for the delegates from the Federation of Planets to sign the drafted agreement once it's sanctioned by the Senate. Thanks again.

'And I'd like *you* present when we come to Nujhar so we can have a familiar person there when the agreement is signed by Kelfas and his Council of Elders. And I'll bring Grant Thompson along so they can meet the engineer who'll be organising and overseeing the excavations. We're checking with MERIC and we should have this organised within the next two weeks. I'll contact you when we're ready. Over and out.'

* * *

After arranging a meeting with the Senate, who approved the signing up of Nujhar to the Federation of Planets and the mining of the Xytrinium on their moon, Dakhar contacted General Kal Zawkon on Terra Major with an unusual request.

'Greetings Kal,' came Dakhar's voice from the holographic image projected in Zawkon's office.

'Greetings, Ehrane. This is an unexpected visit.'

'Yes, it is. I have an unusual request to make. Let me explain.' Dakhar paused for a moment. 'As you are aware, the Nujharenes have now become our allies and Yarron has negotiated with them to join the Federation of Planets. The Senate has sanctioned the agreement.'

'That's good news,' said Zawkon.

'Yes, it is. And the other good news is they have agreed for us to mine their Xytrinium and to trade with Tzurac. What I'm asking is for you to approach MERIC – well, Lauren – and ask if they will permit Grant Thompson, who is still in their employ, to help set up and oversee the mining operations on Nujhar. And by the way, the Senate have made Grant an Honorary Sentinel for his great work in developing the devices that saved our planet and our lives against the Rozakian invasion. He was awarded a silver medal for his hard work and effort in his role as the engineer.'

'I bet he was thrilled,' said Zawkon, smiling. 'I'll talk with Lauren as soon as possible and get back to you, Ehrane. Over and out.'

Several days later, Dakhar contacted the Irish engineer who was on planet Iota still decommissioning the Diutrons to put into storage.

'I s'pose this ain't a social call, General?' Grant sounded his usual cantankerous self.

'No, Grant, I have some good news.'

'The only news ya give me, is usually bad news.'

'You have been chosen to organise and oversee mining operations on Planet Nujhar. I've sought permission from MERIC and they have approved it.'

'Holy Mother of Jesus! I just got settled back on Iota and ya want to send me out in the middle of nowhere to live amongst these giant, green rabbits. Dat's not a reward, dat's punishment.'

'You only have to stay there for about six months, Grant, and you'll be paid double for the time you're there.'

Grant thought for a moment. 'I'll do it on t'ree conditions. When I've finished the job, I want to return to Terra Major to live there permanently with me relatives. I want an all-expenses-paid holiday to one of d'em tropical islands on Terra Major for a week. And I want a doz'n bottles of pure malt Irish whiskey.'

'Done! I'll let you know when to start, but first I'll need you to come to Nujhar with a delegation when we sign the agreement with the Nujharenes. I want to introduce you to their king.'

What had begun as a terrifying threat to Tzurac and the Federation of Planets, had ended in the defeat of the Rozakians, the Treldarians and the Kyroni, and seen a new member, Nujhar, with its own Xytrinium deposits, welcomed to the Federation. Peace would reign once more in the Grekadian Domain, though for how long, was anyone's guess.

About the Author

In the early fifties I emigrated from England to Australia as a youngster with my "ten pound pom" family. I spent my boyhood and teenage years reading Marvel and DC comics and followed all the sci-fi TV series of Star Trek, Lost in Space, Dr Who and Time Tunnel. Then, in my adulthood, I watched sci-fi movies including Star Wars, Battlestar Galactica, and Star Gate, and continue to watch new release sci-fi movies. I have always loved English literature and started writing romantic poetry, graduating to my first non-fiction book in 2003. After retiring from a career of forty years in the public service, I am now writing full time and applying my past martial arts training and my interest in science as well as science fiction, to write believable and exciting sci-fi stories. Readers from Amazon Books who read my first sci-fi novel published in 2012 "Sentinels of Tzurac –Terra Major Under Threat" have asked for more in the space opera adventure and I have now made the series into a quadrilogy.